让日常阅读成为砍向我们内心冰封大海的斧头。

一个人的朝圣 3

莫琳去往事花园

[英] 蕾秋·乔伊斯 Rachel Joyce / 著　万洁 / 译

北京联合出版公司

图书在版编目（CIP）数据

一个人的朝圣 . 3，莫琳去往事花园 / （英）蕾秋·乔伊斯著；万洁译 . -- 北京：北京联合出版公司，2025.4. -- ISBN 978-7-5596-7758-7

Ⅰ . I561.45

中国国家版本馆 CIP 数据核字第 2024GP1300 号

北京市版权局著作权合同登记　图字：01-2025-1166
Maureen Fry and the Angel of the North
Copyright ©2022 by Rachel Joyce
Published by agreement with Conville & Walsh through The Grayhawk Agency.
Simplified Chinese translation copyright ©2025 by Beijing Xiron Culture Group Co., Ltd.
All rights reserved.

一个人的朝圣 . 3　莫琳去往事花园
作　　者：（英）蕾秋·乔伊斯
译　　者：万　洁
出 品 人：赵红仕
责任编辑：管　文

北京联合出版公司出版
（北京市西城区德外大街 83 号楼 9 层　100088）
三河市中晟雅豪印务有限公司　新华书店经销
字数 160 千字　880 毫米 ×1230 毫米　1/32　印张 9.25
2025 年 4 月第 1 版　2025 年 4 月第 1 次印刷
ISBN 978-7-5596-7758-7
定价：55.00 元

版权所有，侵权必究
未经书面许可，不得以任何方式转载、复制、翻印本书部分或全部内容。
本书若有质量问题，请与本公司图书销售中心联系调换。电话：（010）82069336

献给苏珊娜

去年你栽在你花园里的那具尸体,
开始发芽了没有?今年会开花吗?

* * *

《荒原》
T.S. 艾略特

我以为我看见一位身着蔚蓝长袍的天使从草坪那端向我走来，但其实我看见的只是欧椴树羽毛般的树枝间透出的蓝天。

* * *

《基尔弗特的日记》

1873 年 7 月 21 日

目录

01
冬日之旅 /001

02
世界的客人 /013

03
煎蛋 /021

04
人们的嘴 /029

05
海上花园 /041

06
事故中的意外 /051

07
北方和更北的北方 /063

08
卡车 /069

09
遗物花园 /083

10
糟糕的一夜 /097

11
安娜·杜普里 /103

12
咖啡豆 /113

13
月光鸣奏曲 /123

14
冬日花束 /133

致中国读者 /141

致谢 /149

CONTENTS

01
Winter Journey /157

02
The World's Guest /168

03
Fried Egg /174

04
Human Mouths /181

05
Sea Garden /193

06
Accident-Accident /201

07
North and Further North /213

08
Truck /217

09
Garden of Relics /231

10
A Bad Night /244

11
Anna Dupree /250

12
Coffee Beans /259

13
Moonlight Sonata /269

14
Winter Bouquet /279

Acknowledgements /287

01

冬日之旅

Winter Journey

太早了，鸟儿都还没开始歌唱。哈罗德躺在她身边，双手整齐地放在胸前，格外平静。她不禁想知道他在睡梦中游荡到了何处。反正不是她去的地方：她一合上眼，就会看见道路施工的画面。天哪，她想。这可不是个好兆头。她摸黑起床，脱掉睡衣，换上她最合身的那件蓝色衬衫，搭了一条舒适的宽松长裤和一件开襟羊毛衫。"哈罗德，"她唤道，"你醒了吗？"可他一动不动。她拎起鞋子，悄无声息地关上了身后卧室的门。此时不走，她恐怕永远都走不成了。

在楼下，她打开烧水壶的开关。趁烧水的空儿，她搬出她的金盏花，还简单擦了擦家里的灰。"莫琳。"她大声对自己说，因为她不是个傻瓜。她知道自己在做什么，哪怕她的双手不知道。她在瞎忙乎，就是这么回事。她冲了一保温杯速溶咖啡，做了一份三明治，把它用保鲜膜包了起来，然后给他留了张字条。接着，她又在一张纸上写了"马克杯！"在另一张纸上写了"平底锅！"没等她反应过来，厨房里已经到处都是便利贴了，它们仿佛一个个小小的黄色警示标志。"莫琳。"她又说了一遍，然后把这些便利贴通通取了下来。"现在就出发。走吧。"她把哈罗德的木拐杖挂在椅子上，只为了方便他看到，然后把保温杯和三明治一起装进包里，穿上她开车时穿的鞋和冬季的大衣，拎起手提箱，迈出家门，走进了美丽的清晨中。清朗的天空上点缀着几颗星星，挂着一弯月牙，就像是指甲上的白色部分。唯一的灯光是从隔壁雷克斯家透出来的。依然没有鸟鸣。

即使在一月，这天气也还是冷了些。碎石板拼砌的路上一夜之间就结了冰，她不得不抓着栏杆继续往前走。石板之间的车辙里是星星点点的冰碴儿，房前的花园里只剩下几丛被冰包裹的荆棘。她把车打着了火，一边热车，一边擦车窗。目之所及，路面都结了霜，粗糙得像砂纸，在福斯桥路的路灯下看起来滑溜溜的，但外面一个人影都没有。毕竟今天是周日。尽管不知道雷克斯起没起床，她还是朝他家的方向挥了挥手，就这样吧。她要上路了。

撒盐车已经经过了福尔街，撒下的盐粒形成了一张粉毯，一直往山上铺去。她驾车一路向北，途经书店和其他周一才开门的商店，但她并没有多看。她有好长一段时间没逛商业街了。这些天，她和哈罗德大部分时间都在上网，这不仅仅是因为疫情。车窗外，寂静无声的一排排店铺变成了灯火通明的一排排住宅。接着，它们退出视野，取而代之的是一片空荡荡的黑暗，中间某处坐落着一家关门的加油站。然后，她路过一个岔路口，该路口通往她每月都去一次的火葬场；她没拐弯，而是径直开了过去。终于，她开到了大路上，可她并不感到兴奋，更多的是一种感觉，但她不知道该如何解释这种感觉,只觉得自己正在做对的事。哈罗德一直都是对的。

"莫琳,你得去。"他说过。她其实想到了一长串不去的理由,可最后她还是同意了。于是她主动为他演示了如何使用洗碗机和洗衣机,因为他有时候会犯迷糊,不知道该按哪个按钮。后来,她还在一张纸上写下了详细的使用说明。

"你确定吗?"几天后她又问了他一遍,"你真觉得我应该做这件事?"

"我当然确定。"当时他坐在花园中,她在忙着把落叶耙成堆。他把大衣穿得一边高、一边低,显得他左、右两边的身体像是错位了一样。

"可是谁来照顾你呢?"

"我会照顾自己。"

"吃饭怎么办?你得吃东西啊。"

"雷克斯可以帮忙。"

"这主意可不怎么样。在做饭方面,雷克斯还不如你呢。"

"那倒是。我们俩凑在一起,活脱脱两个老傻瓜!"

说完他笑了。他的微笑总能传达出一种圆满的意味,正是这份感觉让她还没走就已经开始想念他了。所以说,在这个问题上,他再怎么确定都随他的便,反正她不确定。她放下耙子,走过去帮他把扣子系好。他耐心地坐着,抬起头,用他那双仿佛出自代尔夫特陶器的蓝眼睛凝望着她,除了哈罗德,再没有人像这样看过她。她轻抚他的头发,他则抬起指尖,将她的脸凑近他的脸，吻了她。

"莫琳，不去的话，你永远有心结。"他说。

"那好吧。我去。我要去了，什么也拦不住我！不过，如果你不介意的话，我就不走着去了。多谢你，我还是用更常规的法子去吧。我会开车去。"

他们一起大笑起来，因为他俩都清楚，她说这话是在尽力掩饰内心的纠结。聊完这些，她回去继续耙落叶，他则继续看天空，可他们之间的这份静默里填满了她不知该如何开口说的话。

就这样，她坐在车里，满脑子都是哈罗德，但距离却与他越来越远。就在昨晚，他为她刷了开车穿的鞋，把它们并排放到椅子旁边，椅子上搁着她这次出行要带的衣物。"早上我不会叫醒你的。"在他们准备睡觉、互道晚安时，她保证道。睡着之前，哈罗德一直紧紧握着她的手，她也紧贴着他蜷起身子，听着他那节奏稳定的心跳，想努力汲取他的平静。

尽管路上没什么车，莫琳还是开得很慢。如果对面驶来一辆亮着前灯的车，她有充足的时间看到，就会把车停在路边合适的位置上。她甚至会礼貌地挥挥手表示感谢，看着车道重新被黑暗吞没，眼前只剩下她经过时摇摆的篱笆和树。在那之后，她开上了一条双行道，路况就更好了，因为这条路笔直、宽阔且依然十分空旷，偶尔会看到停在路旁泊车处的卡车。可随着她离埃克塞特越来越近，出现了不少施工的路段，和她晚上梦见的一模一样，她只好绕路而行。这下她糊涂了。她已经不在A38国道上了，而是行驶在一连串的支路和住宅区的道路上,中间有许多迷你环岛。莫琳又开了二十分钟,突然想起已经有一会儿没看到黄色的临时绕行标志了。现在她来到了一个住宅区的边缘,眼前只有成片的公寓楼和长在地砖之间的瘦骨嶙峋的树木。天还是黑的。

"好吧,可真行,"她说,"棒极了。"她不只是在自言自语。她有对着空气说话的习惯,就好像空气在故意跟她作对一样。后来,她都分不清自己仅是在想,还是真的把想法说出来了。

莫琳又经过了几栋公寓楼、矮小的树和到处停着的汽车,还经过了几辆上早班的送货车,但始终没看到A38国道。因为看到远处有一排明亮的路灯,她拐上了一条很长的辅路,结果发现自己来到了一条死路的尽头,左侧有座大仓库,仓库周围是一组敞开的大门和带尖刺的围栏。

她只好把车停到路边,拿出地图,可她压根儿不知道该从哪儿看起。她打开手机,可这也没什么用,因为哈罗德此时应该还在睡觉。她没辙了,在车里呆呆地坐了一会儿。哈罗德肯定会说"找个人问问呗"。可那是哈罗德才会干的事。她选择开车出行本就是希望不用和不认识的人打交道。"好吧。"她定了定神说道,"你可以的。"她决定带着地图,学学哈罗德,去仓库那边找个人问路。

莫琳下了车,立刻感到一股寒风扑向她的脸和耳朵,直往她鼻子里钻。当她穿过停车场时,左、右两侧的安防灯突然亮起来,差点儿把她照瞎了。她依稀看到主楼左边的一间预制小屋的窗户透着灯光,但她必须小心翼翼地走过去,还得伸出双臂保持平衡。莫琳开车穿的是平底仿麂皮鞋，有脚背带和特殊的防滑鞋底。穿这种鞋在湿的路面上可以走得很稳，但在黑冰[1]上就不行了。这里四处贴着有狗的照片的警示牌，说这片地方定期有狗巡逻。她挺担心撞见狗的。在她小时候，当地农民的狗都是放养的。她下巴上至今还有那时留下的一小块疤。

莫琳敲了敲小屋的窗户，里面值夜班的年轻人还没醒。他弓着身子窝在一把折叠式野营椅上，脑袋上的包头巾[2]牢牢抵着墙壁，嘴半张着，两条腿伸展开来，几乎占据了整个地方。她又敲了几下，这次更使劲儿了，喊道："打扰一下！"

他吓了一跳，揉着眼睛从椅子上慢慢站起来，好像在不断生长一样。他太高了，得略弯着腰才能磕磕绊绊地走到窗口，然后才想到要把口罩戴上。他留着浓密的褐色络腮胡，有着拳击手那样结实的肩膀，双手大到无法灵活地扳开窗户的锁扣。最后，他终于拉开窗户，歪着脖子，眨着眼睛，以俯视的姿势看着她。

"我就不绕弯子了。我迷路了。我想上 M5 高速，可 A38 国道上的几个施工点让我开错了方向。"她的声音有点大，因为窗户太高了，她得往上够着说话，也是因为她担心他听不明白。此外，她讨厌承认自己出错了。毕竟她又不是真不认识路。

他又盯着她看了一会儿，努力让自己完全清醒过来。然后他说："你迷路了？"

---

1 指冬天气温低于 0 摄氏度时在道路上结成的难以发现的薄冰。
2 turban，主要指锡克族、穆斯林、印度教徒等用的包头巾。

"都怪道路施工。平常我好着呢！一般情况下我认路没问题。我只想知道怎么开上 M5 高速。"她又提高了音量，这回是喊的了。

他从窗户前走开，打开了旁边的门。她不知道他希望她做什么，所以只是站在原地等，同时担心着会有狗突然蹿出来。直到他说了一声"不进来吗？"她才戴上口罩，走了过去。

现在她进到了小屋里，面前的年轻人显得更高大了。她的头顶才将将到他的胸口。他歪着脖子，哈着腰，才让体形显得小了些。就连他的鞋子——纯黑的德比鞋，那种用来给孩子矫正脚形的鞋——在这个空间里都觉得挤。难怪他会睡着。窗下有个散发着橘色光的、暖烘烘的老式电暖炉，让人感觉脚踝以上的身体就像被穿在扦子上烤一样。任谁挨着它都会睡着。莫琳忍下了一个哈欠。

他说："你可别随便冲着陌生人嚷嚷说自己迷路了。那可不安全。他们可能会欺负你。"

他的英语说得非常好。非说有什么瑕疵的话，就是他带点儿德文郡的口音。这下好了，又有一件事她判断失误了。"我想应该没有人会欺负我。"

"这谁说得准呢。林子大了，什么鸟都有。"

"是的，你说得没错。那你到底能不能帮我？"

"能啊。好吧。应该能吧。"他在手机上点了几下，然后举着手机给她看。没什么用——那是一张地图，但非常小。他给她看了她在什么位置，以及她要想去 M5 高速应该走哪些路。"看懂了吗？"

"没有。"她说，"没懂。我看不懂。看得我一头雾水。"

"怎么会这样？"

"不知道。我就是看不懂。"

"你有卫星导航吗？"

"有倒是有，但我不用那东西。"

他似乎有点困惑，但她不准备跟他解释。实际上，她早就拔掉了卫星导航的电源。她受不了那个催促她转向、总是在最后一刻告诉她错过了转弯的友好的声音。莫琳属于电话放在大厅桌子上、地图放在杂物箱里的那代人。就连网上购物对她来说都很勉强。她明明只想买两个柠檬，网店却送来二十个，这种烦心事总让她碰上。

他说："如果我告诉你该怎么走，你能记住吗？"

"我觉得我记不住。"

"那我就不知道该怎么做了。你想让我怎么帮你？"

"我希望你能把你手机上的路线说给我听，我把它们记在一张纸上。之后我就可以按照这个路线开了。"

"哦，好吧。"他说着摸了摸络腮胡，挪动了双脚的位置，就好像要换个完全不同的站姿才能继续帮这个忙一样，"那行，我明白了。"

他耐心地告诉她，应该先沿着这条路走到头，左转，再右转，从环岛的第二个出口出去。她把这些都记在了他从笔记本上撕下的一张纸上。他每念完一条路线指示都会停顿一下，以确保她都记下了。到最后，她一共记了二十条，还在每一条前面都写上了数字编号。

"你知道再往后的路怎么走吗?"

"知道。"她指着她那张路线图上的一个地方说。

"去那儿可是要开很长一段路啊。"

"我知道。"

"不过这么一趟至少能让你看看不同的风景。"

"我可没打算看什么不同的风景。我只想抵达那里。"

"你知道下了 M5 高速之后的路吗?"

"知道。"

"交叉路口的编号呢?"

"应该知道。"

他一言不发地看了她一会儿。她觉得他应该是不太相信自己说的。然后,他开口了:"你为什么不把后面的路线也写下来呢? 在高速公路上迷路可不好玩儿。"

他把手机拿得离脸近了些,微微眯起眼睛,慢慢念出了她需要知道的高速公路出口,还有在那之后的路线。他的声音不急不躁,只是有一点,他似乎有点担心自己会念错其中一条,耽误了她。他摇了摇头,就好像无法相信她将孤身一人开那么远的路,还是在一天里。"太远了。"他一直重复着这句话。

"谢谢。"他一念完,她就对他说,"很抱歉把你叫醒。"

"没关系。反正我也不该睡觉。"

她觉得他应该是在隔着口罩微笑,所以她也笑了。"你真是个好心人。"

"哈。"他把手插进裤兜里,转过身向窗外望去。她在小屋的一侧，他则在另一侧，但他们在窗玻璃上的倒影映衬着外面的黑暗，就像两个透明人，他那么高大，她却那么瘦小，顶着一头银发。"大多数人可没这么说过我。"

这句话来得猝不及防。她没想到面前的人如此直率。她挺想说些什么，让他感觉好点——她想成为这样的人，说完之后她就可以回到车上，不带丝毫失败感地按照他指的路继续前进。可她做不到。她想不出该说什么话。这是一个稍纵即逝的善意时刻。人们总是想象自己可以与他人建立联系，但事实并非如此。人与人的悲喜并不相通。没有可以让人一眼看穿的透明人。

莫琳噘起嘴。年轻人伤感地注视着黑暗中的什么，又或许什么都没看。沉默似乎要一直继续下去。她看着地板，视野中再次出现了他那双黑色的德比鞋。这是一双多么严肃的鞋，像是一个格外上进努力的人。

"好了，"他说，"我想你的问题应该解决了。"

"是的。"她说。

"怎么称呼？"

"弗莱夫人。"

"我叫兰尼。"

"兰尼，再见。"

"弗莱夫人，很高兴认识你。以后迷路了别再冲人嚷嚷了。还有，开车小心点。外面太冷了。"

"我要去看我们的儿子。"她说完便离开了，上了车，掉头回到了公路上。

02
世界的客人

The World's Guest

十年前，哈罗德没带莫琳，孤身一人出发。他离开家本是为了给生命走到尽头的朋友奎妮寄一封信，结果一时冲动，他决定步行 627 英里[1]去看她。一路上，他遇见了许多人。他连钱包都不带了，在野外过夜。这件事甚至登上了报纸，让他做了一阵子的名人。落单的莫琳也经历了一段旅程，但不是人们会聊起或者在路上买明信片往家里寄的那种旅程。她始终在家。这才是整件事的关键。哈罗德为了救一个曾与他共事的女人，步行穿过整个英格兰，莫琳却在家清洁厨房水槽。清洁完水槽后，她就上楼，对着他卧室的家具绕着圈喷出抛光剂。在完全无事可做的情况下，她还要尽可能让自己保持忙碌。她甚至开始洗已经洗过的衣物，只为了从中找到更多可洗的。还有一些日子——除了她自己，谁还会知道这些日子呢？——她早上醒来都不知道要如何起床。终于挣扎着爬下床后，她又会花上数小时的时间盯着待洗的衣物和水槽发呆。她问自己，这番擦洗的活儿做与不做没有丝毫

1　1 英里约合 1.61 千米。

区别的时候,做这些又有什么意义呢?她是如此孤独,不知道该看些什么、想些什么。她甚至不确定哈罗德还会不会回家。一种陌生而骇人的恐慌吞没了她。

可那都过去了。莫琳不想再提及那段时间。她知道,她那会儿的经历听上去挺可悲的,但其实不是那么回事。还有比那糟糕的事情呢。哈罗德结束了他走向奎妮的那段旅程。奎妮去世后,莫琳赶去陪伴他。在莫琳的照料下,他的身体状况慢慢恢复。莫琳为他做了他们刚结婚时他爱吃的各种饭菜,为他包扎脚上的水疱与伤口,这些事其他人都不知道。的确,他们一开始同床共枕时都有些害羞,因为毕竟他们已经习惯了分床睡。她依然记得他第一次叫她"甜心"时腼腆的样子,就好像她会当着他的面笑出来一样。她当然没有那么做。她很喜欢这种感觉。他们每天都会到码头散步,一边散步,他一边听她聊拾掇出新菜畦和重新装修房子的事。有时,人们会停下脚步来跟他握手,因为他们听说过他的事迹。遇上这种情况,她都不知该作何表情,甚至拿不准双手该往哪儿放,所以干脆稍稍站到一边等着,既为他感到骄傲,又为他如今能如此轻松自处而感到不知所措。现在,他七十五岁,她七十二岁,他们的婚姻到达了一个美好的新境界,像是只属于他们两个的私密小溪。隔三岔五,哈罗德就会收到曾经与他同行的女人——凯特——的明信片,但莫琳并不在意,他们继续过他们的日子。然后,五个月前,他们收到了关于奎妮的新消息。这个女人再次回到了他们的生活中。

前方出现了路灯,这说明兰尼给的路线完全正确。就这样,莫琳重新开上 A38 国道，然后驶过古坟一样的土方工程，并入了 M5 高速。东方已经不是全然一片黑暗了，藏青色的地平线镶上了粉色与金色的边儿，明亮的金星依然高高挂在天上。万物又开始看得出轮廓了，树木缭乱的线条渐渐清晰；至于那些黑影，她猜应该是架线塔。眼前涌现出越来越多的仓库。路边毫无生命迹象的小圆包可能是一只獾或麂子。沿着路边有一片片覆着冰的地面，它们仿佛一面面彩色玻璃，反射着新一天的曙光。在它们之外的地方，土地依然平坦、黯淡而空旷。莫琳想象着哈罗德在家熟睡的画面。过一会儿，他就会赤着脚悄声走进厨房，就像他每天早晨做的那样，然后打开后门，看看天。他可以一连好几个小时什么都不做，只是凝望天空。他连表都不戴，因为他不想知道时间。天气好的话，他会取出木手杖，因为他腿部的力量太弱，再也走不到那条路的尽头，更不用说去码头了。他会给菜畦浇水，然后痴迷地看着水在泥土之上形成的银色弧线；他还会和雷克斯支起国际跳棋的棋盘，随便聊聊；但他最爱干的还是坐在露台上看鸟。每当烦躁的情绪袭来，莫琳就会告诫自己，要以大局为重。至少这件事能让他开心，至少他是安全的。再有就是他的健康，至少他的身体没什么问题。这并不能说明他的头脑不清晰了，而是他有意地将不再需要的思绪从脑子里赶出去。

  莫琳打了左转向灯，换到了旁边的车道上。路上的车越来越多了。这让她倍加紧张，她开得太慢了，结果后面的大货车纷纷亮着大灯从她旁边呼啸而过，卷起沙砾。卡伦顿。蒂弗顿。布莱克当丘陵上大头针一般大小的威灵顿纪念碑。汤顿。之前有个住在汤顿的斯洛伐克女人帮过哈罗德,但几年前她联系哈罗德时说她要被驱逐出境了。哈罗德因为此事心情格外低落。雷克斯还组织当地人签请愿书来着,可惜最后也没什么用。不管怎么样,他拿到了整整三页看起来都一样的签名。"弗莱夫人,说到底,那女人不属于这里。"一位邻居对莫琳这么说。还有一位邻居说,他不是种族主义者,对当事人也没意见,可现在是时候顾好自己了。当然,那是在她还能不戴口罩逛商业街也不觉得羞愧的时候。

太阳升起来了,在冰封的大地上盛放,将一切都染成了天竺葵的红色,就连海鸥和车流也不例外。月亮还挂在天上,但已经淡得像粉笔画的幽灵了,它既不想坚定地留下,也不愿决绝地离开。在布里奇沃特,她经过了巨大的"柳条人"[1],它伸展着长长的鱼鳍般的双臂,做出大步流星地向南进发的姿态。一座混凝土大桥的桥底喷着反对疫苗接种的口号。新闻是假的,病毒也是假的。如今的英格兰已经不是哈罗德曾经徒步纵贯的英格兰了。有时,他会讲述那段时期他遇到的某个人的故事,或者描绘山那边的风景,她听着就像在闭着眼睛看电影一样,找不到合适的画面。现在是安全的高速公路和优步(Uber)的世界。这年头,人们都用手机支付,注意保持安全距离,更不用说新冒出来的播客、燕麦牛奶、植物肉,以及一切都在网上直播这个现实了。朝

---

[1] 位于英国西南小镇布里奇沃特附近的 M5 高速公路旁的一座巨型雕塑,高 12 米,臂展 5 米,创作者为英国雕塑家塞丽娜·德·拉·埃(Serena de la Hey)。

报春花盛开的河岸上望去,你十有八九会看见叶子中夹着一个蓝色旧口罩。十年前,她可无法想象现在发生的所有变化。

莫琳打开广播,里面正在播一则新闻报道,讲的是一个电影明星为了提升他在照片墙(Instagram)上的知名度,自导自演了一出仇恨犯罪的戏码。她关掉了广播。人们对这个世界有太多期待了。

我想做世界的客人。

她突然想到这句话。这是她儿子说过的话,不过她已经好多年没想起过了。说这话的时候他应该只有六岁。他仰头用那双深褐色的眼睛看着她,那双眼睛里似乎藏着她不曾了解的悲伤。

"你说这话是什么意思?"她问。

"我不知道。"

"你是想要一块饼干吗?"

"不是。"

"那你想要什么?派对?"

"我不喜欢派对。"

"可人人都喜欢派对啊。"

"我不喜欢。我不喜欢派对上的各种游戏。我只喜欢蛋糕和伴手礼。"

"那你是什么意思?"

"我不知道。"

她有种被刺穿了的感觉。关于戴维的一切都让她伤心——他严肃的凝视、缓慢的步伐,以及他和其他孩子保持距离的样子。

"你怎么不去玩儿呢?"她带他去公园时会这样说,"那几个孩子看着挺不错的。我敢说他们肯定愿意跟你玩儿。"

"不用了。谢谢。"他说,"我还是和你待在一起吧。我觉得他们不会喜欢我的。"

但她有种感觉,在那时就有,那就是他其实知道他所说的"做世界的客人"是什么意思。他只是在等她赶上。她总是在追赶这个孩子,直到现在都是这样。

莫琳突然觉得头晕,这感觉就跟晕船似的。她需要喝杯咖啡,再去趟洗手间。

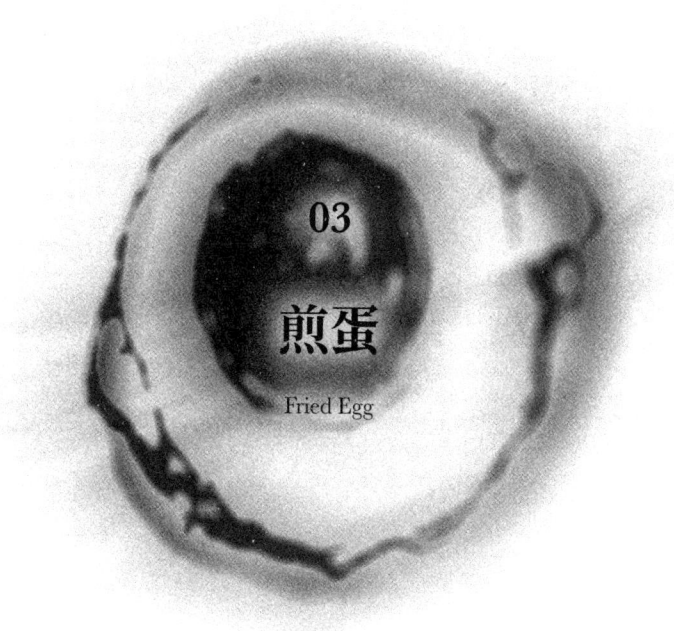

服务员说她可以用自带的杯子接咖啡喝，但她得去吧台买点儿吃的东西。莫琳问服务员能否就在餐桌前为她点餐，因为她已经坐下了。结果服务员说不可以。时间还早，服务站空空荡荡的，客人只有莫琳和用颤抖的手端起杯子的一个老人。在鲜食餐吧对面，一个戴着希贾布[1]的女人正在拖地，还有一个女人正在拉开店铺的百叶窗。

"在这儿和在柜台为我点餐有什么区别吗？"莫琳说，"给我菜单吧，我点份吃的。"

服务员说这里没有菜单，没有可以拿到她面前让她点菜的菜单。总而言之，这里不提供在桌边点餐的服务。服务员穿着一件松松垮垮的黑色上衣，前胸上有一只亮片穿的兔子。她的指尖有啃过的痕迹，头发油腻，整个人了无生气。她全身上下能跟快乐沾点关系的也就只有那只兔子了。

"真荒唐，"莫琳说，"你就站在我桌子旁边。为什么就不能

---

[1] 穆斯林妇女戴的把头发、耳朵和颈部完全遮住的头巾。

为我点餐呢？"

"我是在擦桌子。"服务员说着又用消毒喷雾喷了一下，以此来证明她的说法，"我只能在柜台为您点餐。这是新规定。"

莫琳只好跟随服务员去柜台。可到了那儿，她只能排在刚到的一个五口之家后面，他们正看着咖啡菜单点跟咖啡毫无关系的大杯饮料。等轮到莫琳点餐时，服务员念了一遍所有的早餐。在莫琳看来，她是在故意拖延。这里有酥皮点心、松饼、冰甜甜圈和三明治，和柜台下面展示的一样。她一个个指着看过去，发现这里还有全份英式早餐或无麸质的纯素食英式早餐，不过这些就得在厨房里做了。菜单上还有冬季温暖特惠套餐，但是已经售罄了。

"如果你们没有了，就该把它从菜单上去掉。"莫琳说。

"您到底想点什么？"

莫琳跟她说，自己肯定不想点全份英式早餐，因为那就太多了，吃不了。"我来个鸡蛋吧。"

"不要全份英式早餐？"

"对。"

"那您是否希望鸡蛋旁边有全份英式早餐？"

"不，"莫琳说，"我不希望我的盘子里有全份英式早餐。"

"好。"服务员拿起一个 iPad，"您想吃哪种鸡蛋？"

"水煮。"

"我们可以做煎蛋。"

"只能做煎蛋？"

"对。"

"如果你们只有煎蛋,那何苦要问我想怎么吃呢?"

"因为通常客人会说想要煎着吃。"

"你没开玩笑吧?"莫琳说。

"没开玩笑。"服务员说。

"好吧,我要煎蛋。"

"吐司呢?"

"你是不是要问我想吃哪种吐司,然后再告诉我你们只有白吐司?"

服务员的脖子上腾地泛起一片红,这片红马上就蔓延到了她的发际线。"不是。我们有全麦吐司。我们还有恰巴塔和无麸质吐司。"

"我要全麦的。别切得太厚。得好好烤一下,我不想要温热的面包。黄油放在旁边就行,我想自己抹黄油。"

服务员在 iPad 上记了些什么,似乎比写"煎蛋和吐司"花的时间长得多。她递给莫琳一把带编号的木勺,然后就拿着她点的单往厨房去了。莫琳拿着木勺坐回到桌旁。外面,六只海鸥停留在孩子的游乐场地上;一棵树的枝条上,一条长长的塑料胶带在风中扑打。这时,一个和莫琳年纪相仿的女人从餐吧的另一端走来,她身边还跟着一个推着婴儿车的年轻女子,应该是她的女儿。那女人朝莫琳点了点头,像是在打招呼,于是莫琳也朝对方点了点头,不过她没笑。年轻的女人抱出一个婴儿,把她举起来,莫琳看到她穿了一件粉色儿童防寒服,兜帽上装饰着一圈毛边。她们给孩子穿多了,莫琳想。年轻女子说让她妈妈帮忙抱着孩子,她去取咖啡。她妈妈说:"安排得不错啊,卢。"然后就接过婴儿,把她放到了腿上。莫琳看着她趁女儿不注意给孩子拉开了粉色防寒服的拉链,摘掉了兜帽。她看着那个女人把婴儿的头揽到嘴边,吻了吻。即使没凑到近前,莫琳也知道婴儿头上那股面包般香甜的味道,还有头发那绒毛般柔软的触感。有那么一会儿,她放任她把自己想象成这个带着外孙的女人,她能感到一股爱意从身体里倾泻而出。随之席卷她全身的就是痛苦,也可以说是一种嫉妒。她像是被注入了黑暗而难解的毒药。她能做的只有一动不动,默默忍受。她又回去了,再次被打回原点。她以为自己已经处理好了过去,可最近——即便过去了三十年——还是有那么几次,她因为最喜欢的人被夺走而恨透了这个世界。要是她能多跟哈罗德学学就好了,让过去的伤心事一点一点地真正过去,就好了。

"十三号桌?"服务员将她点的那盘早餐放在她面前,然后说,"小心安全。"

小心安全?莫琳想问这是什么意思。怎么个小心法?但她没问,而是看向盘子里的鸡蛋说:"这是什么?"

鸡蛋硬得像是用塑料做的,看上去跟笑话商店里卖的那种恶作剧煎蛋一样。吐司完全没有烤过的痕迹——看着甚至没有热过,而且黄油并没有放在旁边,而是厚厚地涂在吐司上。"不行,"她说,"这东西我可不吃。"

服务员低下头,油得连成一体的头发垂到了前面。她发出一种令人不悦的动静，像是打了一连串嗝儿。

"你还是把它端走吧。"莫琳说，"你可别指望我为这种东西买单。把钱退给我吧。"

她从自己的大杯里又倒出一小杯咖啡，揭开她带的三明治上的保鲜膜，吃了起来。服务员捏着盘子边儿，把它从莫琳面前端走，就好像莫琳是个危险人物似的，然后她把盘子端回了厨房。

没过一会儿，另一个女人走了出来。她径直走向莫琳桌前。她的年纪是那名服务员的两倍，头发剪成一绺一绺的，染成了不同色调的红色，精心描好的眉毛纹丝不动。

"听说您想要退款。"她把一堆零钱丢在桌上，其中连整镑的硬币都没有，只有现在已经没人用的小额硬币，比如五便士和其他金额的便士。她没有为鸡蛋的事道歉，而是说："我现在得请您离开了。"

"什么？"

"您不可以在本店食用自带食物。店里有告示。"说着她指向入口处的一个告示牌，它旁边还有一个告示牌，上面要求顾客遵守社交距离、佩戴口罩，并要始终礼貌对待店员。

"可那个服务员说我可以。"

"您太粗鲁了。"

"我没说什么啊。"

"我指的就是您说话的这种语气。那个可怜的姑娘刚才都被您说哭了。如果您想吃自带的食物，可以去店外吃。"

莫琳无言以对，只能静静地坐在那里。那个带着外孙女的女人和她的女儿都转过头看莫琳接下来怎么办,那个手抖的男人也在看她。"你当真要请我离开?"她终于张口说话了,声音尖锐而颤抖。她被刺痛了就会这样,一直如此,从她还是个孩子的时候就这样。她的父母很晚才有了她,而迟到的她无法让一段已经冷却的婚姻重新燃起热情。她的父亲很宠她,至于她的母亲,尽管她经常批评莫琳,但她决意让莫琳过上自己不曾有过的生活。

"哎呀,小莫琳,"她的父亲过去常常用湿润的双眼看着她骄傲地说,"这世界上就没有小莫琳干不成的事。"

那个红头发的女人直勾勾地盯着她。"对,"她说,"我就是在请您离开。"

莫琳用一张餐巾纸擦干净她的小杯子,将它扣到大杯子的杯口,拧好。她的手在抖,没法儿用保鲜膜将剩下的三明治重新包好;穿大衣的时候,她的胳膊好几次都伸不进袖子里。她离开服务站时,想着那个女人轻轻拢住婴儿的小脑袋的画面,想着自己永远都没有这样的机会了。她真不应该告诉戴维人人都喜欢派对,那真是一句蠢话。她就很讨厌派对,而且一向如此。你对孩子撒谎,只因为他们的忧愁你无法承受。

莫琳找了条路穿过停车场,只觉得自己单薄而脆弱,孤立无援。她站在寒风中,似乎所有的温暖善意都已经成为过去时。她努力宽慰自己,没关系的,但是她喉咙里像是堵了什么东西,就像有块咽不下去的芝士。她不会认输。她不会落泪。一只海鸥把一个麦当劳的袋子踩在黄色蹼足下,用喙撕扯了几下,然后衔着一根炸薯条飞走了。她想给哈罗德打电话,可如果她打了,就会吵醒他，他会从她的声音中听出悲伤，然后开始担心她。接着，她又突然想起了刚才那个餐吧里的人，他们惊骇地盯着她的样子围着她不断旋转，又一股羞愧像弹片一样打穿了她。

"莫琳，"她大声说，"别为已经发生的事纠结，莫琳。"

那个带着外孙女的女人肯定会接受那份煎蛋。她会微笑着对那个服务员说："亲爱的，谢谢你。"然后把那个塑料一样的玩意儿吃掉。

再开三百五十英里。这段旅程就能结束了。

04
人们的嘴
Human Mouths

"你知道我最想念什么吗?"

"不知道,"莫琳说,"我怎么会知道。"

"我最想念的是嘴!人们的嘴!"

"不是吧。"莫琳说。太阳依然很低,但阳光很足,薄雾齐刷刷地向同一个方向升腾,消失在清冷的空气中。路边的树木像是画笔勾勒出的根根银线,阳光在树枝间跳跃,像辐条一样频频刺出。前方,车流载着菱形的光斑,大地铺展开来,闪闪发亮,呈现出冰冻的白色。莫琳翻下遮阳板。阳光让她头疼。

"熬了几个月,还要再熬几个月,口罩戴起来就摘不掉了!你是知道的,我就是讨厌看不见人们的嘴!"

"我明白你的意思。"另一个人说,这个声音听起来比刚才那个年长些,也更沉稳。莫琳脑海中浮现出一个头发花白的女人,还有那种可以修饰身材的亚麻直筒连衣裙;第一个说话的人应该更苗条,金发还没变白。她说的每句话都像是以感叹号结尾的。

她又感叹了一句:"人们常说可以根据眼睛判断一个人的情绪!但事实并非如此!"

"你说得没错。"花白头发说,"我以前没那么想过,但现在听你这么一说,我就明白你的意思了。"

"暴露一个人心情的其实是嘴!"

"是啊,你说得太对了。"

"你知道我发现了什么吗?我发现我特别想拥抱别人!我看见他们为各自的生活忙碌着,我就想拥抱他们!拥抱跟我完全不认识的陌生人!"

"说到点子上了。"花白头发说,"非要说这场疫情让我们懂得了什么,那就是人们是善良的。我们会感觉到来自陌生人的善意。正是这一点使得我们能够继续……"

莫琳朝收音机伸出手。"哼,全都是废话。"说着,她把广播关了。

莫琳不是个好相处的人。她很清楚这一点。她不怎么招人喜欢,也不善于交朋友。她曾加入过一个读书小组,但她很反感那些人读的书,所以最后干脆不去了。她和别人交往从来都需要有人来当桥梁,那个人就是她的儿子。要是他还活着,今年就五十岁了。

三十年前他自杀后,她悲痛欲绝,甚至以为自己会伤心得死掉。真的,她至今不明白自己当初怎么会没死。她想让时间停下来,让生活陷入瘫痪,但是事与愿违,她每天还是要照常起床,面对儿子的卧室,面对他以前在厨房坐的椅子,还要面对将永远挂在那儿的儿子那件超大的外套。更残忍的是,她不得不出门面对那些身边有孩子的女人、嗑药嗑得正嗨或者醉醺醺的年轻小伙子,她从他们身边经过时必须忍住尖叫。身上背着如此难以承受的重担,心里藏着几乎要把她生吞的难以置信的愤怒,她该怎么做?她收到过几张吊唁卡——对于您痛失至亲,我们深表遗憾;致以最深切的哀悼——卡片上画着一朵白色的百合,字是华丽的金色斜体浮雕字。哈罗德从这些卡片中找到了些许慰藉。他还把它们放到壁炉架上,想让莫琳也从中得到慰藉。但莫琳鄙夷地瞪着卡片上的字,只觉得这些话都毫无道理,就像她每天照常入睡也是件没道理的事一样。她盯着这些话的时间越长,就越觉得这些卡片是在谴责她——就好像他们没真的说出那种话,但也一定认为她应该受到谴责。最后,她把那些卡片剪成了上百张参差不齐的碎片,结果她却并没有因此感觉好一点。于是,她又用同一把剪刀剪掉了自己美丽的褐色长发。哦,她气坏了。简直是暴跳如雷。她都认不出自己了。她变成了另一个人,一个失去了儿子的狂怒的母亲,人们瞥到的网纱窗帘后的朦胧身影。她原本规划好的未来成了泡影。那段日子里,她像个幽灵一样,什么都做不了,只能眼睁睁看着那个取代了她并且恨着她的人继续过活。她都不知道自己当初是怎么挨过来的。她只想要她的儿子,只想见到戴维。

"想要我丈夫的话就把他带走吧。"她对奎妮说。那是在葬礼结束几周后,奎妮来探望他们时她说的。哈罗德过去常常跟她讲起奎妮在工作中的事——他们似乎有着相同的幽默感,有时候她还会在车里闻见奎妮的气味,那是一种混合着紫罗兰和廉价香水的味道。尽管如此,那却是她们第一次见面,也是唯一的一次。奎妮看见莫琳正在花园里晾衣服,便沿着小径向她走去。奎妮递给她一束花。她却把花直接放进了洗衣篮里。"但如果你不想要他,"她对奎妮说,"那就从我们的生活中消失吧。"她们两个站在晾衣绳的两边,莫琳继续把洗干净的T恤一件件地搭在上面,那是她儿子永远不会再穿的T恤。奎妮擦着眼泪。"你怎么还没走?"莫琳喊道。

因为悲伤,她说了最不堪的话。奎妮是哈罗德的朋友。她绝不会夺走他。可那段时间,莫琳不在乎把谁惹生气了。她想让别人难过。她想把别人推得越远越好,可以的话,赶到地球的另一端去才好。就连哈罗德也不例外。"你算什么男人?"她斥责他,"你算什么父亲?都是你的错!我看都不想看你一眼!"

直到哈罗德那趟远行之后,莫琳才终于能表示歉意。"原谅我。"她说。他抓起她的一只手,攥了一会儿,就好像他从来没有握过这么珍贵的东西。然后他说:"哦,莫,我永远不会怪你。你也原谅我吧。"她以为这回他们终于能鼓起勇气,聊聊戴维和他们搞砸的那些事了。还有那些影影幢幢、半遮半掩、她想提却不知道怎么措辞的事。可哈罗德结束那段旅程后歇了数周,乃至数月,好久都没歇过来,所以那些话题他们压根儿就没聊起。在她的印象里,他似乎释放了心中的郁结,又像是获得了赦免,而她——哪儿都没去的她——则陷入了困境,孤立无援。于是,她重拾园艺,因为他以前就爱看她在花园莳花弄草,几乎像他对她的褐色长发一样喜爱。她用带图案的墙纸重新装饰了起居室,换掉了厨房的亚麻油毡地面。她新挑了一种颜色粉刷卧室,还做了跟床罩配套的窗帘。她甚至清空了戴维的房间,把他的东西用包装纸一件件包起来,放进纸箱,准备之后堆到阁楼上。但她仍然在身体里为儿子留了一个空间。毕竟,那是他的故乡。她身体里的那个小篓子。

滨海韦斯顿。克利夫登。清晨的天空呈现出温柔的蓝色,这蓝色在地平线上逐渐褪为奶白色,冰冻的大地伴着溢出的白色天光起起伏伏。海鸥时而盘旋,时而摇摆,发出刺耳的尖叫。海鸥的数量惊人,它们在空中形成一道道支离破碎、纵横交错的线。在比它们更高的地方,一道道蒸气尾迹划过天空。一排树上倒挂着的成簇的槲寄生,像是一个个超大号手提包。在离布里斯托尔越来越近时,她驶上了一段建在高架桥柱上的高速公路,公路下方是森林与谷地。她跨过埃文河,远眺波尔特布里码头,看到那片地方停着成百上千辆车,车顶在阳光下闪闪发亮。远处是塞文河口高大的起重机和班轮。莫琳在另一个服务站停下,不过这回她只是为了接水和上厕所。这里的卫生间不如以前干净,她不得不在马桶圈上垫了一层纸。事后,她非常仔细地洗了手。

一个满大衣都是硕大花朵图案的女人边哭边说:"我不知道我为什么要操这份心。我不明白我怎么总是重蹈覆辙。"她的朋友抱着她安慰道:"你的问题在于你是个圣徒。你最大的敌人就是你自己。"说着她从自动出纸机中拽出几张纸巾递给她哭泣的朋友。莫琳设法绕过她们,因为她们挡在了她和烘手机之间。

"你的母亲是个圣徒。"莫琳的父亲常常这样说,"我说她是个圣徒，是因为她特别能容忍我。"每当听到他这么讲，莫琳就暗暗希望他别说这话，因为这让他显得年纪很大，像是要破罐子破摔。

服务站人来人往，到处都是举家出行的人，因此哪里都能看见乱跑的孩子。她中途有两次不得不停下脚步。一个穿着印有"用餐区主理人"字样T恤的男人正在回收放着剩饭的托盘，一次只收一个，然后步履维艰地端着托盘往中央一处被屏风遮挡着的区域走去。莫琳不知道这个词是什么时候冒出来的。她不明白，为什么"主理人"就比"清洁工"这个词来得高级。她经过一台幸运币街机和一个卡卡圈坊的柜台，柜台旁摆着一排大大的灰色塑料扶手椅，就是那种你投币就可以享受按摩的设施。一个老头儿在那排椅子上蜷着脚睡觉，把口罩当眼罩遮住了眼睛。莫琳第一次戴口罩的时候特别难受，因为她感觉脸就像被压扁了。但很快她就习惯了。她喜欢在人群中保持低调，喜欢大家都客客气气地保持距离。毕竟，她从来不是个喜欢以拥抱传达问候的人。她甚至不喜欢别人直接叫她的名字——这是除了他们选的书是垃圾外，她不喜欢那个读书小组的又一个原因。一举办活动，大家就满场黛博拉、爱丽丝地叫着，好像彼此有多熟似的。因此，如果余生都得戴着口罩莫琳也不在意，因为她觉得这并非世界上最糟糕的事。

"有兴趣买本书吗？"一个女人说，她面前摆着满满一桌子二手平装书。这是个帮助英雄慈善基金会筹款的书摊。

"我没兴趣。"莫琳说。她甚至都没有停下来扫一眼。谁也不知道她停下来会有什么发现。眼下心里七上八下的感觉已经够难受的了。

她走进商店,拿了一瓶水。地上的脚丫形蓝箭头指示顾客排成一纵列,莫琳照做了,不过向她走来的那对穿着有动物印花抓绒卫衣的情侣却没有照做。她只好给他们让路,他们却连声谢谢都没说。"好吧,那我谢谢你们。"她说,声音几不可闻。

这里的告示牌更多了,有的提醒大家保持社交距离,有的提示杀菌洗手液的位置。地板上还有斑斑点点的洗手啫喱。可到现在为止,还没有什么事让她想到处拥抱她完全不认识的陌生人,或者对人类有更深的理解。她买了瓶装水、一本填字游戏杂志。没人问她要去哪儿,也没人问她一路上开不开心。

这儿的收银员长着美丽修长的手指,涂着绿色的指甲油,胸牌上写着"月光"。

"是否需要我介绍一下我们的特惠活动?"

"那得看是什么了。"莫琳说。

"车用空气清新剂买二赠一。"月光指着货架上的样品说。

"可我只有一辆车。"莫琳说。空气清新剂让她有点迷糊。清新剂的包装上画着一堆霓虹色的热带水果,有菠萝和各种瓜,它们全都戴着墨镜。

"但价格很划算。就算你丢了一罐清新剂,到时候车上还有两罐。"

"可如果我有三罐清新剂,那就说明我弄丢一罐也无妨。如果有什么东西弄丢了也无妨,那我肯定会弄丢。"

"买不买由你。我只是跟你说说店里的优惠。你不必非得买。"莫琳还没转身离开,收银员就翻了个白眼,把目光投向了队伍中排在她身后的四个年轻姑娘。

哈罗德在旅途中收获了不少善意,或者说他激发了人们心中的爱。可莫琳的情况就不同了。"真是个难相处的孩子。"母亲这样说过她。现在她回想起来,那句话依然字字清晰,她甚至能看到母亲穿着那双有三条带子的漆皮鞋。因为外面有泥,她总是擦那双鞋。她还记得母亲的味道,恒久不变的味道,总是让人联想到最渴望拥有和最难以捉摸的一切。她的母亲曾经很漂亮,很有气场。她家世好——这一点她很喜欢拿出来说,但她丈夫身体不好,又没什么钱,所以后来他们家不得已搬去了乡下。她母亲讨厌乡下的一切,不管是那里的气味、尘土,还是闭塞。他们请不起帮佣,这让她十分窘迫。她手拿拖把,一字一顿地说:"你以为房子会把自己打扫干净吗?"那口气就好像她和拖把之间有私人恩怨一样。莫琳看着她,暗暗发誓,我永远不要成为那样的人。她还是更像父亲。

然而,这些天当她看到自己在镜中的模样时,倒是微微吃了一惊。虽然莫琳现在是白色的短发,但她的嘴巴和下巴分明和母亲一样。就连她昂着头的样子也和母亲如出一辙。基因摆在那儿,你以为自己跟父母的样子会有多大差别?莫琳看着镜子,她仿佛看到母亲的幽灵正在镜中盯着自己。

上午过去了一半,她驶过了斯特劳德的路标,接着又先后经过了格洛斯特和切尔滕纳姆的牌子。科茨沃尔德丘陵地带就在她的右手边，仿佛灰蓝色的肩膀。她还从一辆坏掉的重型货车旁边经过，看到它的驾驶室向前弯折，就像一截断掉的脖子。天开始没那么晴朗了。前方堆起大片云层，空气中弥漫着冰冷的气息，太阳尚未照到的紧急停车带上依然结着深色的冰。起雾了。一辆长途客车驶到了她的前方，车窗上插着英格兰国旗，车上的球迷也挥着国旗。她超过了一个货车车队，这些货车运送的是现成的预制房屋，每个小房子的窗户上都有网纱窗帘。她还超了另一个女人的车，那辆车里的垃圾袋堆到了车的内顶。在她即将到达M42高速时，雾已经非常浓了，她都能看到雾气在挡风玻璃前摇曳，像是一颗颗小糖粒。现在，她眼前唯一的颜色就是前方车辆尾灯那抹模糊的红。路边被风吹折的树好像是从水里长出来的。整个世界变成了由路与泥滩组成的一片古怪空旷之地，在这里，任意两个事物之间都没有联系，它们先是消融，而后凝固。由此她想到，可能她的思想也是如此，脑子里总有一系列永远也拼不到一起的拼图块。

注意：M42高速已关闭。莫琳只得退回到当前这条路上。高速公路上方闪过一个指示牌，橘色的字在雾中转瞬即逝。前方排队。她又开了几英里，努力将注意力集中到路面上，但她感觉自己好像开进了一片虚无，精神总是集中不起来。她再次出神，开始想戴维和他在火葬场的墓碑，她每个月都会去看看，拿一块布擦拭它。至于墓碑周围那圈绿色的小石头，她会用一把手掌大小的耙子将它们整平。其他人并不收拾小石头，所以它们总会跑到戴维的墓碑旁，于是莫琳还得清理那些石头。她想到了一个浓妆艳抹的胖女人，最近莫琳刚刚跟她打过交道，因为她那块墓碑周围的石子儿跑得哪儿都是，骨灰瓮也锈得很严重。莫琳建议她好好打理那块地方，还说这应该不是一件难事。可那女人却告诫莫琳少他妈的管闲事。一时失措，莫琳表示，如果那女人饮食健康一些，火气就不会这么大了。她真的说了这句话。从她嘴里冒出来的正是这句话。上一秒，这句话还好好地待在她的脑袋里，虽说的确挺冒犯人的，但似乎也没那么过分——因为那女人确实胖，这一点毋庸置疑，她有好几层下巴，每一层都盖着可怕的厚重的粉；下一秒，这些话就像大幅海报一样在风中呼啦作响了。虽然莫琳意识到她说错了话，但她意识到得太晚了。那女人逼上前来，近到莫琳都能看见她皮肤上被堵塞的橘色毛孔和紫色眼影覆盖的褶子。她大喊莫琳是个该死的疯婊子。所以，现在她再去火葬场，没法只想戴维，还要想着那个化浓妆的胖女人，但愿不会碰上她。在她看来，那里被彻底污染了，和几年前商业街上的那家书店一样被污染了。要是继续如此，这世上就剩不下几个她能安心去的地方了。

为了让自己不再胡思乱想，莫琳哼起了歌。开车就这点不好。她脑袋里可以用来想事的空闲太多了。她得手上忙起来，脑子里才能消停点儿。她希望哈罗德能用得了洗碗机，希望他能找得到咖啡和杯子。她真应该在厨房里贴上便利贴。到下一个服务站时，她就得给家里打个电话。另外，她还需要再上一次厕所。她现在满脑子只有上厕所这一个念头，她真的很着急。事实上，她越想就越难受。烧灼感给她带来了不适的压力。她不能再想这事了。她决定开始想哈罗德，想他背上光滑如旧的肌肤，想她第一次看到他赤裸的身体时的情形，当时她很想要他，却竟然因此不敢碰触他。她都没怎么见过自己的父母接吻。前方的路向左拐去，莫琳一直迷迷糊糊地跟着前方的红色尾灯开车，她的心思都在哈罗德身上，后来她才意识到情况不妙——前面的尾灯不动了，而她还在往前开。她的车逐渐向那些尾灯靠近，那些尾灯却丝毫未动。

她踩下刹车。车没有任何反应。她又使劲儿往下一踩，但踩偏了，脚没落到刹车踏板上。车继续前进。她用力压下脚，可这次动作太快了，导致车似乎失去了牵引力，不但没有停下，还突然向左转去。然后，尽管她做了各种尝试，她的车还是非常缓慢地以错误的角度朝着紧急停车带挪过去。有那么一会儿，她都记不起怎么让车停下了，甚至连应该踩哪个踏板都不清楚。她只知道车失控了，她正在滑向公路护栏，而且她周围全都是车，没一辆在动。除此之外，她面前还有一堵雾墙。总之，无论她怎么转动方向盘，猛踩刹车，都没什么效果。

一个奇怪的时刻降临了，她一动不动，几乎是欣然地意识到，她极力阻止的事情已经发生了。此时，除了静静地坐着，看看接下来会发生什么，她什么也做不了。她真的非常需要去趟洗手间。

05

海上花园

Sea Garden

奎妮在她位于恩布尔顿湾的家中建了一座海上花园。因为人们喜欢把东西留在那儿,现在当地人管那儿叫"遗物花园"。不过,我最近才听说,她设计了一个物件纪念你的儿子。我觉得你应该想知道这个消息。爱你,凯特。吻你。

事情缘于他们在夏天收到的一张明信片。哈罗德大声读出了卡片上的内容,然后他们就各自忙上午的事了。莫琳给草莓地除草,他则坐着晒太阳。不过,莫琳的心思总是回到那张明信片上。"我都不知道奎妮有这么一座花园。"她想这样跟哈罗德聊起,尽量避免声音变得尖锐。他应该会微微一笑,说他也不知道。其实那不过是一座花园,一座距离他们四百五十英里远的花园。就算那里有个纪念戴维的物件,那又如何?奎妮和哈罗德共事了那么多年,他们一定聊起过戴维。可是,想到这儿,那座花园给她带来的不适渐渐明显,就像没有及时处理的、扎在肉里的小碎片。奎妮为什么要纪念戴维?她有什么权利做这件事？那个用来纪念他的物件是什么？奎妮认识戴维吗？莫琳不管是在晾衣服，还是在菜畦里耙地，总是想到这些问题。刷牙的时候，给哈罗德做早餐的时候，还有夜里躺在哈罗德身边，他睡着了，她却醒着的时候，这些疑问都萦绕在她心头。时间一天天过去，白昼变得越来越短，树叶都变了颜色，但她脑子里那些事没变。她还是惦记着那座花园，想起它的频率越来越高。聊或不聊，那座花园都在，既坐落在恩布尔顿湾，又压在她的心上。

"你真不知道奎妮的花园吗？"一天，用过晚餐后，她问哈罗德，"就是凯特在寄给你的明信片上说的那座。"现在已经是秋天了。她想用一种随意的姿态问这个问题，就好像这是她刚刚想到的事情。

"奎妮的花园？我不清楚。应该不知道。"

"可她是个园艺爱好者，不是吗？"

"我不记得她是什么园艺爱好者。我们从来没聊过园艺的话题。至少凭我的印象，我们没聊过。"

"那为什么她会在花园里纪念戴维？奎妮认识戴维？我怎么不知道她认识他？"

她不耐烦的语气暴露了她的心思。她问得太多、太急了，哈罗德面露难色，就好像他疑心自己做过什么理应记得的可怕的事，可他就是想不起来。"天哪！"他说，"天哪！"他用手掌根轻触脑袋，然后又轻轻敲了敲，试图唤起某段记忆。"我会想起来的，我会想起来的，给我一点时间。"但他到最后也没想起来。

她端起晚餐的盘子,将他的剩饭倒在她盘里的剩饭上面。然后她把这些盘子拿到水槽里,用热水冲洗。

"莫琳,需要我帮忙吗?"

"不用。你坐着就行。"她本不打算这样聊的,这一招实在不高明。哈罗德走到她身后,双臂环住她的腰,把下巴搁在她的肩膀上。他累了,她能感觉出来。她又提了关于戴维的话题,这就是她对他做的事。

他柔声说:"这是很久以前的事了,你知道的。"

"我知道。"

"那座花园没什么可担心的。"

"我知道。"

"我们过得很开心。"

"是的。"

"那我们不要操心了。"

"好,哈罗德,听你的。"

他吻了她,话题就此终结。她虽然答应了,但还是做不到。她就是操心。而且,他不想操心这件事让她加倍操心——就好像她还得把他该操的心扛到自己身上。奎妮去世后,疗养院的院长将奎妮的信寄来,她也是这样操心的。哈罗德也不想为那封信操心,倒是莫琳仔仔细细地读过那封信,想搞懂字不成字、句不成句,只有破折号和弯弯曲曲的线条的那封手写信里写了什么,想知道奎妮迫切想跟他说的都有什么事,想试着了解哈罗德不愿知道的事。最后,她把信折好,放进一个鞋盒,然后把鞋盒和戴维的东西都放到了阁楼上。可她现在老了，老到无法再这么做了。他们都老了。她不想前尘往事再次翻涌起来。可已经晚了。幽灵已经进入了房间。

莫琳独自在电脑上搜索了那座花园的照片。她震惊了。有很多人去参观过，都是她不认识的人。这些人有的在那儿自拍，有的照全家福，还有的用广角镜头拍摄了颇有艺术气息的照片。那么，他们一定看到过奎妮为纪念戴维设计的那样东西。他们都见过，莫琳却没有。它在哪儿？是什么样子？是他的一幅画像？还是更现代的东西？她找啊找啊，把照片放大了找，可哪儿都没找到。她没找到一件看着跟她的儿子有半点关系的东西。

事实上，她不仅没找到代表戴维的东西，还对那座花园大感迷惑。花园似乎连道栅栏都没有，就直接出现在沙丘上。那里有一片片碎石滩，上面点缀着用小石头和花摆出来的圆圈，各种形状的金属雕塑——漏斗形、管道形、螺旋形、纺锤形和旋涡形。那里还有若干浮木，有的跟木勺一般大小，有的却和柱子一样高，其中最显眼的是位于中央的一根巨大的木料。那里有一些挺奇怪的雕塑，制作材料五花八门，包括塑料瓶、雨水槽、马口铁罐头、旧家具、绳索和刷子——总之就是莫琳不假思索就能扔掉的东西。此外，那里竟然立着几根柱子，柱顶是经风雨而褪为白色的动物头骨。她看着这一切，就像隔着一扇怎么也擦不干净的、蒙着水汽的窗户凝视着生活。用海草做的旗帜与软木浮子或是挂在树枝间，或是像项链似的挂在单独的某样东西上。那里有系着丝带的枝丫,轮廓鲜明堪比铁艺品的种子头[1],还有喷泉大小的片片草地。到了夏天,所有这些都会被金雀花的黄色、金盏花的橙色和罂粟花的红色等斑斑点点鲜艳的色彩映衬得更加突出。(你能看出有的照片是夏天拍的,因为里面的天空是蓝色的,参观花园的人都戴着太阳镜,穿着T恤。)在有的照片里,花园中亮起数以百计的小蜡烛,蜡烛后面立着一座油漆斑驳、屋顶坍塌的老木屋。

冬天到了。哈罗德和莫琳继续过着他们的日子。虽说他们同桌吃饭,同床共枕,但他们再一次分属于不同的活动圈子。哈罗德喜欢观鸟,和雷克斯玩国际跳棋;莫琳则成日守着电脑,在网上搜索奎妮的花园,并且越看越恼火。此外,在莫琳看来,花园就是花园。它是用来种东西吃的。你可以种芜菁、甘蓝、洋葱、土豆、菠菜和水果,可以把它们冻起来,或者装到瓶子里,方便你冬天吃。花园不是用来放垃圾、木头和破铜烂铁的。她如此关注那座花园并非只是因为那里有戴维,更重要的是,他成了花园的一部分,莫琳却被这个世界排除在外。她认为这种感觉就像又看了一遍那些吊唁卡。后来,她做了个噩梦,醒后依然深感不安。因此,她下楼把家里的每一盏灯都打开了,就这样一直等到天亮,哈罗德醒来。

"莫,甜心,发生了什么事?"他伸出双臂搂住她。她把头靠在他的肩膀上,开始给他讲她的梦。

---

[1] 某些植物在开花或结果后发育的含有种子的部分。

梦里，她在挖一片菜地，结果发现戴维孤零零地埋在地下。不过，她没有提从他嘴里和耳朵里涌出的蛆虫，也没有提他的脸腐烂到像一层黑色烂树叶。即使过了这么久，她还是无法忍受说关于他们唯一的儿子的那些话。最好还是把这些不堪的画面藏在心里。

"对不起，我做不到像你一样，哈罗德。我忍不住一直想奎妮的花园。"她讲了她在网上看到的所有她无法理解的照片。

这时，他露出了那种能让她稍稍放松的微笑，并告诉她，他错了。她得去亲眼看看才行。

"哦，不要。"她赶紧说。她站起来，将几样东西摆正，一只手贴在椅子上抹了几下，查看并不存在的灰尘。"不，不。没有必要。不，不。太远了。谁来照顾你？不，不。我只是说说而已。如此而已。"

"当然，你说得对。这是一段很长的路。但你为什么不考虑一下呢？你可以花上几天的时间去看看。凯特是个善良的女人。她住在大约二十英里外。你至少可以在她那儿住一晚。"

"哦，不，不，我不想那么做。我不想和凯特一起住。我跟她又不熟。她是你的朋友，不是我的。"

她说了很多她不能去的原因。不只是距离问题。家里离不开她，洗洗涮涮等家务活儿都得靠她。她甚至想着把旧的粉色卫浴套装换成颜色更中性的套装。实话是，虽然她从未见过凯特，但她有点怕凯特，就跟她害怕奎妮的花园一样。凯特快六十岁了，算是个激进分子。和哈罗德一起徒步之后，她决定再给自己的婚姻一次机会,但那段婚姻还是结束了,现在她独自生活。莫琳只知道这些。在哈罗德遇见的许多人中,他最关心的就是凯特,这也是莫琳一想到她就没有安全感的一个原因。莫琳甚至不确定自己知不知道该跟一个激进分子聊什么。

可她把自己逼到了绝境。一如既往地,她单枪匹马就把事情做到了这个地步。最后,她不得不同意哈罗德的建议。他说得没错。是的,她要去看看那座花园,但她决定开车前往,而且要在一天之内赶到目的地。雷克斯答应在她离开期间照顾哈罗德,不过莫琳私下里觉得他并不靠谱,因为以哈罗德的健忘和雷克斯的心肠,他俩更像是两个小男孩手牵手。

"我就不去拜访凯特了。我可不想让别人知道我这次出行。你和雷克斯需要什么的话,我可以在网上给你们下单。另外,我还要演示给你看怎么使用洗碗机。操作并不难,只要记清该按哪几个按钮就行。我会在便利贴上写明白……"

这回他笑了。"就算我们俩再笨,洗几个盘子和碗总不成问题。"

她还是写了洗碗机的使用说明,而且在恩布尔顿附近找到了一家名叫"棕榈树"的不错的家庭旅馆,这个旅馆可以在傍晚时分提供一顿饭。她订了两晚。她准备第一天就去那儿住下,第二天上午去参观花园,第三天一早就动身回家。她给哈罗德和雷克斯做了好多顿饭,冰箱里都快放不下了。只要她一直忙碌,就会有较强的掌控感。前一天晚上,她收拾了几样要带的必需品,然后将她最合身的那件蓝色衬衫压到跟剪纸一样薄;哈罗德找到一把钢丝刷,帮她刷了开车穿的鞋子。一个想法掠过,她觉得自己像是在准备盔甲,尽管没人要上战场。那只是一座有几根浮木的花园,没什么大不了。

他向她露出微笑,也许他猜到了她在想什么,因为他说:"没关系。没什么好害怕的。"

"我知道。"

但后来等他睡着了,手从她的手中松开,整齐地放在胸口,她就在一旁看着他,听他发出规律的呼吸声——她羡慕这给他带来的平静。她想,他是个勇敢的人,完整的人。我不是。

06
事故中的意外

Accident-Accident

行至塔姆沃思,雾气分外浓重,几码之外的东西她都看不清了。树木浅淡的轮廓缓缓揉进空气,树枝上栖息的乌鸦仿佛一个个巨大的黑色树芽。这里看不到地平线,也看不到天空。你可能会感觉这里——M42高速公路上的一个服务站——是世界上仅存的地方。莫琳在停车场一换好衣服,就给哈罗德打了一通电话。那辆长途客车上载的球迷从入口处四散涌出,一个个把旗子举过头顶,唱着:"英——格——兰!英——格——兰!"

哈罗德说:"事故?你说出了事故是什么意思?你受伤了吗?发生了什么?"

"没事。车没事。保险杠上连个凹痕都没有。"空气好似一卷潮湿的绷带,围着她缠来绕去。

"我不关心车怎么样了,我一点都不关心车。"

"好吧,那是因为你不再开车了。"她说。

他发出了轻柔细微的咯咯声。她知道,那是他在笑。"不,莫琳。才不是这个原因呢!车不是我的妻子,你才是。车就只是车而已。"

"总之，我只想说我没事。哪儿都没受伤。"她用一种她不喜欢的轻快的声音说道，但她不忍心告诉他当时停下的另一辆车或者下车帮助她的那个年轻男子。这时，她听到高速公路上飘来警笛声，隔着雾气看到那边有蓝灯闪烁，警车和救护车向北驶去。"现在，他们彻底把 M42 高速公路关闭了。那里出了事故。"

"还有一起事故？"

"是的。和我的事故不一样。我只是遇上了一片黑冰，车子溜到了紧急停车带上。另一起事故出事的是一辆卡车。我绕了一段路才到服务站。"

"太倒霉了。"

"可能要再等一个小时。也许更久。我说不准。"她紧紧握着手机，她不想让他挂电话，起码现在不想。可她又不知道该怎么跟他说。她脑海中不知怎的突然浮现出一个画面：一次，哈罗德走在一条杂草丛生的小路上，他把黑莓丛多刺的枝条向后扎起，以防过路的人被划伤。哈罗德就是这样一个人。她有点想哭，但她还是忍住了。"雷克斯怎么样？"她说，"他和你在一起吗？"

"是的，雷克斯在这儿呢。我们在下跳棋。"

"莫琳，你好啊！"

"问问他吃药了吗？"

"莫琳问你有没有吃药。"

"吃了，莫琳！"

"你们有没有好好吃饭？"

"好好吃了。"

"别只吃三明治。"

"知道啦。"

这时出现了一阵沉默,时间感觉比实际的还要长。

哈罗德慢慢地说:"莫琳,你还好吗?"

"当然好了。我只是受了点儿惊吓,其他什么事都没有。"

"你确定吗?"

"我确定。"

"你确定就好。不管什么时候你需要我,我都在。"

"我也是,莫琳!"

"谢谢,"她说,"也替我跟雷克斯说声谢谢。"

"我们知道你一定可以的。"

"莫琳,你一定可以的!"

"开车千万要小心。"

"我会的。别忘了吃饭。"

"我们不会忘的。"

"跟我保证:不能一天只吃三明治。只吃三明治是不够的。那种东西可不是像样的饭。"

他说好。他保证道:"一定不会只吃三明治,我们会好好吃饭。"

*

接下来是她没告诉他的事。事实上,她说不出口。关于停下车来帮助她的那个年轻男子的善意。那份善意让一切都变得糟糕了一百倍。因为当时她的车头笔直地撞在紧急停车带的护栏上，她被吓蒙了，但并没受伤，也不觉得有什么丢人的。然后后面有辆车停下来了，一个年轻男子跳下车。他打手势示意她把车窗摇下，并俯身问她是否需要救护车。惊魂未定，她不知怎的竟然还注意到他没穿外套，但看起来干净利落，刮了胡子，所以有着柔软的粉红色下巴；另外，他头发中间有着笔直的分缝，套衫是熨过的——这正是母亲曾经希望莫琳嫁的那种年轻人。她反复告知对方，她没事，可他就是不肯离开。他就是一心想帮忙。突然，她就只剩下了那种膀胱紧绷的感觉。

"你可能是吓坏了。"他说，"用不用我帮你给谁打电话？你确定你的腿能动？"

"我要上厕所。"她用她最标准的讲电话的声音说道。

"什么？能再说一遍吗？"

太迟了。她已经尿了。就在这位没穿外套、干净和善的年轻男子面前，她尿到了裤子上。她原本只是想动一下腿，让他满意，结果一切就这样发生了。她的身体先是不自觉地松弛下来，给她带来了短暂的愉快，随之而来的便是大腿间一股可怕的暖流。车流又动了起来，只不过动得很慢，莫琳不得不倒回到等待的队列中。与此同时，那个男子坐在她后面的车里，非常清楚她刚才是什么情况，而她还得坐在湿答答的车座上，在这缓慢行进的车流中开上二十英里。她觉得很恶心。她大声地说："莫琳·弗莱，你可真恶心。"后来，她带着从行李箱中拿出的东西，用手提包挡在自己身前,走进了服务站。她径直走进洗手间,拽出一些纸巾,将其浸了水,这才把自己锁在一个隔间里。

"噗——那个老太太可真臭。"她听见一个孩子说。

她要死了。她简直要羞愧死了。她等别人用完烘手机离开后,才把那条湿透了的内裤塞进那种装用过的卫生巾的袋子,扔进了垃圾桶。此时,她已经换上了本该明天穿的内裤和休闲裤。刚才在狭小的隔间里换衣服的时候,她始终努力保持平衡,尽力不让衣物掉到瓷砖地上,因为地上也是湿漉漉的。与此同时,她发现这里到处贴着经期防渗漏内裤的广告海报。哦,这个世界真是没有道理可讲。她扬着下巴走出了卫生间,但内心焦灼得很。在商店里,她找到了消毒湿巾,拿着它走到了自助收银台前,因为她现在最不愿意做的就是和其他人类有任何形式的对话。

现在,她回到了车上,开始清洁驾驶座椅。她真应该听那个涂着绿指甲的店员的话。她应该买那三盒空气清新剂。

"好吧。"一个男人从她车旁经过时,对他的妻子说,"好吧。也许我是不知道我在讲什么,但任何有点脑子的人都会同意我的说法。"他们每个人怀里都抱着一条小狗。

莫琳继续开车。车流从塔姆沃思驶向阿瑟斯通,但中途又有道路施工,所以她开上了另一条临时绕行道路,也就是在一条绕行道路上绕行。她以前都不知道还能有这种路。比绕路更糟的是,她身上还是有那股味道,车里也一样,所以她现在只想洗个热水澡。她努力把注意力都放在前面的路上,不让自己的思绪飘到别处。可外面的风景毫无变化,不走神太难了。"我想养条狗!

我想养条狗！"戴维过去常说。有一年圣诞节，他们送了他一个毛绒玩具，按下按钮，它就会"汪！汪！"甚至还能坐下，就好像在乞求什么。戴维看见玩具说了一句"哦！一条狗！"但是后来，她发现那个玩具狗被搁在包装盒里，戴维望着花园发呆。莫琳的心沉了下去，她知道，他失望了。

双车道上，车流陷入了停滞。路边的坡上到处都是塑料垃圾。乱丢垃圾：有人将十个垃圾袋排成一条直线放在了那里。她又排到了载着那些球迷的长途客车后面，他们把旗子伸到车窗外摇晃着。她紧张地看着他们，不想让他们注意到她。人们纷纷从轿车、卡车上下来，在不允许行人逗留的地方走动。他们爬过中央分隔带，想去前面看看是什么情况。他们还掏出手机，甚至彼此交谈起来，与完全不认识的人交谈起来。接着，那群球迷从长途客车上跳下来，拿着啤酒，挥舞着旗子，敲着其他人的车窗。莫琳僵直地坐在座位上。一辆车上坐的全是年轻女人，上身穿的小背心看起来更像是胸衣。她们朝那些球迷挥挥手，大笑着也下了车，开始和球迷们一起喝啤酒，就好像他们是在一个俱乐部里。年轻人啊，莫琳想。他们的眼睛里闪着光，透着对什么都无所谓的样子。曾几何时，她也这样。虽然很难相信，但她的确曾经以为自己站在未来的浪头上。她曾真的认为历史不过是一种演习，真正的生活才刚刚开始，而莫琳就是这生活的中心。她会出色地通过学校的考试，然后进大学读法语——她所在的那个村子里还没人上过大学呢——生活就这样展开。她会遇上其他人，和她一样有天赋、充满激情且聪明伶俐的人，也戴贝雷帽，抽法国香烟，谈论哲学。她倒是还没有读什么哲学书，但她以后会读的。她父亲不是一直这么跟她说的吗，只要她用心，世上就没什么她办不到的事。

前方的车辆开始缓缓挪动了。人们纷纷回到各自的车上。隔着雾气，她只瞧见了飞机库一样大小的工业装置。

挪啊，挪啊。车流移动的速度太慢了，恐怕只比走路快那么一点。雾气散去了片刻，太阳向大地伸出它肤色浅淡的长臂，好似即将被淹没在云中一样。一丛金雀花灌木中闪现出星星点点的黄。又过了半个小时，莫琳把车停到路侧停车带，伸展一下双腿。那里有一辆卖汉堡和烤串的车，可车上卖的东西闻起来好像过热的橡胶制品和滚烫的油脂。她累得都没有胃口吃东西，但她把杯子里剩下的咖啡喝光了。

在停车带对面，一个男人独自坐在他的汽车后座上，车窗蒙了一层水汽。他似乎什么事都不准备干。莫琳甚至觉得他也许是睡着了。突然，他打开车门，走到垃圾桶旁，把一个塑料袋里装的水瓶和聚苯乙烯食品托盘倒了进去，然后他把那个塑料袋捋平整，折成近似于方块的形状。接着，他从口袋里抽出一把牙刷和一管牙膏，开始刷牙，把牙膏沫吐到地上，然后回到车上，又坐进了后车座上。他穿着一身时髦的休闲装。就算他刚才看见她了，也没有打招呼的意思。

莫琳继续往前开。她琢磨着那个坐在车里的男人，心想，也不知道他到底在车上待了多长时间了。可能得有好些天了。可能他没家。可是，要想不迷路，你对其他人的问题的关心程度就只能到此为止。一辆卡车缓缓超过了她，车上摞得高高的都是被丢弃的圣诞树。一群乌鸦飞了出来，活像被烧焦的废品。

莫琳的思绪又回到了戴维的房间里。哈罗德那次出行之后，她决定重新装修那个房间。她选用色调明快的黄漆粉刷墙壁，撤下了蓝色的窗帘，换上了花朵图案的印花棉布窗帘。这感觉很对路，就像书本新翻开的一页。这感觉甚至可以说是平静。她在屋里放了一张书桌，想着她可以尝试写诗，不过她尝试了几次之后就放弃了。要么是她想要的神来之笔总是不出现，要么是她把词组合成句的那一刻，那些词就失了神韵。怪不得她在学校里的考试会不及格，最后没上成大学，只上了个秘书学院：原来她并没有那么特别。

戴维的房间几年来都是这个样子，果汁冰糕颜色的墙面，空荡荡的。每每经过这个房间紧闭的门，她都忍不住感到心痛，甚至有像过去一样走进去跟他说说话的冲动。是疫情改变了这一切。人人都得待在家里。她发现自己又开始一次次走进这个房间，哪怕只是为了换一个空间待着。结果，她猛然意识到，这个房间是那么空旷，那么可怕，那么黄；还意识到她有多不喜欢那幅花朵图案的印花棉布窗帘，可以说是一点都不喜欢。这突如其来的发现让她顿觉虚弱无力。于是，她开始从阁楼中取出戴维的东西，包括他的书、小摆件和照片，将它们一一放回原处。她甚至找到了他的蓝色旧窗帘，重新将其挂好。对此哈罗德什么都没说。也许他压根儿没留意。有时候，她觉得自己和哈罗德正向着相反的方向前进，就好像现在她要为搬回他觉得可以放手的这一切而负责。可就算这样，房间里的一切看起来依然不对劲。尽管她把房间又刷回了蓝色,她依然能看到之前的黄色。她还是想着自己曾把戴维的东西打包放了起来。这让她有种苦涩的感觉。她仅剩下的戴维的东西就是他的房间了,可是看哪,她竟然肆意破坏了这个房间。

从久远的过去,她找回了一段鲜活的记忆:她注视着还是个小婴儿的戴维,他还那么小,头发那么黑;当时,一种责任感油然而生,把她吓坏了,但同时也让她意识到,在他和这个世界的孤独之间,只隔着一个她,还有她所有的爱与恐惧,但最主要的还是她的恐惧,因为不管他出了什么事,她都无法承受。她一定挺不过来。她发现他死了的那一刻,感受到了一种前所未有的安静。

莫琳想着她放回戴维房间里的那些小摆件——一匹瓷斑马、一匹木马、一只玻璃鹿,还有他婴儿时期的一张照片。她全部的、充沛的爱都堆在这些微不足道的遗物上了。放在架子上的它们之间拉扯出一种空荡的感觉。她从未想过,怎么会有一天她只剩下这么一点他的东西了?那些他对她说过、她却一定已经忘记或误解了的话,那些故事,那些念头,它们如今都去了哪里?她要如何背负这么多她仍然无法理解的事物的重量?

车流如倾泻一般涌回了 M1 高速公路。她先后经过了拉夫堡、凯格沃思,最后到诺丁汉郡了。欢迎来到罗宾汉之乡![1] 莫琳摇

---

1 诺丁汉郡是英国家喻户晓的民间传说中的英雄人物罗宾汉的故乡,《罗宾汉传说》的故事发生地。

摇头。她咕哝了一声。她明明不间断地思考了这么多，回忆了这么多，可她竟然还有两百多英里的路要赶。她如今被困在车上，没有哈罗德来分神，注意力都放在了自己身上。烟雾从烟囱里袅袅升起。载着球迷的长途客车又驶到了莫琳旁边，球迷们指着下面的她嬉笑不止。尽管他们肯定不可能知道她之前做了什么，但她忍不住觉得他们什么都知道。她想起了家，想到家里的一切都干干净净，放在妥当的位置，还想到粉色的卫浴套装，以及黄铜水龙头和配套的粉色瓷砖，这些都不需要更换，也根本不必全部更换。她想到哈罗德赤着脚在楼下轻手轻脚地行走，那双脚上还有他走去找奎妮时留下的疤。她想到住在车里的那个男人，还有她有多不想沉耽于别人的悲伤中。

莫琳从下一个出口下了高速，把车子停入她见到的第一个车库里。她都没把车子端端正正地停到停车位上，就伸手拿出了手机。哈罗德一接电话，她就告诉他，她下定决心要往回走。

"可是，为什么啊？"他问，"为什么？"

"哈罗德，我出事故时还发生了一个意外。不只是车的事，我尿裤子了。真的。我现在身上穿的是我本来准备明天穿的衣服；哈罗德，我想洗个澡。我没法儿继续往前开了。我和你不一样。眼下我刚过了诺丁汉。我甚至都没法儿及时赶到那个小旅馆吃晚餐。我要回家了。"

他们的对话中止了片刻，他什么都没说。然后，电话那头又传来了他的声音和那熟悉的、轻柔的咯咯声。

"哦，莫。我们老了。就是这个缘故而已。可你是真心想去看看那座花园。不去的话,你总会记挂着这件事。眼下你的行程已过半,不如找找凯特的电话号码,问问她是否方便让你在她那儿住一晚?就算你晚点到她家也无妨。莫琳,做不成这件事,你就无法安心。"

听着他的话,她感觉心里豁然开朗。他懂她,也接受真实的她。许多年前,她看着还是个年轻小伙子的他跳舞,手舞足蹈,无知而笨拙,完全不得要领,但她就像现在的他一样,对他全然接受。直到遇见哈罗德,莫琳才知道自己想做什么:她想要做的就是站在他和这个世界之间,体验爱与被爱。这时候如果说雾散了,恐怕十分勉强,但她觉得天上的云似乎变得稀薄了些,这是她以前从未见过的。尽管眼下还看不到蓝天,但她觉得有望见到。

于是,莫琳按照他说的做了。她重新回到路上。雷克斯给她发了去凯特家的详细路线,还附上了一个微笑的表情。

十分钟后,她放在副驾驶座位上的手机又响了一声,雷克斯又发来了消息。这次他发来的是一张地图,上面的箭头标出了她可以停下洗澡的一处服务站。

这次,他选用的表情是一只心形眼的独角兽。虽然她看不懂这是什么意思,但她还是笑了。

07

北方和更北的北方

North and Further North

指示牌上写着"北"。一直往北。到了下午,雾终于散去了。切斯特菲尔德,谢菲尔德。远处是打着一块块"白色补丁"的峰区[1]。风力发电机布满了原野,它们就像巨型打蛋器上壮观的刀片,靠近了看特别古怪,一点都不真实。大地起起伏伏,大片的土地过去后是房屋与货栈、石板灰的屋顶,还有远方内陆城镇的轮廓线。莫琳驾车前行,天空断断续续地漏下阳光,仿佛缕缕金丝,与钢青色的天空相映成趣,景致丰富多彩,直让人觉得好似在从乌鸦背上眺望。哈罗德说过,世界上有多少个国家,就有多少种鸟鸣。他常这么说,就好像以前从未说过这话似的,语气中总是带着惊奇。有时候,雷克斯会用手机录下一段他们没听过的鸟鸣,然后回家在电脑上进行辨别。"听听!"之后他会兴冲冲地跑过来,举着手机让她听。"莫琳,你觉得这是什么声音?"

"在我听来,这就是鸟叫而已啊。"她会说,"你们谁要喝

---

[1] "峰区"(Peak District)是英格兰中部和北部的高地,英国最大的国家公园之一。它的中部和南部区域,临地表处为石炭纪石灰岩,被称为"白峰"。

咖啡？"

"莫琳，给我放两块糖可以吗？"

"哦，雷克斯，"她会边笑边说，"都这么多年了，你当真以为我记不住你喝咖啡的偏好吗？"

在蒂布谢尔夫，莫琳冲了个澡。这就是她高兴的原因。之前谁知道呢？谁知道在服务站里有淋浴间呢？她以前从未注意过——但真的有，在一扇有莲蓬头图片的灰色的门后面，有一个干净的小隔间，里面有一组挂钩，可供挂衣服。这里竟然还有一台自动售货机，从里面可以买到可能需要的各种卫生用品，不过都是小包装的，包括洋娃娃大小的一瓶沐浴露、一小袋洗发水、一个避孕套和一个卫生棉条。她站在热气腾腾的水流下，感觉和在家洗澡一样舒适。

她沿着 M18 高速行驶，最后终于上了 A1 国道。她先后经过了唐克斯特市艾德威克村和庞蒂弗拉克特镇的指示牌。接着，她看到了费里布里奇发电站，其废弃不用的冷却塔像是一个个扣着的花盆。莫琳飞驰在进入北约克郡的路上，利兹市的出口和韦瑟比镇的指示牌一闪而过。太阳在云层间洒下银色和金色的光，一只苍鹭腾空而起，就像一个毛毡旅行袋突然飞起来一样不可思议。当她在服务站下车时，着意提醒自己要讲礼貌。她特意给了正在卫生间拖地的年轻人一个微笑，跟他说卫生间打扫得真干净。她买茶的时候还跟吧台的服务员说了好几次谢谢，尽管她的热饮不过是一个盛着开水的纸杯，再加上一个用独立小袋装的茶包。之后，服务员问她是否还需要点别的，她说："谢谢，不用了。一杯茶就够了,谢谢你。"她发现一张靠窗的空桌子,显然没人坐,而且它和邻座之间还隔着一张塑料隔板,但她还是向隔板后面的那对夫妻确认了一下才坐下。她拿出她的填字游戏杂志,在没有任何人打扰的情况下,喝着茶完成了一个扑朔迷离的填字游戏。她甚至对另一张桌的四个孩子露出了微笑。那四个穿着超级英雄服装的孩子正在吃肯德基全家桶,他们的妈妈一边刷手机,一边喝着气泡饮料。

"我喜欢你的大衣。"她离开时对另一个女人说道。

"这件旧衣服吗?"女人这样说着,拽了拽大衣的翻领,开心地笑了。

"是啊,这件大衣很漂亮。"莫琳说。

回到车上,她才意识到,那件大衣其实相当普通,是因为她的心情变得格外美好。她打开广播,里面传来熟悉的一首歌,于是她跟着哼了起来。一群大雁从空中飞过,它们修长的脖子奋力探向北方。

白天结束了。一月低垂的天空暗了下去,只剩下一抹红彤彤的冬日残阳。大地在车前徐徐展开,打开双臂,像是在做深呼吸。里彭。比代尔。斯科奇科纳。达拉谟。等她到达"北方天使"[1]的时候,夜晚再次降临,头上已是满天星辰。这座雕塑意料之外地出现在她面前,从前方一座小丘的顶上探了出来。虽然

---

1 一座室外现代钢铁雕塑,高 20 米,翼展 54 米,也是北英格兰的著名地标,由著名雕塑艺术家安东尼·戈姆雷于 1998 年创作。

光线不佳，但月光照在雕塑的翅膀上，让她清楚地看到了它们伸展开有多宽、有多平，和一般人印象里那种优雅轻灵的翅膀区别有多大。一个念头转瞬即逝，她想，如果说这个天使是从别处来的，它一定不是来自天堂或天空，而是来自某个属于人间与世俗的地方。莫琳绕过纽卡斯尔，跨过泰恩河，最后拐下 A1 国道，向西行驶。她看到了零零星星、孤单矗立在这片大地上的一座座花岗岩农庄，农庄房屋的窗户透出黄油色的灯光。然后，她从树木形成的一段隧道下驶过，街灯的光透过树梢洒在前方的路面上，形成了斑驳的像水晶一样闪烁的光亮。最后，她终于看到了赫克瑟姆的指示牌。

莫琳已经在路上行驶了将近十四个小时。她累坏了，又看了那么多风景，只觉得精疲力竭，"遍体鳞伤"，她的脑子也似乎整个被汽车发动机的声音占据了。

她把车停下，再次查看了雷克斯给的路线，然后涂了一点口红，便开车去见凯特了。她一定能行。她可以的。

08
卡车
Truck

莫琳还是个孩子的时候,她的母亲喜欢用连衣裙和白袜子来打扮她。那一件件连衣裙都是母亲用她的电动缝纫机做出来的。她还会手工给裙子加上一些细节,比如给裙子的上身缝上装饰用的抽褶,或者做上一对泡泡袖。莫琳唯一一次真切地记得母亲开怀大笑,就是她的手指拂过一卷新的欧根纱时。莫琳也的确喜欢那些连衣裙。她父亲说她看起来像个公主,当时她是相信的,就好像一个生活在偏远农村的五岁女孩像公主是件好事似的。直到开始上学时,她才渐渐明白,她被严重误导了。

如果一个孩子裙子上有白色蕾丝花边、腰间系着玫瑰花蕾装饰或青苔绿的绸带,上面缀着跟她的脑袋一般大的蝴蝶结,那她对于没她幸运的孩子而言就是一个"活靶子"。当她穿着小女孩穿的那种连衣裙蹦蹦跳跳地往家走时,他们会埋伏在路上,逮住机会就往她身上甩泥巴或者更恶心的东西。同样地,如果一个孩子背着书包去上学,铅笔总是削得尖尖的,并按照颜色从深到浅的顺序将它们摆放在书桌上,或是说起话来嘴里像是含着一颗李子,或是坚持讲那种让她父亲听得高兴的长篇故事,那她永远都不会受欢迎,而是会成为笑柄。

随着她离凯特家越来越近,莫琳产生了与她多年前还是个孩子时相似的那种担忧,她害怕自己犯自以为是的毛病。那时候,她穿着精致,拥有漂亮整齐的铅笔,而且她相信自己知道一切问题的答案,哪怕她其实不知道;她认为其他孩子一定会羡慕这样的自己,但直到那一天她才明白,事实并非如此。之前她怎么能想得到呢?现在,她又同样认为,凯特会住在一座可爱的乡村小别墅里,因为莫琳即将到访,她还会特意打扫一番。她想象着,凯特家一定有雅家炉,上面已经放了一锅炖菜——因为就算是激进分子也得吃饭——而且凯特还一定在餐桌上铺了块干干净净的白色桌布。抱着这样的期待,莫琳停下车,进商店买了红酒和一盒巧克力。

想到去凯特家的路线,她现在很清楚自己确实搞错了状况。地址里没有宅邸的名称,也没有写是多少号。仔细想想,甚至连街道的名字都没有。上面只是说沿着一条小路往前开,结果她发现那条小路更像是野径。此外,路线说明里还有几处不靠谱的地标,比如一座废弃的电话亭、一座农场的旧大门。为什么凯特从来没有在她寄给哈罗德的明信片中提过,她的家不是传统意义上的家,别说什么乡村别墅了,恐怕实际上只是一辆经过改造的卡车?她为什么不曾透露这里并非只有她的移动住宅,而是有其他野营车与卡车组成的社区的一部分,住在那里的全是莫琳在报纸上读到过的那种女人,比如她们为了防止树被砍伐而住到树上,或是坐在桥上对全球变暖表示抗议?

她感觉自己沿着那条野径开了好几英里，小心翼翼地在黑暗中绕过一处坑洼，结果却让车从一块石头上轧了过去。就这样，她没有多加考虑就从一些拖车和篷车旁开了过去，最后开到一道写着"严禁擅闯"的大门前。她不得不倒车，因为路太窄了，她无法掉头。于是，她再一次轧过了坑洼与石头，只不过这次的颠簸更厉害，因为她在黑暗中无法透过后挡风玻璃看清它们的位置。话说回来，倒车从来不是她的强项。后来，她在靠近那些篷车和野营车的地方停了下来，但手机没信号，她无法给雷克斯打电话。

"有什么需要帮忙的吗？"一个披着彩虹披肩的蓝色姑娘敲了敲她的车窗。莫琳稍后才意识到，她之所以看起来是蓝色的，是因为她有大面积的文身，"彩虹披肩"其实是她的头发。

莫琳摇下车窗，但没有摇到底。她跟对方说她在找一个叫凯特的人，但她恐怕找错了地方。

"不，你没找错地方。凯特的确住在这儿。"那个年轻姑娘说。她的声音如孩童般甜美，年纪大概还不到三十岁。

"这儿？"莫琳说，她难掩震惊。

"没错。"

"我不知道该把车停在哪儿。"

"哦，停这儿就行。"

"这儿？"莫琳又说了一遍。

"对。"年轻姑娘说。

于是，莫琳把车身摆正，停下，然后又调整了一下车身，因为她没有其他参照物，比如车库的墙壁，所以很难调正车的位置。然后她从车上下来，穿着开车穿的那双鞋，直接踩进了泥里。接着，她打开后备厢，心想也不知那个彩虹色头发的年轻姑娘会不会帮她搬一下行李箱，但显然不会，因为她已经走到前头去了。

莫琳跟着她从其他篷车前经过。她不想弄脏行李箱的轮子，所以只能提着箱子。她们总共经过了大概十辆篷车，她能看到车里透出的灯光和其他女人的影子。她只盼着别有人出来，因为她可不想再和陌生人打交道了。

"就是这里。"那个年轻姑娘说。

"就是这里？"莫琳重复了一遍。

"是啊，我妈妈就住在这儿。"

"你的妈妈？"

"没错。"

"凯特是你的妈妈？"

这么说眼前这位是凯特的女儿。凯特有个女儿。又是一件没人跟莫琳提过的事。她把头发染成彩虹色倒是没什么，可好歹洗一洗啊。莫琳随后想起自己决意要表现得友善一些，于是她说："我挺喜欢你的头发的。"

"谢谢。"

"我可不可以直接进去？"

"当然。"话音没落她就已经飘走了。

莫琳穿着她那双开车穿的鞋经过一堆空塑料椅和一个地灶，

绕过一摞木托盘，又从一辆紫色的儿童自行车旁挤了过去。她想到昨天晚上哈罗德才为她刷了这双鞋，就觉得一阵强烈的疲倦袭来。福斯布里奇路似乎是在另一个国家。

还没等莫琳敲门，门就开了。这是个意想不到的好事，若非如此，莫琳还不知道那是一扇门呢。卡车里传来一声高呼："莫琳！"一个女人出现了，一头乱蓬蓬的花白头发里编着丝带。她穿着一件厚厚的绿色开襟羊毛衫，戴着一对用羽毛和珠子做成的硕大耳饰，脖子上挂着很多条项链，还有一条捕梦网似的东西。

"莫琳，你这小可怜！"女人大声说着，从一截陡峭的台阶上重重地走下来，一把将莫琳抱住。"我是凯特！"她亲了亲莫琳一侧的面颊。这不请自来的热络让莫琳畏缩。

"看到你真是太开心了。快进来，亲爱的，进来吧。"

莫琳跟着她走上木台阶。凯特扭头对她说，这么多年过去了，终于见到莫琳本人感觉是多么惊奇，还说她是多么爱哈罗德。她说哈罗德给了她很大的启发。她为卡车上空间狭窄表示抱歉，说希望莫琳不要觉得诧异。莫琳赶紧说不会、不会，这个地方很好。"这是个不同寻常的地方。"她说。凯特听出了对方口气中的矫揉造作，也看到了她那双开车穿的鞋上溅得都是泥点子。

卡车里放满了东西，没有一处能让眼睛休息的，简直看一眼就要患上偏头疼。这里有装饰用的极小的佛像、脉轮石、石英吊坠、水晶、蜡烛、劝告人们寻找内心女神和天使的训词，还有用一条紫色布帘盖着的架子。这里所有东西都蒙着一层薄薄的灰尘，不是坏了，就是快坏了。还有就是那股味儿。老天爷啊。她以为自己闻见了什么难闻的味道，原来是每个角落里都点着香。她几乎无法呼吸。这里没有雅家炉，也没有炖菜。

莫琳从包里拿出红酒和巧克力，把它们递给凯特。凯特说："你太客气了！太客气了！"然后把它们放在一个放着许多其他物件的家具上。莫琳怀疑她的礼物可能永远无法重见天日了。她为它们感到一阵懊悔。

这地方是个肮脏简陋的窝棚。她尽可以像她表现出友善那样在措辞上努力，但这种话怎么说都不会好听的。戴维小的时候，他们每年都要去伊斯特本，住在一座度假小屋里；的确，那地方后来不太成样子了。一推开前门就能闻见一股霉味儿，为了掩盖地板上的污渍，上面还铺着泥土色的地毯。在哈罗德完成那次长途跋涉后回家的路上，他们住进了一家汽车旅馆。后来她才意识到，那地方属于红灯区，发现的时候他们已经住下了。不过，他们住在哪里都没什么区别，因为他一直在房间里睡觉。只有莫琳独自一人在汽车旅馆的餐吧里吃饭，那里还有几个看起来不像是为了用餐之乐而坐在那里的女人。可眼下的情况与彼时不同。莫琳从来没想过，给哈罗德寄明信片的人竟然会住在这样的环境里。这里连整洁都达不到。或者说，这里最突出的特点就是不整洁。

这辆卡车被设计成一个开放式的工作室——莫琳从来都对这种设计不感兴趣，靠近门口的位置有个微型厨房，里面是硬质纤维板做成的碗橱，中间有一个小小的水槽；对侧是能放下一个衣柜的空间，挂着另一条紫色布帘；再旁边是用塑料帘子隔出来的淋浴间，狭窄到人只能斜着身子站在里面。然后，卡车里出现了又一条紫色帘子，帘子后面的东西似乎是世界上最不舒服的沙发——比起沙发来更像是壁架，还有一张富美家的桌子和两把椅子、一个凳子。除此之外，卡车上有一张大得不协调的翼背椅，上面盖着莫琳不敢轻易碰触的一床旧羽绒被。"真是个可爱的地方，"莫琳又夸了一句，"多迷人啊。"

她脱下大衣，但因为无处可挂，只好又把大衣穿上了。

"你准备花多长时间在这儿度假？"她说。她的声音调整到了最欢快的状态。

凯特匆忙地走到卡车的另一头。她念叨着，似乎在告诉莫琳，这里就是她的家，不是为了度假临时租住的居所，这里也是她女儿的家，以及住在这片地方的其他女人的家。她们决意结成一个社区，什么东西都与大家共享。她说，这是她做过的最好的决定。当然了，这得除了与哈罗德同行。莫琳现在看到了，卡车前面有两个座位和一个方向盘。

莫琳还提着她的行李箱。凯特和那个住在车上的男子只有一两步的距离。她实在不明白，怎么会有人抛下好好的家，偏要住在交通工具上，这份疑惑让她有点发慌。她和哈罗德在同一栋房子里一住就是五十多年。一想到不住在福斯桥路13号，看不着她的东西都安然无恙地放在正确的位置上，她就感到害怕。凯特打开电热水壶的开关，伸手取来两个有缺口的马克杯。

"那么你到底怎么样？"她说这话就好像有两个莫琳，一个浮在面儿上，一个藏在底下，而且她并不相信眼下站在她面前的这一个。

"我挺好的。"莫琳说。

"哈罗德跟我说,你开了一天的车到了这儿。我真不敢相信你做到了。你一定累坏了。他说你要去参观奎妮的花园。我想,你一定不太好受吧?"

"确实不好受。"莫琳说。

"亲爱的,你一定饿了。"

的确如此。莫琳饿得要命。她四肢几乎发烫,烫得在发抖。从吃过带的三明治之后,她就再没吃过什么东西。但她嘴上还是说不饿。"我没事,谢谢。我连杯茶都不用喝,直接睡觉就行了。或许你可以带我去我的房间?今天可真够累的。"

她说这些话的时候,内心的疑惑并没有减少分毫,同时她还觉得自己有点蠢,好像她又一次说错了话。卡车上除了她们所站的这个房间,显然没有其他房间了。另外,这里也没床。

"我觉得今晚你可以睡我睡的地方。"凯特说。她指着那个像壁架,但肯定不是床的东西,解释说它是折叠的,可以展开。然后她又表达了她终于见到莫琳本人是多么开心,遇见哈罗德给她的人生带来了多么大的改变,而莫琳一直盯着那个"壁架",想着她家里那张床,上面铺着可爱又平展的床单,还躺着哈罗德。凯特滔滔不绝,她现在开始给莫琳讲她的婚姻,以及封城是如何导致这段婚姻结束的,不过她和她的前夫之间关系还不错,他还住在他们的老房子里。

"我不明白。"莫琳说,"你把你的房子给他了?"

"是啊,莫。我想有个全新的开始。"

莫琳可不觉得这辆卡车算什么"全新"的开始。她努力挤出一个微笑。

"而且我想和我的女儿、外孙女一起生活,你知道吧?"

不,莫琳不知道。直到凯特指着外面,莫琳在其他卡车和篷车的灯光下看见她刚才遇到的那个年轻姑娘,她才知道。年轻姑娘抱着一个留着黑色长发的瘦小的孩子。那个小女孩的双腿盘在她妈妈身上,脑袋枕在妈妈的肩膀上。莫琳只觉得身上一阵寒冷,仿佛内心被什么击中。这么说,凯特也有孙辈。

"梅普尔。"凯特说。

"什么?"

"她是我的生命之光。"

"她的名字叫'梅普尔'?取的是枫糖浆的意思?[1]"

凯特露出一个不太自然的礼节性微笑,她似乎不太确定莫琳说这话是不是有意冒犯。"不,不是枫糖浆,而是枫叶。"

哦,莫琳已是筋疲力尽。她觉得自己像是被疲惫掏空了。这疲惫缘于她开车开了这么长时间,也缘于她见到的那些人,包括染了绿指甲的人、住在轿车和卡车里的人,以及用大自然的一部分给孩子取名的人。哈罗德给她讲过他在旅途中遇上的种种奇事,但他从未提到过这类事。她头疼起来。"有时间你应该去我们家做客,"她说,"哈罗德一定非常希望见到你。"她想象了一

---

1 "梅普尔"是枫树的意思。

下凯特的卡车停在福斯桥路 13 号外面的画面，便立刻清楚自己这话并非当真的。

"好，我会的。"凯特说。

莫琳清楚，凯特这话也不当真。

尽管如此，凯特还是演示给莫琳看如何展开折叠的壁架，让它变成一个更大的壁架，然后递给她虽然没熨过，但闻起来还算干净的床品。她道了晚安，不过这次没有上前拥抱莫琳的意思。独自一人，莫琳取出睡衣穿上，刷了牙。之后她拿出填字游戏杂志，却又不小心把杂志掉在了地上。她太累了，懒得弯腰把它捡起来，直接躺到了床上。

床是一种恩惠。眼下这拉出式的东西和床毫无相似之处，但现在莫琳只能躺在这凹凸不平的床垫上尽力放松。她已经累过劲儿了。就这样，她身体僵直地躺着，一点都不舒服，但她应该还是睡着了，因为她中途被车外的声音吵醒了，同时听到远处的钟声响了十下。

"凯特，你还好吗？"说话的是凯特的女儿，那个嗓音甜美、满身文身的女人。莫琳睁大眼睛，想听得更清楚些。

"很好啊。"凯特说。

"你要在哪儿睡呢？"

"我和别人挤挤就行，这不成问题。"

"什么情况？我是说莫琳。"

"她的日子有点难过。"说到这儿，她的声音低了下去，莫琳再没能听清她后面说了什么。后来，莫琳听见了关门声，还有其他女人互相打招呼和欢笑的声音,她们问候凯特母女并询问她们需要什么。

"亲爱的,晚安!晚安啦!"

周围又恢复了安静,莫琳局促不安,难以入眠。小时候,她打扮得与环境格格不入,用的东西在别人眼里过分讲究、傻里傻气,但她又无法改变这一切,因为她没有别的选择。现在,小时候的感觉再次涌上心头。她想到营地里的女人们彼此之间打招呼时的友好,那份轻松自在的亲昵;想到凯特竟然愿意把自己的床让给她,尽管那只是个壁架;还想到自己永远也变不成那样。她坐起来,打开手提包,想从里面拿张纸巾,结果却摸到了一张纸,上面是她记下来的兰尼说的路线。又一个证明她失败了的证据。

为了不把翼背椅上的羽绒被弄乱,莫琳僵直地坐在上头。她不知道自己该怎么办了。要是她在自己家的厨房里就好了,那里的一切都干干净净、井井有条,就连杯子的把手都冲着同一个方向。她在脑海里支使自己蹑手蹑脚地沿着铺有米黄色地毯的走廊前行,经过她和哈罗德用来挂大衣的挂钩,来到起居室;这里贴着带花纹的墙纸,椅子的布面上也有着与之相衬的花纹;如今,她在这儿的壁炉架上摆放着结婚照片和戴维的一幅肖像画,与之相伴的是一个瓷制的牧羊女小摆件,那以前是她母亲的。想到这里,她的思维又跳跃到她小时候住的那栋房子,那里总是很冷,她脑海里突然浮现出母亲在她的缝纫机前忙碌着的样子,她的父亲则不停地为自己成了家里的负担而道歉,又因为他常常道歉,最后真的成了负担。

要是她能更像其他孩子就好了。要是她能学会在穿着打扮、言谈举止方面跟他们一样，而不是与之相悖就好了。她现在还记得和父亲一起步行穿过田野的情景，管理那片田野的农户没有给狗拴绳，几条狗朝他们跑过去，冲着父亲狂吠；父亲伸出双手想安抚它们，还告诉她别跑，要保持冷静；可她看到狗向她逼近时，什么都听不进去，最后还是决定逃跑；就在父亲挡在她身前时，一条狗跳起来咬了她下巴一口，还咬伤了父亲的手。母亲再三责骂父亲，父亲却满怀悔恨地坐在那儿，甚至都不敢看莫琳一眼。母亲骂他软弱可欺、一无是处，他只是摇着头承担着一切，莫琳却希望这次他能站起来为自己辩解几句。父亲死后，母亲对生活失去了兴趣。三个月后，她也死了。莫琳惊讶地发现，另一个时期的自我竟然可以化身牢笼，将一个人困住，而完全无法享受近在咫尺的幸福。

莫琳设法睡了几个小时，醒来时全身僵硬，但还好到了早晨。她穿上休闲裤和一件新衬衣，捋直开襟羊毛衫的袖子，然后套上大衣，蹬上开车穿的鞋，拎起行李箱。要不是一时间找不到她带来的红酒和巧克力，她肯定会把它们都带走。

外面已经有了灰蒙蒙的光，但并没有多亮堂，只是驱走了些许黑暗。营地中有种迟滞的寂静。所有卡车和拖车小屋都门窗紧闭，灯光全无，只有一辆除外，莫琳听见那里传来一个女人轻柔的吟唱。有一瞬间，她非常渴望让一切都停下，她好回到车里，再出来一次。可她怎么做得到呢？她做不到。她生来就不是这样的性格。没有别的办法,她只好像小时候学过的那样,高昂着头走开了。远处,车流沿着地平线散发出朦胧的光向北驶去。莫琳按了一下车钥匙,车便亮了起来。在她看来,汽车表现出的这种热情愚蠢而无聊。但她还是上了车。

莫琳走时连张字条都没留下。她也没说谢谢或再见,就好像她决意再也不见凯特或者凯特那辆糟糕的卡车一样。她就这样离开了。

09

遗物花园

Garden of Relics

清晨的天空被风撕裂，金光从破碎的天幕透出，一闪而逝，但她已然看清了一切，大地、阳光，还有云，甚至隐约看到了前方的海。不过，它们都与她隔着别样的雾，因为她现在唯一能想到的只有戴维。三十年了。三十年的等待与寻找，现在她终于要见到他了。他是她唯一的念想。

莫琳驱车从凯特家直接向恩布尔顿赶去。在此之前，她还给哈罗德打了个电话，他已经醒了，不过她一点都没向他透露发生的事，甚至连她住的那辆卡车都没提。她留心着只跟他聊路况和天气。当他问莫琳觉得凯特人怎么样时，她告诉他，她一到凯特家就上床睡觉了，没有时间去了解她。

"哎呀，那太可惜了。"他说，她能从声音中听出他的惋惜，"我一直觉得凯特人特别好。"

"我现在该出发了。"她说。

到了恩布尔顿。莫琳找到棕榈树旅馆，停车办理了入住。前台是个亲切的年轻姑娘，她坐在一个小隔间里，身前的桌子上摆着一棵塑料的玩具棕榈树。她说莫琳的房间已经收拾妥当，可以入住了。但莫琳解释说,她只是想先把行李放下,然后她要去参观一座花园。"奎妮的花园?那座遗物花园?"女孩操着唱歌一样的诺森伯兰郡口音说,"过了高尔夫球俱乐部就是!你一定不会走错的!我母亲去世后,我们就把她的骨灰撒在了那儿!从这儿散步过去,一路上风景很美!"

尽管散步看到的风景可能很美,但莫琳并没有这个打算。她把车先开到高尔夫球俱乐部,发现前方再没有公路后,她尽量把车停到了离花园很近的位置,然后才下车步行走完了最后这段路。她一直往前走,没有回头,一次都没有。她戴上了头巾,但海风依然吹得她的裤腿一摆一摆的,拂过她的脚踝。沙丘的另一边是一望无际的大海,海上是广阔无垠的天空。

她沿着高尔夫球场旁的一条小路向海岸走去:前面的沙丘上矗立着几座木屋,因为建在海边,所以显得格外小。她朝着这些木屋走去。在高尔夫球场的尽头,小路向左拐去,拐弯处有个手绘的胶合板路牌,写着"奎妮的花园",紧接着是另一个路牌,它指向一座小桥。这些路牌让莫琳很恼火。她知道它们存在的目的是给人指路,但她觉得即使没有路牌,她也应该本能地知道该往哪儿走。可事实上是她没有这个能力,她确实需要这些路牌——这让她更讨厌它们了。

踏上沙地后,她就得小心脚上那双开车穿的鞋了,因为这双鞋很容易突然陷入松软泥泞的沙地里,她的脚会随之被弄湿。潮水离她还有很远的距离。天上飞着三五成群的海鸥和蛎鹬,风吹起海中成团的泡沫,它们翻滚着从大地上掠过,最后破碎,消失于无形。在她左侧遥远的地平线上，邓斯坦伯城堡残破的废墟静静地矗立着，它的轮廓就像一片让人难以判断放在哪里的拼图。与此同时，她脑子里想的就只有戴维，戴维，戴维，你在哪里？

沿着沙丘脚下立起的路牌向每位来者表示欢迎，每张路牌上都装饰着横幅似的海草、塑料花和贝壳项链。Bienvenue！Willkommen！ Bienvenido！ Välkommen！ Hoş geldin！Witaj！[1] 她不明白为什么要写这些外语。这不过是在显摆。

莫琳在这些路牌的指引下踏上一段嵌在沙丘边缘的木台阶，台阶尽头是一组木屋。这台阶太过陡峭，说是梯子也不为过，而且上面散落着沙子。尽管台阶旁有一根蓝色的绳索当扶手，按说这已经足够，但为了稳妥起见，她还是伸手去抓地上浓密的杂草。已经有人前来悼念了。一个塑料花环，上面点缀着各种鲜亮的红色小玩意儿，还有一捧假的百合花。海风越来越大，四面八方都传来呜呜的风声。莫琳来到第一栋木屋前。这座木头房子的台阶东倒西歪，像是要散架的样子，底层竟然还带有半敞的游廊，窗户都被百叶窗帘挡得严严实实，门上挂了把锁。第二栋木屋外面被刷成了绿色，窗后是同样颜色的窗帘，另外一栋木屋更像是平房，房顶铺着石板瓦。这里还有奎妮的花园的路牌，它们依然指向前方。现在她看到了在电脑上见过的图腾柱一样的东西，于是她放慢了脚步。她突然不知道自己该干什么了。一直以

---

[1] 从前到后分别是法语、德语、西班牙语、瑞典语、土耳其语和波兰语的"欢迎"。

来,她心心念念的就是见到戴维,却从未想过,这到底意味着什么呢?当她终于站在奎妮的花园前,之后要怎么做呢?

虽说莫琳在网上也看了些照片,但它们都不足以让她准备好迎接她亲眼见到的画面。这些也都是她不曾想象到的。现在她到了这里,花园这个谜团却似乎更难解了。她不知道该去哪里找戴维。

她脚下是坑坑洼洼的草地,但前方地面上出现了鹅卵石、碎石和五颜六色的小石子儿组成的复杂图案,这些石头或摆成方形,或摆成圆形,其间还夹杂着没能活过冬天的植物,以及外形宛若烛焰的金雀花丛。其间放着几块浮木,最高大的那块放在正中央,它周围的其他纪念物大小都不超过勺子,由各种各样的东西做成。螺旋状的铁片、扭曲的环链、生锈的铁链、钥匙做的风铃、多孔的石头、废塑料和烂木头。这里还有在杆子上飞扬的旗帜、许许多多盛放蜡烛的玻璃罐。但最让她吃惊的还是参观者的人数。

花园最后面站着两个男人,他们对花园中的各种景物指指点点,一边看一边点头,好像在肯定这里的美丽。一对年轻情侣手牵着手,无言而专注地欣赏着一座用石子儿堆成的金字塔。还有一个女人坐在她的大衣上,手上拿着笔记本和铅笔,正在画她眼前的景象。还有一个穿机车夹克的男人正往粗铁链上挂一把锁。现在,莫琳看到了一条她未曾留意到的小径,它穿过整个花园,直通后面一间简陋的彩绘小屋。这感觉就像是你看到了这辈子都没见过的风景,比如海底,那儿的自然广阔无垠比你想象中的更加独特美妙。因为自己原本对这里的期待并不高，此时的她竟然深感羞愧。

花园的一角突然有什么一动，莫琳猛然发现，离她很近的地方有个弯着腰的女人，她戴的帽子上两侧各有一个绒球。她的年纪大概刚过六十，好像正在用一把小泥铲挖石子儿。

莫琳待在场地边儿上，既不愿再往里走，又无法说服自己离开。不管他人如何沉浸其中，她都像是在盼着只要她目不转睛地盯着花园看，就能看出个所以然来。后来，那女人放下小泥铲，问道："需要帮忙吗？"

"谢谢，不需要。"莫琳说。

于是，那女人没有上前，莫琳也待在原地没动。她试着从诸多雕塑中寻找戴维，但看了半天依然不知道自己在寻找什么——这儿没什么看着像戴维的物件。现在她是真的需要指点，却没有一个标示牌可以帮到她。况且，花园里有这么多参观者，莫琳只觉得尴尬别扭、局促不安。她试着往左走了几步，可依然摸不着头脑，于是她又回到了她刚才站的地方。那个戴着有绒球装饰的帽子的女人再次放下小泥铲，站起身。"请问，你是不是迷路了？"她问道。

"没有，我很好。"

"你是想找什么东西吗？"

"没事，我自己能行。"

女人打量了莫琳一会儿。她的帽子似乎让她脸上的皱纹更显眼了，它们好似她脸颊上的一道道伤痕。"你干吗不进来呢？"

她说,"进来好好看看吧?"

花园内外并没有栅栏隔着,所以她这句话听起来有点奇怪。但凭着直觉,莫琳听懂了这个女人的意思。这里有块被大家神圣化的空间,也就是花园,而其他地方不属于花园——那些地方都是普通的沙丘和沙茅草。莫琳定在原地,双手紧紧握在一起。只见那女人径直走到她面前,然后往旁边迈了一步,做了一个手势,仿佛在邀请莫琳踏入一扇看不见的大门。

"这边走。"她说完转过身,自顾自地向花园深处走去。

莫琳低头跟在她身后。这又是一件她无法理解的事情,就好像人走进教堂时要画十字,只不过她并不经常去做礼拜。她甚至不知道这个女人要带她去哪儿。

她们走的并非一条笔直的小径,它蜿蜒于大卵石、浮木和石头摆成的圆圈之间。有些物件在风中飘动,像是一件件晾起的小衣服,她经过时发现这些物件原来是许多不同面孔的照片,还有一些手写的留言和其他奇怪的纪念品,比如鞋与十字架、夹在石头之间的钥匙与锁。此外,这里摆满了蜡烛,还有更多用瓶盖和五颜六色的塑料与泡沫做成的雕塑。从海上吹来一股劲风,几根丝带和缕缕海草随之飞到半空,铃铛和许许多多的风铃也叮当作响。

莫琳走得很慢,就好像她不信任脚下的石子儿——就好像它们会毫无预兆地凭空消失。她脑子里想的只剩下奎妮带着花去拜访她的那天,当时她正在晾她死去的儿子的衣服。她经过时,花园里的其他人纷纷抬头看她,有的还向她微笑。她再次产生了过去的那种感觉——她与周遭环境格格不入,她像是个闯入者。虽然那么多年过去了,但她真心希望当初自己对奎妮的态度能友善些。

那女人开口说道:"我叫凯伦,是这里的志愿者。我每周会来这儿工作两次。你是第一次来,对吧?"

"对。"

"我猜也是。我还记得我第一次来的时候,没完没了地哭。这里就是有这种影响力。"

凯伦带着同情的笑容看着莫琳,似乎认为对方很快就会发出呜咽声。但莫琳转过了身。阳光再次冲破云层,直射花园,照得一块块浮木尤其明亮,它们的侧面呈现出金色与紫色。串串风铃反射出银光。

"你是园艺师?"

莫琳说她是,但专攻蔬菜种植。

"奎妮也种蔬菜。她尤其喜欢观赏南瓜。"

"哦,我从来没种过那些。我种的都是比较……普通的,比如说豆类什么的,你应该懂,还有土豆之类的。"她紧了紧头巾的结。

"大多数人都会选择夏天来参观,因为那时候天气好。不过,奎妮最喜欢冬天的这里。我和她一样。当然了,要是一个人常年在花园里劳作,他就会像了解一个人一样了解它。花园的每一部分都有它自己的故事。你见过她吗?"

"没有。"她飞快地回答。

"她是个很特别的女人。她把这座花园留给了恩布尔顿湾的人。起初,没人知道该拿这地方干什么,但后来这里成了一个旅游景点,吸引了来自世界各地的参观者,甚至还有从中国来的。"

莫琳没想到还有人从那么远的地方来。还有,除了父亲在她小时候说过她特别,再没有别人这样形容她了,可这个词让她落得如今的处境。她想挤出一个微笑,但终究失败了。

"随后人们便开始在这里留下他们的东西。起初是一些挂锁。我们这儿的挂锁特别多。后来,人们开始带来比较私人的物件,比如照片、放在漂流瓶中的诗,甚至还有他们自己的雕像。我们把那些物件都收了起来。但我们随即开始觉得,奎妮应该会希望留下它们。毕竟,她才是这里的策展人。"

她们经过几块镌刻着人名的大卵石和一只玻璃碎片做成的鲜亮的蓝色小鸟。凯伦说:"曾有人告诉我,这座花园的主题是爱。从那之后,我又听人这么说过几次。他们说花园会发出它自己的声音。不过,人啊,什么都信。要我说,那不过是风罢了。"她的声音很低,就像是在自言自语一样。"又多了一只小鞋子?"

她指着一只童鞋,那只鞋子很小,想必是孩子人生的第一双鞋。因为风雨侵蚀,鞋上的皮子已经看不出原来的颜色了,它用常青藤挂在一个大些的浮木十字架上。那里还有一些贝壳,它们也都是用常青藤挂在上面的。"我很高兴有人觉得可以把它留在这里。"

凯伦指给莫琳看另外一座雕塑,那是一个用铁丝网做的心形雕塑。"我真想知道这背后有着怎样的故事。"她说。

然后,她移步到一排照片前,伸出一根手指,挨个触摸照片上的每一张脸,标记他们的存在。这里有种种以浮木和园艺工具做的图腾,其中一个做成了小狗,还有一个做成了鸟类颅骨的样子。她谈起带纪念物来到此处的人们,比如因为一场车祸失去了丈夫的男人,因为二十世纪八十年代的疯牛病而流离失所的农妇。她说来这里的人各行各业的都有。"我非常喜欢听他们的故事。"

"你是说他们会把自己的东西留下?"莫琳依然不太能理解为什么大家会认为这座花园是美丽的。但让她更无法理解的是,为什么人们会欣然将他们的东西留在这儿,那可是特别私人的、私密的、无可取代的一些物件。

凯伦说花园里还有奎妮最初放在这儿的东西。奎妮还专门为她的父母留了个地方——她指着一座铁锹做的纪念碑和一根结实的树枝。之后,她指向一片羽毛帘子。"这些代表与她一起生活过的几位女性艺术家。不过这些东西太轻了,总是被风吹走。"她笑着说,"所以我们老是得找新的换上。"

此时她们来到了花园中央,旁边就是最高的那块浮木。凯伦仰头望着它说:"奎妮心里应该有个挂念的男人。对,我想这块浮木代表的就是他。"

莫琳已经听不见后面的话了。她感觉到了自己脸上的震惊。她微微睁大双眼,张开嘴巴,一时仿佛灵魂出窍。

她看着那个女人指的地方。那是一根巨大的方木,有十英尺[1]或者更长，而且特别结实，很可能以前属于一条旧船。不管怎样，她清楚凯伦说的是真的。如果要把哈罗德比作什么，那他就是那根木头，坚定而可靠。如果可以，她想去触摸它的表面——那些褶皱与扭结；她想靠在他高大强壮的身上，感受他的善良。

"但她只给一件作品起了名字，就是她称作'戴维'的那件。"

莫琳措手不及。她的思绪原本都在哈罗德身上，结果遭到这句话的一记重击，就好像在完全不设防的情况下挨了一闷棍。听见戴维的名字从一个陌生女人的口中说出，她震惊的程度不亚于她在殡仪馆与戴维的遗体告别时。

"戴维？"她说。

"他年纪轻轻就死了，好像是自杀。"

莫琳不知道该说些什么，不知道该如何调整表情，甚至不知道该往哪儿看。

"哪个？"她说，"哪个是戴维？"

"说到这个，"凯伦微微一笑，"很长一段时间我都搞错了。曾经我以为那边那个是他呢。"她指着没有和其他浮木摆在一起的那块，那上面有一个贯穿的洞，它大概有四英尺高，但十分纤细。任谁看了都觉得难以理解，它为什么没有因为中间的洞而断成两半，毕竟能通过那个洞直接看到另一边。"这不是我见过的最悲伤的物件，"凯伦低声说，"但算是其中之一。"

---

[1] 1 英尺 =0.3048 米。

"那不是戴维?"

"不是。我觉得那可能谁都不是。它只是奎妮曾怜惜的一块浮木而已。戴维是那一块。"她指着另一个被一堆小鹅卵石围起来的物件,"你看见了吗?"

莫琳只觉得一阵痛楚。天哪,这实在太骇人了。甚至比殡仪员努力用化妆品遮住他脖子上的那圈瘀青还残酷。她看着那块可怕的浮木,一时间难受得说不出一个字。她感到头晕目眩,像是突然遭到了重创。这个戴维的纪念物是一块上面带着节疤的V形浮木,高度只有约两英尺,已经风化成了深灰色,曲里拐弯,外形复杂,好似一把断掉的七弦竖琴,而且两端都被磨出了锐利的尖。这和凯伦刚才指给她看的那块中间有洞的浮木不同,造型并无悲剧性可言。但它愤怒、暴虐,与其他物件之间有石头相隔,是一个不争的存在。莫琳想到了她错刷成黄色的戴维的卧室,火葬场的墓碑和她常常收拾整理的那些绿色小石头,想到不管她如何努力寻找,都无法在这两个地方再见到他。可这就是戴维。这就是他,脆弱到不足以面对这个世界,有青春朝气,也满怀心事,喜欢讲排场、要面子,而且傲慢自大。她不知道这样一块木头是如何经受住风雨,最后在奎妮的花园里安然保存下来的,它一定在这里扎得很牢。她呼唤了戴维那么多年,等了他那么多年,原来他一直都在这儿。是奎妮收留了他。

"你想再走走看看吗?"凯伦说,"还是说你已经找到了你要找的?"

莫琳的心似乎在胸腔中紧紧缩了一下,它想保护自己。她还是个孩子的时候,哈罗德远行的时候,还有在凯特的卡车里,被别人用她不理解、也永远无法达到的标准衡量的时候,她都有这种感觉。

"你没事吧?"凯伦说。

莫琳说不出话来。她点了点头。

"我要不要给你拿点什么?要喝水吗?"

她先是努力挤出一个"不"字,然后又挤出了一句"谢谢"。

她慌忙地在沙丘间疾走,匆匆下了台阶,来到沙滩上,整个过程中她几乎连直线都走不成。与此同时,她能感觉得到,凯伦始终在盯着她看,让她产生了一种从远处注视自己的奇怪感受,就好像她变成了一个远离一切,甚至远离了自己的孤零零的人。

10

糟糕的一夜

A Bad Night

那天晚上，在棕榈树旅馆，莫琳早早点了一份便餐。看过奎妮的花园后，她就开始朝邓斯坦伯城堡走去，因为她不想停下来，可一路上并没遇上什么能让她稍微开心起来的事。什么都无法把她从纷乱的思绪中抽离出来。她甚至觉得自己无法专心做填字游戏。餐厅里灯火通明，装点着各种各样、大大小小的塑料棕榈树，令人眼花缭乱。在另一张桌子旁，坐着一对穿着考究的夫妻，他们正在嘱咐儿子好好学习，争取期末考个好成绩。莫琳尽量专注于吃自己的饭，不去听他们的对话，可偏偏说话声不断传来，这情形跟与他们同桌吃饭没什么区别。他们的儿子把手插进他蓬乱的头发里，梳来拢去，直说没关系，不用担心。他妈妈则用她那穿透房间的声音说道："我真是不明白。要是你期末考试考砸了，你也觉得没关系？彼得，告诉他。你要是不努力上进，最后什么都得不到。"莫琳心想，我的天哪，我还要再忍多久？她折起餐巾，将几乎没怎么动的晚餐留在桌子上，起身离开了，因为她的嘴放弃了张开吃饭。

她的房间和她在网上看到的完全不一样。这里狭窄逼仄，还有过堂风,那俗艳的地毯肯定是二十世纪五十年代铺上的。她冲了个澡,然后找出一条包在塑料袋里的、红得过分的毯子,把衣服穿上后,又裹上了那条毯子。她看起来就好像刚从一场事故中获救的人。她完全不知道自己该如何入睡。客房的小冰箱里空空如也。

莫琳给哈罗德打了个电话,告诉他,她今晚要早点睡,好明天一早起来就离开恩布尔顿。

他说:"跟我讲讲吧,你去过奎妮的花园了吗?"

"我去过了。"她说。

"怎么样?"

"嗯,你知道的,就是……还行吧。"

"那你看见……了吗?"他说不出口。他无法说出他的名字。她只能替他说出来。

"没有。"她说,"我没看见戴维。凯特搞错了。他没在这儿。"

"这样啊。"她能听得出他声音中的悲伤。失望再次降临。她一开始就不该没完没了地说起花园的事。她早就应该放手。要不是她,他会很开心地忘掉那些事。"好吧。"他说。

"说实话,我都不明白我为什么要来这一趟。"

"因为你想看看奎妮的花园啊。"

"好吧,是这样。"她说,"可是我不知道我为什么当初会觉得这是个好主意。我不知道我当初以为这趟会有什么收获。"

"不妨跟我说说花园的样子吧?"

莫琳想到了那座高大的浮木雕塑,以及近旁的那块 V 形浮木。她想到自己是多么渴望碰触那块高大的木头,感受它坚实的力量。奎妮肯定也有过这样的渴望。她还记得奎妮给哈罗德写的最后一封信,上面尽是斑斑点点的潦草字迹,不时还有因为笔尖过于用力戳出的洞。莫琳想到自己将那封信放在一个鞋盒里,将它妥帖地保存了起来,但她本该将它撕得粉碎。哦,她应该用剪刀来处理那封信。那天她在晾衣绳旁说的是对的:奎妮一直都想把哈罗德从她身边抢走。莫琳又感觉到了那针刺一样的酸楚,那由来已久的醋意。她斩断思绪,深吸了一口气。

"莫琳?"

"哈罗德,我现在不想聊奎妮和她的花园。我知道当初是我说我想来这里的。但我错了。这趟旅行纯粹是浪费时间。我们还是把整件事都忘了吧。"

就在她说这些话的时候,她心里跟明镜似的——自己说的都不是真的。哈罗德或许能忘,但她没有这样的出路。她或许能忘掉自己一生的故事;忘掉冲过来咬她和她父亲的狗(那次是因为她没听父亲的话造成的,但后来担下责任的却是父亲);忘掉她没上大学的耻辱和后来扔掉的贝雷帽;忘掉第一次见哈罗德时,他像疯子一样跳舞,而她呆呆地望着他,清楚自己就此改变了人生,再也无法回头了;她甚至可能忘掉——上帝保佑啊——自己最近犯下的错误;但奎妮为纪念哈罗德和戴维选的浮木将永远立在她的眼前。因为它们是那么美。莫琳有多不愿意看到这一幕,就有多清楚这一切的真实性,清楚得就像这一切烙刻在了她的骨头上。奎妮把他们两个都带走了,还找了那么美的物件来代表他们,而莫琳费力得到的只有一间空荡荡的卧室和一块周围铺着绿色小石头的墓碑。当你走到人生的尽头,回望过去,你希望不会满怀惊惧与怨恨地回忆自己做错的事,这自然不是什么过分的要求。可你仍会一遍又一遍地想自己犯下的错误,就像反复掉进同样的洞里。

"你还在吗?"

"我还在。"她说。

"你怎么不说话?"

"我只是累了。"

"你和凯特相处得好吗?"

"我告诉过你了。我没在她那儿住多久。"她噘起嘴,换了个话题,"你吃饭了吗?"

"什么时候的饭?"

"今天的。"

"都吃了。我们吃得很好。"

她再次顿住,不知道该说什么。"好吧,哈罗德,那就晚安了。"

"晚安。"

这才过了两天,莫琳却感觉自己像是老了十岁。她只觉得内心苍老、荒凉、空空落落。

这是一个不眠之夜。她已经连续三个晚上没睡好觉了。她像是一直在休息之外徘徊,却始终无法真正进入。她躺在那儿,睁大眼睛,就是无法入睡,像困在自己思绪中的囚徒,警醒地听着暖气片的每一声嘎吱和一扇门哐哐作响的动静。这让她想到了戴维去世后的那几个月，当时她觉得睡觉就相当于背叛，晚上她会在他房间里待上好几个小时，像结茧一样把自己裹在他的蓝色窗帘里，拒绝接受她其实明明知道的事实。不过，最后她一定还是打了个盹儿，因为她迷迷糊糊地听到风吹窗户的声音，懵然不知自己身在何处。黑暗中浮着几个红色的数字，告诉她时间是 5 点 17 分。她知道发生了一些让世界从此不同的事情，但她不知道具体是什么，直到她感觉到身上裹着的毯子，才随着一阵新鲜的剧痛反应过来，她之前开车来到恩布尔顿湾，想在奎妮的花园中找到戴维，释放自己的某种情绪，就像拔出一根刺，但没想到她找到的东西非但没帮她拔出那根刺，反倒又在她心上扎了成百上千根刺。

没用的，她就是睡不着。她打开灯，伸手去拿填字游戏，可她脑子里只有那座花园。她感觉眼睛酸涩不适，头皮发紧。"这不是我见过的最悲伤的物件，"她听见志愿者凯伦指着那块有窟窿的浮木说，"但算是其中之一。"

莫琳回想起多年前她晾衣服时奎妮看她的眼神。那眼神充满了怜悯，让人觉得耻辱。她打了个冷战，匆匆穿上衣服，把胳膊伸进大衣，把脚塞进鞋子，勉强抽出空来关掉了灯，然后就拉着行李箱走出了房间。可随即那可恶的滑轮卡在了地毯和楼梯平台的交会处，她不得不用力把它拽出来。她往前台隔间里看了看，想找人办理退房，但所有的灯都熄了，她只好把房间钥匙放在棕榈树摆件旁边，拉开了前门。

莫琳迫不及待地要离开这家旅馆。

11
安娜·杜普里
Anna Dupree

愤怒，无以复加的愤怒，她胸口像是被劈出了一道熊熊燃烧的火沟。奎妮凭什么这样做？她凭什么？自退出那个读书俱乐部之后，她就再没有过这种感觉。月亮像一个银白色的碎片，放任清冷的光漫过大地。她踩着自己的影子向前走，因为脚上穿着那双开车穿的鞋，她在沙地中走得磕磕绊绊的。前方的海面起起伏伏，波浪从黑暗中翻滚而出。一股咸味儿刺痛了她的鼻子，风扑面而来，发出可怖的声音。她走到海湾尽头，一边沿着陡峭的木台阶向上爬，一边伸手抓住沙茅草，可草割得她的手生疼。她从那些关门闭户的木屋中穿过，朝花园走去。她的车停在了高尔夫球场上，车上放着她的行李与手提包，随时可以出发。奎妮想为其他人做什么都随她，就算夺走哈罗德也无妨，但她决不能霸占莫琳的儿子。她不能霸占戴维。

夜色中，花园变了个模样。当你知道东西长什么样子后，它们通常在你眼中会小一圈，但月光照在浮木上，却好像放大了它们。风发出她从未听过的声音，仿佛嘶鸣或者沸腾，随之而来的是短暂的静默。莫琳摸索着在雕塑之间前进。有什么飘动的东西撞到了她的手，吓得她一缩。她周围赫然耸立着一座座雕塑和一块块浮木，她害怕极了，感觉那些东西好似在盯着她。她得赶紧做完这件事，离开这儿。她得加快速度了。

莫琳朝着代表她儿子的那个物件走去。她伸出双手，紧紧抓在V形浮木的两侧，就好像抓住了一对角，然后开始用力拉拽。浮木纹丝不动，从她的手指间滑过，还擦伤了手指。她再次尝试，还是一样的结果。要是她有一副手套就好了。

"好吧。"她说，"看来我得动真格的了。"

这次，她俯下身去，将它罩在身下，让V形的两个尖正好位于她身体的两侧，然后她攥住浮木根部再次猛拉，非常用力地往外拉，可惜她没掌握好平衡。这回，她不但没能把它拉出来，还再次失去控制，踉跄地倒退了好几步。脚下的地面似乎在飞速撤离，她摔到了地上。一声刺耳的断裂声传来，同时她感觉到一阵难忍的痛楚。哦，天哪，她想，可千万别是我的儿子出事了。

她花了好一会儿才弄清楚发生了什么事。这些瞬间并非接踵而至，而是断断续续的，像一串句号。一切都错位了。她仰面躺在地上。天空。她看着夜空。星星，小小的，一闪一闪的。她后颈猛烈地撞上了什么东西，脊椎顿时感觉麻木了。她试着喘息。疼！她便屏住呼吸，开始尝试挪动自己的腿，可她都不确定挪动的是不是她的腿，或者说那条腿好像已经不是她的了。还是疼。她不知道自己的脚趾还在不在。她尝试着挪动身子，却听见像是动物被困在地下时发出的动静，然后才意识到那是自己发出的声音。于是她便不再试着坐起来。她一动不动地平躺在原地，做了次深呼吸，然后再次深呼吸。她开始觉得冷了。

"莫琳，"她说，"动一动。"

可她就是动不了。她无法挪动双臂或双脚，连头都动不得，因为她只要一尝试转动头部，脖子就会感到惊人的疼痛。一瞬间，她只想闭上眼睛睡觉。

"莫琳，"她再次命令自己，这次声音更大了，"快动一动，你这个笨蛋，快动。"

一点用都没有。无论她怎么不耐烦地催促自己，情况还是没有丝毫好转。她无计可施，因为身上太疼了。

"救命！"她高喊，"救命！"没有任何回音，也没有一个人来救她。

代表哈罗德的那根浮木离她只有几英尺之遥。莫琳依然保持着仰卧的姿态，一点一点地蹭着地面朝它挪过去。她的身体似乎是由几块材质脆弱的积木拼搭成的，而且拼搭的手法还十分拙劣。她脖子僵直着试图伸手去够那根木头，但不时爆出的星星点点的疼痛制止了她。若是她不转动脖子，就无法够到浮木。于是，她翻了个身，先伸出一条胳膊拽住那根木头，然后伸出另一条胳膊，将自己拽起来，跪坐在地上。自始至终，她都没有让脖子转动分毫。就这样，她双手抱住浮木，就好像这根木头焊在她的肩胛骨之间，接着她凭着这样的支撑向上爬，直到最后站了起来，将身体倚靠在浮木上。可只要她牵动脖子上的肌肉，就会出现一闪而过的疼痛。

现在，除了等待天亮，她什么也做不了。她让脊背紧紧贴着

"哈罗德",因为她清楚,要是没有他,她一定会像堆石头一样轰然倒地。她试着想象他像她在厨房洗碗时那样待在她身后,可这并不能宽慰她。她像活着的遗物一样,被困在奎妮的花园里,那些浮木和雕塑则盯着她,窃窃私语。此时她脑子里只剩下在书店度过的那晚。

她是否早就知道了?在她买那场活动的票时,心底某个角落是否就已经清楚当晚会发生什么了?"哦,你一定很爱那本书吧?"书店老板说。她把书紧紧按在胸前,就好像书长在她的重要器官上一样。不。莫琳不爱那本书。她为了新加入的读书小组读这本书,在读的过程中感到非常受伤——因为她不知道该如何自处。这本书讲的是一个女人二十岁的儿子上吊自杀的故事。她能读完这本该死的书的唯一原因是她想融入那个读书小组,不然她早就把它丢出窗外了。这是本可恨的书。

那天晚上,书店里挤满了人。莫琳想一个人待着,所以选择了最后一排的座位。可就在活动开始前不久,一个助理问她是否介意挪下地方,好给后来的人留点空。她只好从其他人身边挤过去,坐到了中间的座位上。于是,她在那个读书小组里新结识的人——黛博拉、爱丽丝,等等,都坐在他们各自的座位上向她投来微笑。莫琳只觉得心里紧绷绷的,就好像心被尼龙扎带缠住了一样。她感觉呼吸困难。

让她吃惊的是,那本书的作者比她想象的年轻。她可能刚二十多岁,身穿一件豹纹连衣裙,脚蹬一双牛仔靴,腰间的宽腰带显得她身段玲珑利落。她面向观众时，做的第一件事就是双手合十，低头做祈祷状。哦，莫琳讨厌这个一身游猎观光／牛仔女郎装束的作家。

尽管那个晚上她有种自己并不在场的奇怪感觉，就好像她在做一场梦，或者说她在回忆梦中的书店。她的心依然有压迫感，但奇怪的是，她的身体却感到空荡荡的，好像一根骨头都没有了。作者聊着她的书和生活，并针对丧亲之痛评说了几句，整个书店因此沉浸在悲痛中，一片寂静。书店老板说，这是迄今为止对她来说最重要、最让她动容的一次采访。然后是读者提问环节，有人问作者是否相信上帝，作者说她相信我们看不到的东西，读者们纷纷点头，还有几个人哭了起来。在此期间，莫琳始终保持着绝对的静止，既在场，又仿佛完全不在。接着，观众席中有个女人举起手，说道："我想问……"

椅子摩擦地面的声音响起。一排排读者向提问的人望去，脸上都带着警惕与困惑。书店老板说抱歉，没听清问题，然后一个年轻男子拿着麦克风，扭着身子从大家的膝盖中挤到了莫琳身边。因为读者中举着手的那个女人是她，靠着颤抖的腿站起来的、声音过分尖锐的那个女人是她——是她却又不像她。

"安娜·杜普里，我想问的是，你凭什么？"

莫琳已经记不得她当时具体说了什么。那段记忆化为她心中的一系列污斑，就好像她大脑中有一扇百叶窗挡在了语言形成和赋予语言意义的区域之间。就这样，她身体僵硬地立在虚空悬崖的边缘。她知道，她问了安娜·杜普里是否真的失去过孩子，是否真的以为自己知道失去孩子是什么感觉；她说当她看到杜普里的时候，发现她太年轻，根本没到生养一个孩子的年纪，更别提有一个成年的儿子了。她问杜普里有什么权利把她压根儿不理解的事情写成书，还把这本书卖到世界各地，卖给了数百万她压根儿不认识的读者——这就是她的原话。她是不是还管安娜·杜普里叫游客来着？好像是。她是不是指责整个书店里的人都是游客？她好像也这么说了。当她开口后，她就觉得无法停下了，尽管她必须得停下来，可停下来意味着她要面对后果；一个女人讲出这样一番话之后，她势必要面对接下来出现的可怕后果，所以她只能硬着头皮继续说，离那处虚空悬崖越来越近。有个戴着可爱圆形耳环的读书小组成员一直在摇头，好像在说：莫琳，别说了，快别说了，求你别让自己陷入如此境地。

安娜·杜普里听她说这番话时，手掩在嘴上，绷着脸。

莫琳想离开。更确切地说，她希望自己一开始就没来。那天发生的一切都不是她想看到的，可她就是被困在了那家书店里，困在了折叠椅与善良的人交织的丛林中。那些人尽量把目光投向别处，因为莫琳的脸涨得通红，她也能感觉到脸在发烫。她想说，对不起，我不是这个意思，可她已经把话都说出来了。太晚了。另外，她其实就是这个意思。这就是麻烦所在。她字字句句都发自真心，包括那些非常刺耳的话。

真是个难搞的孩子。

她奋力向门边走去，一路上膝盖不时撞到椅背，还要推开人们的手肘与肩膀，最后终于扑进了夏夜暖烘烘的空气中，这时她无意中听到有人低语:"对,那是他的妻子。"她知道,他们在谈论她和哈罗德。她知道,她再也不会去那家书店了。她知道,等她收到关于读书小组的邮件时,她会抱着格外矛盾的心情,不等点进去细看就把它们删掉。她不想再拿起哪怕一本该死的书,永远也不想了。她还知道,在超市里,人们看见她都会避开——尽管哈罗德说这不过是她的想象,但这反而激怒了她,因为这话听上去像是在说她多疑又偏执。总之,之后她就在网上购物了。

几个月后,莫琳在一本周日版杂志上读到一篇访谈,安娜·杜普里在上面谈及她写的那本全球畅销书,以及她因为一名读者对她说的话准备就此封笔,不再写小说了。我意识到,我再也编不出来了。莫琳将那本杂志扔进了垃圾箱。"活该。"她说。但她也不知道这话是她说给自己听的,还是说给安娜·杜普里听的。

她那天晚上做的事并不是最糟糕的事,就像在奎妮的花园中,那块无名的浮木并不是最可怜的。但这件事比漏尿的膀胱更糟糕,甚至比一个人在花园里偷东西时摔倒还糟糕。因为此举相当于莫琳把她不堪回首的丧亲之痛堂而皇之地摆了出来,她被孤立的人生处境和她的羞耻感因此得到了确实的印证。失去戴维是她的秘密,是那块让她每每面对都会粉身碎骨的石头。所以莫琳就像一架失控的大炮,向着四面八方开火。她就此无可挽回地、彻彻底底地背离了生活。她再也不会拥有自由了。

天一亮,莫琳就拖着脚穿过花园。这时的浮木和雕塑只是些阴影罢了。她在不转动脖子的情况下勉强能走路,但任何轻微的头部转动都会让她感觉到胳膊疼痛。冉冉升起的太阳发出橙色与粉色的光,照耀着大海与沙地上蜿蜒流过的小河湾。海滩上零星散落着根系像指关节的巨藻,还有浮木与塑料瓶。她感觉十分虚弱,都记不起上次吃饭是什么时候的事情了。远方,阳光洒在恩布尔顿湾沿岸房屋的窗户上,有那么短暂的一刻,它们像是着火了一样。她极度想和哈罗德通话,可他应该还在睡觉,就算没有,她也不知道该如何解释自己之前的所作所为。她甚至不知道该怎么坐进车里。

最后,莫琳缓慢地将身子放低。她发动汽车,以蜗牛般的速度驾车离开了海湾。她可以勉强在不低头看的情况下操纵踏板和挡位杆,不过她不能转动脖子去看后视镜。这些年来,她一直高昂着头,维持着自尊与体面,结果现在她想低头都困难。她尽量把注意力放在前方的道路上,强迫自己保持清醒,可疼痛以旋转的方式向她袭来,让她昏昏欲睡。她知道她应该拐弯,往回开,可她忍不了再在那家旅馆住一晚了。她听到后面有辆小型货车呼啸而至,靠得太近了。那辆车超过她时,车里的司机对她破口大骂,高喊着让她滚出这条路。

这一切让她无法承受。她做不到。她甚至不知道自己要去哪儿。事实是,她尽可以去一个她喜欢的地方,可她永远无法逃离自己。因为莫琳恨的不是安娜·杜普里。说到底并不是她。她恨的不是杜普里那本该死的书,不是很多喜欢那本书的人,而是那个年轻女人竟然能从悲痛中攫取某种美的东西,像全职专业选手一样以悲痛为生、以悲痛为空气的莫琳却没那个本事。现在,她知道奎妮通过那座花园也做到了同样的事,她再次败下阵来。

莫琳把车停在她经过的第一座加油站,然后给她唯一能想到的人打了电话。

12
咖啡豆
Coffee Beans

"莫琳，出什么事了？"

凯特一边叫着莫琳的名字，一边把脚伸出驾驶座的门，匆匆下了卡车。她的外孙女梅普尔坐在副驾驶座位上的母亲腿上。她们把车停在了加油站内离莫琳很近的位置。

"我动不了了。"

"伤到哪儿了？"

"我不知道。脖子。哪儿都疼。"

"让我来帮你，好吗？"

莫琳感觉到凯特朝她伸来双手，开始轻轻把她往车外抬，边抬边问她："怎么样？能行吗？"虽然眼下发生的事让她有些别扭，但她还是没有抗拒凯特的帮助，同时她也在想，自己应该把手放在哪儿。她既不想把凯特推开，也无法做到环抱住凯特，所以只好让手悬在半空中。凯特脸上挂着微笑，但莫琳不知道这是不是在对她微笑，她也不知道该说些什么。她发现凯特的双手温暖而有力。凯特领着莫琳小心翼翼地向她的卡车走去，打开后车门，另一只手还搀着莫琳，扶着她走上台阶，一步只上一级台阶，在此期间依然会问她："怎么样？能行吗？"之后，她扶着莫琳直接走到卡车最里面，那里的床已经拉出来准备好了。坐在副驾驶座位上的梅普尔转过身，越过她母亲的肩膀，忽闪着又黑又圆的眼睛。凯特将莫琳的身子安置在那床羽绒被上，然后又抬起莫琳的双脚。躺下的感觉真好。莫琳僵直地躺在那儿，闭上眼睛。现在我可以死了，她想。真的，我一动也不想动了。

"咱们是要送这位女士去医院吗？"梅普尔问。

"咱们得照顾她。"梅普尔的母亲说，"另外，我们还得安静点。"

凯特的脸离得那么近，莫琳都能感觉到她的呼吸——一种类似牙膏和泥土的味道。莫琳继续闭着眼睛，只听见凯特的声音说："好了，亲爱的。咱们接下来这么办。莎拉先开她的车返回营地，然后再去上班。我带你去医院检查，然后你跟我待在一起就行了。你什么都不用说。"

她缓缓地对莫琳说出这些话。她离得那么近，可她的声音又好像很遥远。莫琳始终闭着眼睛。她用最轻柔的声音呢喃了一句，表示她明白了。不过，她没动弹，也没准备好正经回答什么。疼痛宛如一波波浪涛冲刷着她的内心，她就想像现在这样一动不动地躺着，让对方像对孩子似的跟她亲切和善地说话。

莫琳感觉有个结实的东西放在了她头上，她意识到那应该是凯特的手，正在抚摸她花白的短发。"你经历了一段难挨的时间，但现在没事了。在你准备好之前，你不必再去别的地方。你会没事的。"

她的脖子没有骨折,但肌肉扭伤了,背上有很严重的瘀伤,另外就是血压偏低。莫琳需要休息几天,尽量少走动,显然也不适合开车。凯特陪莫琳在医院待着。她把梅普尔放在腿上,给她讲故事,讲了一遍又一遍。与此同时,莫琳直挺挺地坐在她旁边,恨不得有人能在她脊柱上放上一张烤盘。除非她挪动整个身体,否则一点都不敢活动背部,甚至不敢开口说话。她早就忘了孩子会反复听同一个故事,并从重复的讲述中得到无限的慰藉。

"你是不是很疼?"护士问。

"我还忍得了。"她说。

他笑了,好像看穿了她一样,然后给了她第一片强效止痛药,还给她演示了几套有助于缓解肩颈疼痛的动作。

"弗莱夫人,你很幸运。"他说。她没问他说这话是什么意思,因为她知道,他说得对。

凯特说她已经给哈罗德打过电话了,告诉他莫琳摔了一跤,但休息几天就没事了。她让哈罗德放心,说莫琳伤得不重,所以他不必过来,由她照顾莫琳就行。"他想问候一下你。"她说,然后再次拨打了哈罗德的电话,举着手机,把它放在莫琳的耳边。

"哦,莫,"她听见他说,他的声音中满怀爱意,"哦,甜心。"

她点点头,说:"嗯,嗯,嗯。"因为要想避免疼痛,她就只能说这些。

"你还好吗?你会没事的吧?"

她又应道:"嗯,嗯,嗯。"

"我能去看你吗?"

"不用,"她说,"我没事。凯特在呢。"药物起作用了。

之后,她让凯特领着她回到了卡车上。她觉得她对凯特搀扶自己的方式熟悉了一些,所以她可以更信任地倚靠凯特了。凯特驱车慢慢回到了营地,然后热了一锅汤,跟她一起在桌旁喝了起来。莫琳筋疲力尽,连把勺子举到嘴边都很勉强。凯特取来羽绒被,安顿她躺下、盖上被子。她不再觉得这张床凹凸不平或者陌生了。凯特把羽绒被搂到莫琳下巴处,说:"好了,睡吧,亲爱的。"直到莫琳的眼皮垂下。睡意突然袭来。或许是止痛药的缘故。她清楚地知道她在想哈罗德,想和他再说说话,可她就是无法打起精神睁开眼睛。

莫琳醒来时,感觉自己像是从一个黑洞似的地方冒出来的一样。她不知道自己为什么会在那儿,也不知道"那儿"是哪儿。接着,莫琳的视野渐渐清晰,辨认出了凯特,她坐在翼背椅中,戴着一副大眼镜,在台灯下看一本从图书馆借的书。有那么一刻,莫琳慌了神,就好像自己缺席了一段时间,那段时间发生的事情她通通都不知道。她挣扎着要坐起来,可身上太疼了,她只好继续躺在床上。

"休息吧。"凯特说,她的目光从书后扫了过来,"我后来又跟哈罗德通了电话。他托我跟你转达他的关心。他说他和雷克斯在一块儿呢。"

"他有没有说他们在干什么?"莫琳说。可是还没等凯特回答,她就闭上了眼睛。

第二次醒来时,莫琳看到梅普尔蜷缩在凯特腿上,凯特正在给她讲另一个故事，但声音非常低，更像是在吟诵经文，莫琳听不出她具体在讲些什么。她也不需要听清，光听着这声音，知道身边有人陪伴，就已经是一种安慰了。她拉着凯特的羽绒被蒙到头上，再次睡了过去。她再次醒来的时候已经是早晨了，天空仿佛紫色云霞下的一条银带。卡车里只有她自己。

凯特用托盘端来了咖啡，并且在桌上摆了两个杯子。她搀扶莫琳坐起身，给她垫上几个靠枕，又喂她服下一片止痛药。她们都默契地避而不谈莫琳上次造访期间发生的事，而是选择聊一些无关痛痒的事，比如咖啡。凯特告诉莫琳，这壶咖啡她用的是自己新磨的咖啡豆，莫琳说她总是随身带着速溶咖啡。凯特愣了一下，然后斩钉截铁地说，应该没人喝那种垃圾。她说那玩意儿差劲得很，喝它就跟喝刷锅水一样。说罢，她拿起土耳其市集上的那种银壶，把她煮的咖啡倒进两个蓝色的小杯子里，像在进行某种仪式。莫琳艰难地喝了一小口——她的脖子不能动，所以只能喝一小口——发现凯特说得不假。这咖啡的确相当可口。热气腾腾，加了牛奶，只有一丝苦味，还带着巧克力的香甜。于是，她们通过这种方式避开了分歧，得以继续相处。

"需不需要我帮你端杯子？"凯特说。

"不用，我自己能行。"

"哦，莫琳，你为什么不能让别人帮你一回呢？"

说完她就端起杯子，把咖啡送到莫琳嘴边，还把碟子放在莫琳下巴下面。这次，莫琳终于痛痛快快喝了一口。

"我觉得我欠你一个道歉。"莫琳说。

凯特笑了。"你什么都不欠我的。不过，莫琳，我倒是很高兴你在需要帮助的时候能给我打电话。我很高兴你又给了我们一个好好认识的机会。"

杯子里的咖啡都喝完之后，她们又默默地坐了一会儿。然后凯特伸出一只手紧紧握住莫琳的手，这样她就能感觉到莫琳手的重量和手心的老茧。凯特没有看莫琳，而是望着窗外说："我们要怎么做？我们要怎样才能接受那些让人无法接受的事？"

沉默过后，她的声音和问题回荡在整个空间中。莫琳突然意识到自己有多么疲惫，就好像此时并非早晨，而是又到了晚上，凯特拉上窗帘。"还需要什么吗？"

"没有了，谢谢你。你帮我的忙已经够多了。"

"那你好好休息吧。"

在暗下来的光线中，莫琳躺到凯特的羽绒被下，再次沉沉睡去。

后来，凯特敲了敲卡车的车门，问莫琳有没有感觉好一点。她想找莫琳帮个忙。她和女儿要参加一个女性会议，只需要离开两个小时。她问莫琳是否愿意帮忙带一下梅普尔。"莫琳，我不知道该怎么办了。我感觉挺不好意思的，但还是想问下，你是否愿意考虑一下呢？"

莫琳说："行。我很高兴你能问我。"

"你觉得你应付得来吗？"

"也许可以吧。我不确定梅普尔喜不喜欢我。"

凯特听见这话大笑起来。"哦,莫琳。"她说,"听听你在说什么吧。她还是个孩子。你要是对她好,她自然会喜欢你。"

于是,凯特离开前把梅普尔送来了,梅普尔还把她的书和水彩笔带到了卡车上。凯特涂着莫琳欣赏不来的口红,但莫琳忍住了,什么都没说。梅普尔用力拥抱了她的外祖母,双手环住她的脖子,好像挂在她身上的一条大项链。这让莫琳顿时觉得这个计划行不通,可是凯特吻了梅普尔一下,说莫琳是个好人,然后就跟她们道别了。一开始,梅普尔对莫琳很警惕。她坐在餐桌旁,但是一直抱着她的书和其他东西,就好像害怕莫琳把它们偷走一样。看来此时最好还是给她一些空间。

莫琳去小厨房洗了几个盘子。她想,那些止痛药真是管用。她找了块布,然后拧开水龙头,让热乎乎的肥皂水注入塑料水槽。

坐在桌旁的梅普尔开口说话了。她还在给画上色,说话的时候手也没停,而且是想到什么说什么,也无须莫琳做任何评论。不过,莫琳认真听着梅普尔说的每一句话,听得很入迷,因为她已经很长时间没有像这样与一个孩子独处了。她都忘了孩子们是多么喜欢滔滔不绝了。梅普尔开始讲她的一个女生朋友、一条在农场上汪汪叫的黑白相间的花狗、她的自行车,等等。这些话题之间唯一的联系就是它们都装在梅普尔的小脑袋里。然后这个小女孩从桌边的凳子上滑下来,搬着凳子来到莫琳身边,问自己是否能看看莫琳在做什么。

于是,莫琳在保持脖子不动的前提下,扶着梅普尔站到了凳子上，让她将小手伸进肥皂水里来回搅动，洗了几把勺子。与此同时，梅普尔还在喋喋不休，直到莫琳意识到自己没有再认真听她说话的内容了，而是在听她的语调，因为莫琳在忙着擦拭周围的一切。她擦了水龙头、塑料水槽的边沿、水槽与沥水板接触的边缘、各种厨房五金部件的表面、各种炊具、烧水壶，还有后面的防溅挡板。她甚至擦掉了水槽下水口的塞子和抽屉把手上的污渍，还将挂茶巾的挂钩擦得干干净净。她继续干着活，因为在热水中洗涮抹布、将其拧干的过程，也因为梅普尔那歌唱般的嗓音，她的心情逐渐平静下来。但对她心情平静帮助最大的还是眼看着各种器具的表面变得洁净——尽管这里没有消毒剂喷雾、碧丽珠或希恩先生清洁剂，也没有橡胶手套。她把所有的马克杯整理了一遍，将它们的把手统一朝右摆放。此时，她已经感觉筋疲力尽了。然后梅普尔突然往床上一躺，要求莫琳给她讲她带来的绘本。

绘本讲的是关于兔子的故事。有一群小兔子住在一座大房子里——它们竟然不是住在洞穴里，而且它们都戴着帽子，穿着衣服。刚讲了三页，莫琳就睡着了。梅普尔开始喊她的名字，这让莫琳感觉到一种久别的愉悦，听一个孩子喊她名字的愉悦。"冒——琳——"[1]听起来甜腻而清晰。她只好重新拿起书，强撑着又讲了一页——这些兔子似乎是在做汤——然后又闭上了眼睛，她在梅普尔身边伸了个懒腰后睡着了。

---

[1] 此处为梅普尔的错误发音。

凯特和女儿回来时，看到这位老太太和小女孩都躺在床上。莫琳大张着嘴，鼾声如雷；梅普尔也张着嘴，小脸绯红，头埋在莫琳的臂弯中。莎拉抱起梅普尔，凯特往莫琳身边塞了一个靠枕。她给莫琳留下一盒止痛药和一杯水，以防莫琳醒来后需要。

早晨，莫琳问是否能再看一眼梅普尔的绘本。她想知道故事的结局如何。

"那个故事相当好看，"她说，"我很喜欢。"

就这么简单。一句让人听着开心的话就这么脱口而出。

13 月光鸣奏曲

Moonlight Sonata

莫琳已经很长时间没像这样被人照顾过了。她在那辆洞穴般的卡车上又住了三天，卡车里满满当当尽是捕梦网、佛像、脉轮石和玫瑰灯，还弥漫着一股焚香的味道。这三天都是凯特为她做饭、洗衣服。莫琳向窗外望去，看见她那条舒服的宽松长裤在晾衣绳上随风摇摆，旁边晾着梅普尔的小衣裳。她常常能看到小女孩骑自行车或者摆弄她母亲彩虹色的头发。偶尔，她还能看到其他女人，她们有时会停下来在外面聊会儿天，或一起喝咖啡。有时，梅普尔会拿着她的书蜷在莫琳身边，莫琳则会设法在保持脖子挺直的情况下给她讲书上的故事。外面的世界都装在那扇窗里，它时而晨曦朦胧，时而乌云蔽日，时而会被窗帘遮住。另外，这些天她拥有了从未有过的睡眠，酣甜、自在，一觉醒来，看看表，浑然不知是清晨还是傍晚，闭上眼睛还能继续睡。她经常给哈罗德打电话，他会给她讲他和雷克斯正在干什么，也就是他们平常做的事——玩跳棋和观鸟。她问他们有没有记得好好吃饭，他告诉她，记得，而且他们在这方面做得相当出色，他们刚吃了红烩牛肉和炖菜，但剩下了一盘馅饼和一碗汤。他最希望的还是她的身体能好起来,这是他常挂在嘴边的话。

"我很高兴你和凯特住在一起。"第三天时他对她说,"我就知道你会喜欢她的。在与我同行的所有人里,我最喜欢她了。这我跟你说过吗?"

"嗯,"莫琳说,"也许说过吧。不过,你再说一遍也无妨。"

"我想你。"

"我也想你。"

"你很快就能回家了。"

"但愿明天能行吧。"

"你猜我们看见什么了?"

"我猜不出。"

"我们看见了一只赭红尾鸲。"

"一只鸟,是吗?"

"对,莫。那只鸟就像你一样,是个美人。"

*

那天夜里,莫琳睁开眼睛,是开门的轻响吵醒了她。窗帘是拉开的,月光洒进了卡车里,把这儿照得如同白昼,只不过一切事物仿佛是夜光的,而且蒙着淡淡的蓝色。

他就在那儿,坐在翼背椅上看着她。他把她的衣服放在了地上,不过放得很小心,不会弄出褶子。

"戴维。"她轻声呼唤。

"你好啊。"他说。

他的坐姿还和以前一样,两条腿舒展地伸开,像个高大的人偏偏生在了一副过于小巧的躯壳里。他穿着他那件大翻领的旧大衣,翻领上别满了徽章,脚上穿的是他最喜欢的黑色靴子。他的褐色头发长而浓密,跟他把头发剃光之前一样。他还是老样子,头发略微凌乱,有些衣冠不整,但眼神犀利。他既没有嗑药,也没有喝醉,清醒而平静。他手捧一束冬日的花束,看起来像是有金缕梅、鲜红的山茱萸,一些蕨类植物、结着浆果的常春藤和深红色的山楂。他的指甲是绿色的。

"真的是你吗?真的是我的儿子吗?"

"是我。"

"我还以为永远都见不到你了。"

"可是,"他说,他腼腆地耸了两三次肩,"我就在这儿啊。"

他沉默了一会儿,用那双美丽的黑眼睛注视着她,她也一动不动,不想做出任何会破坏这一刻的事。她想知道,这捧冬日花束是他要送给她的,还是他恰好拿在手里而已?

"你还好吗?"最后她说。

"我一切都好。"

"这么说会不会太荒唐了?"

"我觉得不会。"

"我一度习惯跟你倾诉。那时候我总是找你聊天。我跟你说的话要比我跟任何人说的都多,这是真的。"她说话声音柔和,语速却很急,因为她怕如果没能说出口,这些话就会蒸发掉,"我什么事都跟你说,比如我在忙什么、想什么,而你会倾听。你对我那么有耐心。我知道我说话有些颠三倒四的,但我真的希望我能跟你解释清楚。也许我不需要解释。"

他点点头。然后,他低头看着那束花,摸了摸葡萄叶铁线莲的种球,它柔软而洁白,像是一个小线团。

"后来,我变了。我不再跟你倾诉了。这种行为伤害到你了吗?当时我是不是应该继续找你倾诉?那样的话你会喜欢吗?"

"没关系的。"

"我知道。我知道。我问的问题太多了。这完全是因为我又看到你了,我有太多的话想对你说。"

他把花束放在胳膊下面,伸手从口袋里掏出烟。他用火柴将烟点燃,烟雾飘到窗前投下的月光光柱时,从灰色变成了蓝色。他说:"你的脖子怎么了?"

"哦,没什么。"

"看着应该挺疼的。"

"我吃着药呢,睡眠也很充足。只不过,我吃药吃得有点迷糊了。"

他微微一笑,深吸了一口烟,吐气时稍稍眯起了眼睛。

"这儿还住着一个女人,这些天是她照顾我的。我原以为我不喜欢她,但后来我发现自己错了。凯特是个好人。所以,实话实说,我没事。我只是得在这儿待上几天。有点像人们说的避世隐居?"

她害怕自己一不说话,他就会消失。老天保佑,他现在看起来已经有点要消失的样子了。

"我不知道。我不知道人们会怎么形容这个状态。我从来都不擅长这些。"

"戴维?"她说,"如果我在这里住的时间久一些,你会留下来陪我吗?"

他再次微微一笑,不过这次感觉像是她问了什么让他回答起来痛苦的问题,然后他又用指关节揉了揉眼睛。她还记得他小时候做作业时是如何揉眼睛的,他会揉到脸发红、膝盖抽搐。她还记得她多么担心,像他那样拼命地学习,想要超越别人,会是一种惩罚。她记起自己年轻时是如何有着同样的渴望。她是多么想跳出自己生活的那个地方。他俩是一样的。戴维只是像接力一样接过了她手中的一棒。

"我真希望当时我给你买了狗。"

"狗?"

"对。可我当时太害怕了。我是说,我太害怕狗了。我小的时候,有个农夫放任他的狗追我。可你一直想养狗来着。"

"我不记得了。"

"你聊起狗就停不下来。"

"什么?"他说,"我会那样吗?"

"你难道不记得我们圣诞节送给你的那只狗了吗?"

"什么狗?"

"哦,那是一只会汪汪叫的丑八怪。你把它放在包装盒里,没再多瞧一眼。"

他再次大笑起来，这次她也跟着笑了。能再次像这样和戴维一起欢笑，感觉真好。他们总是能相互理解。

她说："我去看了奎妮的花园。你看过吗？"

"我为什么会看过她的花园？"

"我不知道。我慢慢得出一个结论，那就是我知之甚少。我是个愚蠢的老太婆。我只知道这些。"她想，即使过了这么多年，那种被掏空的感觉还在。现在她终于和他重聚了，她不知道要如何才能狠下心弃他而去。"哦，戴维。我无法继续生活。对不起。我只想着我自己了。我不想过没有你的生活。别再离开我了。留下来。"

他缩了一下，就好像她刚刚打了他。她说得太多了。她又一次没有控制好自己的嘴，说了完完全全、彻彻底底不该说的话。她这张该死的嘴啊！这次，她不是对陌生人说的，而是对她自己的儿子说的。

戴维滑下椅子，放下花束，佝偻着坐在地板上，下巴抵着膝盖。之前她以为那束花肯定是用绳子绑在一起的，结果并不是，现在枝条和花朵全都散开了。这时，它已经没有一束花的样子了，而像是他经过时因为喜爱而折下的一把冬天的植物。或许是他还没来得及考虑拿它们怎么办，也许他只是顺手折了这些树枝。

他开始抱着自己静静地哭泣，摇晃着身子，就好像他不想让她知道他在哭一样。

莫琳下了床，跪坐在他身边，抬起胳膊搂住他的肩膀，把他拉近,直到他身体的重量都落在她身上。她的肩膀扭了一下,但这不算什么。她想,就算身体从内到外翻过来,我都不会动的。他柔软的头发挨着她的脸颊,闻起来有他十几岁时用过的洗发水的味道,有点像医院里的味道。他曾在电视上看到了这款洗发水的广告,便不停地催促她去买。她已经很多年没有闻到这种味道了,甚至连想都没想过,但现在却感觉这是她生命中最真实的东西,甚至比她膝下的地板或窗外的月光都真实。她想把这种气味都吸入身体,这样就永远不会忘记了。她想到了很多她想说的话。我错过了这么多。我怎么能让你走呢?她希望能有机会给他买他喜欢的洗发水,想在早晨问他前一晚睡得怎么样,想按照他喜欢的方式给他煎鸡蛋——单面煎的鸡蛋,想了解他小时候说他想做世界的客人是什么意思。

但这些她都没说,因为他先开口了。他问她能不能听他说。他有事要告诉她,因为这些事让他心里堵得慌,可因为这些事太糟糕了,他之前没说出口。他不停地说:"对不起,对不起,对不起。"几乎每一句话都是在道歉。

"没关系。"她说,"没关系的。你可以告诉我,孩子。我在呢。我当然会听你说。你想说什么就说什么。把一切都告诉我。我哪儿也不去。"

他告诉她,他过去总是从她的钱包里偷钱,他对此感到很抱歉。他真希望自己没有染上酗酒和嗑药的毛病,但那只是因为他曾经一度相信自己可以成为一个特别的人,他需要让脑子里那个说他一无是处的声音安静下来。他说他还记得小时候在班特姆海滩上跑进海里,他不知道为什么要一直跑下去,只知道他以为自己会游泳,他为此感到抱歉。还有一件事他也很抱歉,他毕业那天让他们在烈日下等了两个小时,以致他们错过了整个典礼。

莫琳说:"我知道,我都知道。没关系,儿子。没关系的。可是,天哪,你并非一事无成。你听到了吗?"

他告诉她,他实际上并没有完成剑桥的学业,他被开除了,所以毕业典礼就是个谎言,他是个浑蛋,因为她为了参加典礼买了条新裙子,哈罗德则买了件新夹克,他们都为他感到骄傲。他说,当时他就在远处看着他们,现在一想到他们穿着最好的衣服等在那儿是什么感觉,他就难受得要命。

"我知道。"她说,"没关系。反正那天我穿的那条裙子很糟糕。我都不知道那时候我在想什么。真的。我看起来像一只煮熟的虾。就算是我,也会放我鸽子的。"

他说他希望自己从来没有剃过光头,因为他知道那个举动刺痛了她。他问她是否还记得他喜欢的那顶插着羽毛的帽子,她笑着说:"哦,记得,儿子。是的,我记得那顶帽子。那顶帽子很讲究。戴着跟花花公子似的。你戴着像孔雀。儿子,没关系。我知道,我都知道。没关系。"

他还有很多话想对她说。他恨不能以最快的速度卸下种种负担。她刚刚听完一件事,他就又给她说一件,然而他说的每一件事都契合了她埋在内心深处的某种东西。他说他三岁时有多喜欢自己的第一双鞋("我知道,我知道。"),他问她是否还记得他想种的盆景,她抱着他说,记得。"没关系,儿子。我知道,我都知道。没关系。"

她把他揽近了些。他们若是站着,她都够不到他的肩膀,现在她却张开双臂,把他完全拥在臂弯里。她想,为了这个男孩,我可以变成世界那么大。然后她把他的头发拢到后面,捧起他的脸对着她,但他的脸开始逐渐消失,黑眼睛也更模糊了,就连他的肩膀都薄了。"你是个了不起的人,"她说,"你听见了吗?天哪,你真的很了不起。"

她待在他身边,抱着他,听他说话,虽然她已经听不清了。后来,她听到了第一声鸟鸣,发现自己躺在床上。卡车里除了她没有别人。窗帘是拉上的。她穿着睡衣。戴维没有坐在翼背椅上,她也没有在他身边。这里没有什么冬日花束,也没有任何迹象表明他来过,甚至没有洗发水或烟灰的气味。她的衣服好好地叠放在椅子扶手上,和她之前放的一样。

她躺在床上,太阳出来了,冬日的阳光洒进卡车,鸟儿不停地叫着,唧唧,咕咕咕!吱吱!早上好!早上好!

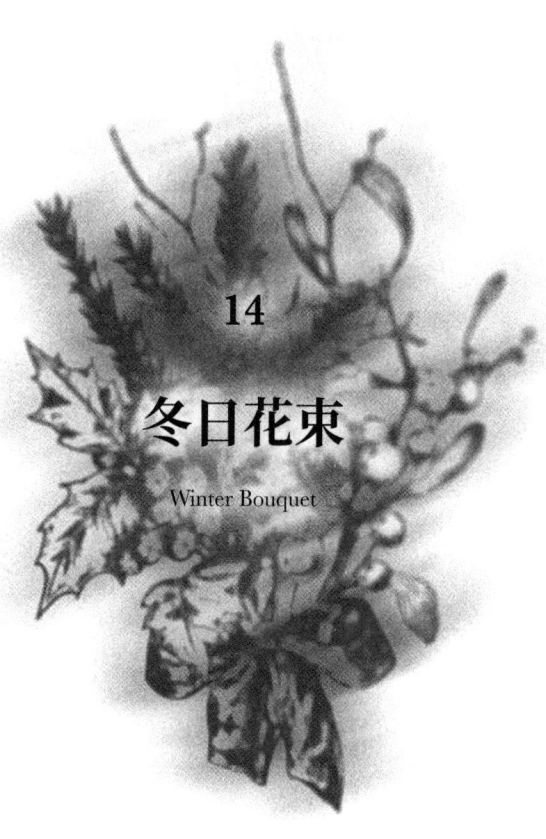

14
冬日花束
Winter Bouquet

离开凯特后,莫琳做了一件她自己都想不明白的事——她就是这样。她开车到赫克瑟姆,问一个陌生人哪里有书店。她买了一本安娜·杜普里的平装书,然后找到一家花店,选了束冬天的花。虽说她想不明白,但她还是去做了这些事。毕竟,整个旅途充斥着她无法理解的事,再多两件也无妨。她把书和花放在副驾驶座位上,然后开回了高尔夫球场。她把它们带进了奎妮的花园。这是她的第三次到访,也是最后一次。

她和凯特的分别不疾不徐,温情脉脉。莫琳没说晚上的事,不过她相信,凯特虽然不完全清楚发生了什么,但她调直翼背椅的靠背后,稍稍停顿了一下,然后抚平了椅套上的褶皱,这时她肯定察觉到了什么。她帮莫琳收拾好行李箱,然后煮了一壶咖啡,一起穿着大衣坐在外面的塑料椅子上喝。她给了莫琳一包新磨的咖啡豆,让她带回家给哈罗德尝尝。她们还说好了要保持联系,以后再见面。接着,让莫琳又惊又喜的事发生了,凯特捧住莫琳的脸,带着一种圆满的意味吻了她一下,让她想起了在信上盖邮戳的感觉。"我不会忘记你在我的卡车里卧床休息的这些日子。"她说,"不管发生什么,我都会永远地保留关于你的这段记忆。"

当她步行穿过高尔夫球场朝沙丘走去时,下午已经过去了一半。尽管太阳破云而出,斜斜地将阳光洒在大地上,投射出一个个纺锤般细长的影子,也洒在近旁的一朵云上,将它照得仿佛海湾上空的一个大橘子。花园里除了她之外只有一个人——一个男人,他坐在远处角落里,礼袍外穿着一件防水夹克,还戴着一顶帽子,低着头,手握一串念珠。空中飘着雨,不过只是牛毛细雨,对她没什么影响。

莫琳艰难地从哈罗德和戴维的浮木雕塑前经过,朝着那块中间有个洞的无名浮木走去。她给那本书找了个好地方,就在一座用瓶盖和软木塞做成的雕塑与一个明艳粉纸花做的花环旁边,她把那本书放在了那里。

"安娜·杜普里,我希望你能再写出一本畅销书。"她说,"我真这么想的。不过,要是届时我没买来看,希望你也不要介意。"

然后,她转身面对人们以为不代表任何人的那块有洞的浮木。它其实代表莫琳。她知道,从住在旅馆那晚她就知道了。她跪下来,把一只手放在洞上,有那么一会儿,这块浮木好像变得完整了。伤痛消失了。随之消失的还有她的愤怒和怨恨。它们终于不见了。之前她一直搞错了:这块脆弱的浮木并非奎妮出于恶意摆在这里的,也不是出于同情。它体现了一颗宽恕之心。她们在晾衣绳旁见面的那天,奎妮懂得了莫琳的悲痛,而且尽力给予了那份"懂得"一个位置,就像莫琳现在明白,奎妮写给哈罗德的信其实是对爱放手的意思。她很高兴自己把那封信放在了鞋盒里。就这样，虽然她们没有任何言语的交流，但还是接过了彼此的失落，并为彼此不堪承受的那份情愫赋予了意义。

莫琳独自一人跪在她未曾理解的花园中。天上的云再次被风撕开，阳光漏下来，洒向海面，照在片片雨水上，空中遂出现了雪白的小小亮点。一只红隼双翼支成钩状，迎着海风翱翔。莫琳久久地注视着它，突然感觉自己似乎能和那只鸟看得一样远，甚至能比它看得还远。

整个诺森伯兰郡在眼前铺陈开来，绵延起伏，涟漪般荡向南方。她仿佛看到了下方片片低缓的丘陵与平原、古老建筑的燧石墙、交织成各种图案的田野、山谷与高地沼泽；还有切维厄特丘陵、奔宁山脉的山脊、峰区的石灰岩峡谷、鲍兰德森林西面天鹅绒一样的尖坡、约克郡谷地、地形起伏的科茨沃尔德丘陵、门迪普丘陵、白垩岩海滩；壮丽的河流——泰恩河、乌斯河、特伦特河、埃克斯河，片片湿地，大森林与小树林，其中各种各样的树在她脚下仿佛苔藓与水藻；此外，她看到了公路、铁路和运河交织而成的网络，工厂与仓库、蔓生的城市、污水处理工程和成堆的有害物质、石棉与塑料、垃圾填埋场；被漫山遍野的石楠花染成紫色的达特穆尔高原，一处蓝色的河口，一条两边坐落着一栋栋小房子的路，每栋小房子都带着一座花园，哈罗德就在那花园里仰头看天、观鸟。她想象着世界的边缘在缓缓转动，她的身体停留在原地，随着这不可思议的运动而运动，思想却蜿蜒深入地表之下，穿过孔洞与沟渠，穿过遮天蔽日、密密匝匝的草地；她的思想沿古老的河道而行,去看地下那花体字般纹路繁复的贝壳;她跟随甲虫钻进打卷的叶子里,一直钻,往深里钻,钻到幼虫藏身的地方。她仿佛化身为黑暗中一个无眼的球,或者说是一层不断向远方探索的根系。然后,那只茶隼飞出了她的视野,她重新回到了奎妮的花园。

"好吧,"她渐渐回过神来,说道,"莫琳,莫琳。现在你终于疯了。"

莫琳凝神望着所有这些浮木雕塑和雨伞一样的种子头。她想,我是世界的客人。她突然想明白了。她明白戴维小时候说的那句话的意思了。因为她失去了儿子,其他的妈妈却没有,所以她一直活得好像这个世界亏欠了她。她想到哈罗德观鸟时的样子,想起他看到一只蓝喉歌鸲时眼睛立刻亮起来的样子。一个活了一辈子的老人,突然开始在重量和一枚硬币差不多、披着一身羽毛的小家伙身上找乐子。如果不是因为丧子之痛,还能是因为什么呢?一股痛苦的喜悦涌上心头,仿佛血液涌进饥饿的肢体。整个故事的主题就是宽恕。哈罗德的朝圣,奎妮的信,还有如今莫琳的这趟冬日之旅。风中摆动的风铃与石头项链,还有那一个个种头,也是在讲宽恕。没错,它们说。没错,莫琳!一切都围绕宽恕而存在。她想到了那些因无法承受失去至亲至爱而为他们寻找安息之地的陌生人。他们在花园里留下了爱的挂锁、纸十字架、照片、钥匙与花朵、自制的纪念物和成百上千根蜡烛、诗歌与留言。原谅我,原谅我,原谅我在你离去之后还继续活着。目光所至,你总能看到人最本质的孤独——不管是在服务区、书店里，还是停在路边的车里。因此，人们为了努力承受失去而做的选择都应当得到尊重。这些出于爱的举动不过是在通过许多不同的方式来表达同一件事，因为这种事的确无法言说。

莫琳站起来，将冬日花束靠在V形浮木上。奎妮把戴维放在花园里是对的。他不是莫琳失去的儿子，他是他自己。他不属于任何人，只属于他自己。

"奎妮，谢谢你。"她说，同时惊讶地发现自己在流泪。

莫琳在停车场给哈罗德打了电话。她告诉他，她要开一夜的车，得很晚才能到家，不过她还想给埃克塞特附近的一个夜班保安送去一张感谢卡，因为那人帮助过她。她说的这些，他只说了一句好。他当然会说好了，天哪，真好。她一定会小心谨慎地开车，不管什么时候，只要她觉得有必要，就停下来。如果她想，她还会找个地方睡一觉。虽然他等不及要见到她，但他知道，最重要的莫过于她的安全。然后她问："你们俩今天吃了什么？"

"哦，我们吃得可丰盛了。我和雷克斯吃了三明治。"

"你们在里面放了什么？"

"三明治里面吗？"

"对啊。"

"我们好像什么都没放。"

"这么说你们吃的是面包喽？说到底就是吃了面包嘛。"

"是的。"他哈哈大笑，就像"面包"是他未曾想到的、一个让人开心的词，"雷克斯，听见了吗？我们吃的三明治其实是面包！"

莫琳朝着海湾对面的奎妮的花园看了最后一眼。尽管她以前没注意过,但这个世界上发生了不少勇敢的事。树枝上发出了成簇的黑色小芽,地面上也冒出了小到不能再小的新芽,绿得仿佛珠翠。风依然刺骨,脖子依然隐隐作痛,但她不觉得痛苦了。

莫琳多待了一会儿,因为她不愿放过白天这最后一点时间。她甚至不愿放过这独处的时刻。眼下如此平和宁静。远方,奎妮的花园若隐若现,明明灭灭。她望着蕨红的天空中那卷着金边的重重云彩,尽管此时挂在地平线上的太阳只有一颗润喉糖大小,但夕阳余晖依然如洪水般涨起。一群褐色的鸟儿俯冲向一片冬天的灌木,叽叽喳喳,就像街角聊闲话的人一样说个不停。它们在说什么?不管它们说的是什么,她都喜欢听。那么忙碌,那么热闹!唧唧,咕咕咕!吱吱!啾啾!她不清楚该怎么解释,但就算清楚,也不需要——总而言之,她知道,此时此刻,她感受到了久违的快乐。

"莫琳。"她轻声说,"莫琳啊,莫琳。"

然后,她上了车,踏上了归家之旅。

致中国读者

——与莫琳·弗莱的电邮往来

亲爱的莫琳·弗莱：

在书的结尾添加一些额外内容已经成了我的一点小执念，所以我想知道你是否愿意接受我的采访？

祝好

蕾秋·乔伊斯

亲爱的蕾秋·乔伊斯：

你是谁？什么书？你说的"一点小执念"是什么意思？

你的莫琳·弗莱

附言：你是记者吗？

亲爱的莫琳·弗莱：

我想通过电子邮件问你几个问题，不过你完全有拒绝回答的自由。我不是记者。我觉得自己更像是一个和你挨得非常近的邻居。

祝好

蕾秋·乔伊斯

亲爱的蕾秋·乔伊斯：

我很抱歉。我还是不明白。你是想跟我丈夫通信吗？

你的莫琳·弗莱

附言：你是那个在封城期间一直敲锅抗议NHS（国民医疗服务体系）的邻居吗？那时候我们其他人都不敲了，只有那个人还在敲，并且打扰到了我们这条路上住的唯一一个真正为NHS上夜班的人。那个人是你吗？

亲爱的莫琳：

不是我。

不过，我承认有一段时间我也敲锅抗议来着。那时候，我不知道自己还能做什么。另外，我也喜欢听别人敲锅的声音。

祝好

蕾秋

亲爱的蕾秋：

好吧，我承认我也敲过锅。

那么，你想问什么样的问题？

莫琳

亲爱的莫琳：

这些问题可能会帮助人们更了解你。比如，你喜欢吃天然黄油还是人造黄油？

诸如此类吧。

蕾秋·乔伊斯

莫琳：我不吃人造黄油。就着那玩意儿还不如连吐司都不要吃了。

蕾秋：这算是你接受采访了吗？

莫琳：我也不确定。再看吧。

  总的来说，我觉得人们对了解彼此的渴望超出了必要的限度。当然，生活并非如此，或者说没那么简单。有些人拍下他们吃的每一顿饭，喝的每一杯咖啡，就好像这样会让他们更透明，而实际上，这些照片只是反映了他们喝了很多咖啡。

蕾秋：你是在说社交媒体吗？

莫琳：我的隔壁邻居最近玩起了社交媒体。有五个人关注了他，其中一个是只叫索尔兹伯里的猫。我说："雷克斯！你被一个伪装成宠物的人关注了。"不过，雷克斯似乎很开心。他发了一些鸟的照片，所以也许我错了。也许他和索尔兹伯里之间有很多事可以分享。

  我想我们看问题的角度都不一样。然而，人们似乎越来越不愿意接受我们是不同的，所以也越来越容易拿自己的标准去评判别人。

  我承认过去我自己也很爱对别人品头论足。毕竟，放下偏见很难，但也很有必要。

蕾秋：那你重视女性友谊吗？

莫琳：我不会只因为一样事物本身的好处而重视它。我重视和所有女人之间的友谊吗？不。我并不喜欢所有女人，正如我并不喜欢所有男人一样。随着年龄的增长，我想拥有更多的念头也越来越淡了，我更想利用好我已知的东西。

我又想起了我的隔壁邻居雷克斯。（你认识这个邻居吗？）我清楚，他明摆着不是做朋友的料，但这么多年来，我们一打照面就礼貌地微笑致意，再加上我会借牛奶给他——他妻子去世后，他失去了判断一个人喝多少牛奶的能力，我几乎什么事情都可以跟他说。我解释不清我们怎么就发展出了这么深厚的友谊。可能就是因为方便吧，因为我们住隔壁，同时我们都需要说点什么。

最近我遇到了一个住在卡车里的女人——实际上她现在还住在那辆卡车里。我错怪了她。我第一次见到她的时候，她的头发里编着丝带，身上简直像套了个麻袋，我觉得她整个人看起来都像是羊毛做的。我以为，因为她有她独特的生活方式（比如住在卡车里），我们聊不到一起去。但事实证明我错了。

通过她，我意识到，有时候，即使你和一个人待在一起不说话，但那仍然算是一种交流。

她和我现在定期互寄明信片。我打算再去看她，不过

  我建议这回我们在海边租一个小木屋，就别住在她的卡车上了。只有吃了止痛药的人才会觉得她睡的床很舒服。

蕾秋：谢谢你，莫琳。

莫琳：我希望我没有多说话。

蕾秋：我喜欢你的回答。

莫琳：我不得不说，友谊这个问题比黄油那个好多了。

蕾秋：那个问题相当于热身了。我承认那个问题不怎么样。我可以认为你是个热心的园丁吗？你想多谈谈这个吗？

莫琳：我一直种可食用植物来着，但是我最近去旅行了。我就是在旅行途中，遇到了我前面提的那个女人——住在卡车里的女人。我还参观了一个花园——这对你来说可能是一件小事——但我不知道如何解释这个女人和这座花园对我的影响。他们改变了我的生活吗？没有。但他们对我的思维方式和存在方式有影响吗？有。正是通过这座花园的奇特语言，我了解到自己的局限。

  那次旅行结束之后，我给我们的花园引进了几种开花植物。比如向日葵，它们比我丈夫还高，而且经常倒向一侧。我过生日的时候，我的朋友凯特送给我一些种子。我哭了。种出来才发现，它们的花太大了！而且完全不能吃。

  我丈夫说我很会种菜，这让他很高兴，但实际上他只是惊讶于这些菜会年复一年地生长。我以前一直不明白植物开花有什么意义，直到我遇见我的朋友凯特，参观了奎妮的花园，我才明白。如今，我看着那些花，就仿佛看见了凯特和奎妮。

蕾秋：我能多问一些关于奎妮的事吗？

莫琳：不能。

（一天后）

莫琳：我真希望当初我对奎妮更友善一些，但我们见面那会儿，我的人生正处于一个对人友善不起来的阶段。

旅行结束后，一个年轻人和我取得了联系。奎妮住在她花园旁边时，他是照顾她的人之一——是他开车把她送到临终关怀医院的，她在那里度过了余生。他告诉我，因为自那以后他再也没有去看过她，他很内疚。这太痛苦了。

你看，我们不可能一直当我们想成为的那个人。但是我们可以吸取教训，朝那个方向努力。

蕾秋：是一个叫西蒙的年轻人吗？穿着粗呢大衣的那个？

莫琳：是的。现在他有时会给哈罗德写信。你怎么认识西蒙的？

蕾秋：说来话长。

这次旅行有没有在其他方面改变你？比如，它是否改变了你对阅读的态度？

莫琳：有一次，我妈妈看到我捧着一本书看，就问我有没有什么正经事要做。那时我还是个年轻姑娘，很难不受那种评价的影响。直到现在，我还总是觉得，我做点什么都比看书强。这并非我对阅读有什么意见，而是说我们会被长辈的影响所累。

蕾秋：旅行结束后，你又去过当地的书店吗？你还喜欢在网上购物吗？

莫琳：我又去了当地的书店。我买了十张明信片，还给我的朋友凯特买了一个钥匙扣。我向店主问好。她问我过得怎么样。然后聊天就戛然而止了。正如幸福有风险一样，悲伤也有风险。如果我们没有体验过二者，就很难产生同理心。我的生活在很长一段时间里没有幸福的体验。

蕾秋：你最珍贵的财产是什么？

莫琳：我的结婚戒指。

蕾秋：你有和你的丈夫，还有雷克斯一起去观鸟吗？

莫琳：我会给他们做三明治。我是说给我丈夫和雷克斯做三明治，不是给鸟。不过我怀疑，那些三明治一半都被鸟吃了。

蕾秋：你会给今天的年轻女性什么建议？

莫琳：去学踢足球。

蕾秋：你还有什么想让我问的吗？还有什么重要的事我没问到吗？

莫琳：你可以在照片墙（Instagram）上关注我的邻居雷克斯吗？

蕾秋：当然可以。我还会关注那只猫呢。

最后一个问题。你觉得你的书封面怎么样？反正我很喜欢。

莫琳：书？什么书？

蕾秋·乔伊斯
于 2024 年 7 月 11 日

致谢

十多年前，我的第一部小说很幸运地落到了双日出版社（Doubleday）的编辑苏珊娜·韦德森的手中。从那以后，我们合作的书便一本接一本地出版，我们的友谊也越来越深厚。所以，我要一如既往地感谢苏珊娜，感谢她的信任、智慧，还有她提出的问题和付出的辛苦，感谢她给我书写那些触动我的人与事的自由。这本书是献给你的。

感谢我优秀的经纪人克莱尔·康维尔，以及康维尔与沃尔什文学代理公司的所有人。感谢黑兹尔·奥姆、凯特·萨马诺和审稿小组、制作部的卡特·希乐顿、艺术部的贝奇·凯利、营销部的艾玛·伯顿和莉莉·科克斯、有声书部的奥利·格朗、国际销售部的劳拉·里凯蒂和娜塔莎·福蒂欧，英国销售部的汤姆·彻肯、劳拉·加罗德、艾米丽·哈维、尼尔·格林、埃尔斯佩思·道格尔。感谢克莱奥·泽拉菲姆、琪拉雅·肯特和兰登书屋团队的全体成员。感谢这么多年来一直支持着哈罗德·弗莱并且始终慷慨如初的人——埃丽卡·瓦格纳、大卫·黑德利、凯西·雷岑布林克、范妮·布莱克。感谢拉里·芬利明确的鼓励。

我还要感谢艾莉森·巴罗，因为没有你的启发、指导和友谊，这一切都无从谈起。

我要一如既往地感谢我的家人，感谢你们的爱。感谢莎拉·艾德希尔当初仔细阅读了本书第一章最初的一版草稿，鼓起勇气告诉我写得不好。（她说得对。所以我重写了。）感谢多年来看过我写的每一个故事、连我写在电子邮件里的故事都看过的尼亚芙·丘萨克。

感谢我的丈夫保罗·维纳布尔斯。按说我应该私下感谢他，但保罗从我写作之初就参与了，没有他，我断然不会有今天的成绩。有时候就是要把谢谢大声说出来，这是件好事，也是对的事。

最后，也是最重要的，我要感谢读者，他们多年来带着如此的善意阅读我的作品，向我提出带给我更多思考的问题，大方地与我分享他们自己的故事。还有书店与图书馆的员工，在我们居家隔离期间，他们还坚持送书上门。你们是阅读的看门人。没有你们，我都不知道自己会身在何方。

MAUREEN FRY

AND THE ANGEL OF THE NORTH

For Susanna

The corpse you planted last year in your garden,

Has it begun to sprout? Will it bloom this year?

* * *

The Waste Land,

T. S. Eliot

I thought I saw an angel in an azure robe coming towards me across the lawn, but it was only the blue sky through the feathering branches of the lime.

* * *

Kilvert's Diary,
21 July 1873

01

Winter Journey

It was too early for birdsong. Harold lay beside her, his hands neat on his chest, looking so peaceful she wondered where he travelled in his sleep. Certainly not the places she went: if she closed her eyes, she saw roadworks. Dear God, she thought. This is no good. She got up in the pitch-black, took off her nightdress and put on her best blue blouse with a pair of comfortable slacks and a cardigan. 'Harold?' she called. 'Are you awake?' But he didn't stir. She picked up her shoes and shut the bedroom door without a sound. If she didn't go now, she never would.

Downstairs she switched on the kettle, and while it boiled, she got out her Marigolds and wiped a few surfaces. 'Maureen,' she said out loud, because she was no fool. She could tell what she was doing, even if her hands couldn't. Fussing, that's what. She made a flask of instant coffee and a round of sandwiches that she wrapped in clingfilm, then wrote him a message. She wrote another that said 'Mugs!' and another that said 'Pans!' and before she knew it, the kitchen was covered with Post-it notes, like small yellow alarm signals. 'Maureen,' she said again, and took them all down. 'Go now. Go.' She hung Harold's wooden cane from the chair where he couldn't miss it, then slipped the Thermos into her bag along with the sandwiches, put on her driving shoes and winter coat, picked up her suitcase and stepped out into the beautiful early morning. The sky was clear and pointed with stars, and the moon was like the white part of a fingernail. The only light came from Rex's house next door. And still no birdsong.

It was cold, even for January. The crazy paving had frozen overnight and she had to grab hold of the handrail. There were splinters of ice in the ruts between stones, and the front garden was no more than a few glass thorns. She turned on the ignition to warm the car while she scraped at the windows. The frost was rough, like sandpaper, and lay as far as she could see, slick beneath the street lamps of Fossebridge Road, but no one else was out. It was a Sunday, after all. She waved at Rex's house in case he was awake, and that was it. She was going.

Road-gritters had already passed through Fore Street, and salt lay in pink mats all the way up the hill. She drove north past the bookstore and the other shops that would be closed until Monday, but she didn't look. It was a good while since she'd used the high street. These days, she and Harold mostly went online, and not just because of the pandemic. The quiet row of shops became night-lit rows of houses. In turn they became a dark emptiness with a closed-down petrol station somewhere in the middle. She passed the turning for the crematorium that she visited once a month and kept driving. Now that she was on the road, she felt not excitement, but more a sense that, even though she didn't know how to explain it, she was doing the right thing. Harold had been right.

'You have to go, Maureen,' he'd said. She had come up with a list of reasons why she couldn't but in the end she'd agreed. She'd offered to show him how to use the dishwasher and the washing machine because he sometimes got confused about which buttons to press and then she wrote the instructions clearly on a piece of paper.

'You are sure?' she'd said again, a few days later. 'You really think I should do this?'

'Of course I'm sure.' He was sitting in the garden while she raked old leaves. He'd done up his coat lopsided, so that the left half of him was adrift from the right.

'But who will take care of you?'

'I will take care of me.'

'What about meals? You need to eat.'

'Rex can help.'

'That's no good. Rex is worse than you are.'

'That is true, of course. Two old fools!'

At this, he'd smiled. Only, something about the completeness of his smile made her miss him without even going anywhere, so that he could be as sure as he damn well liked, but she wasn't. She had put down her rake. Gone to him and redid his buttons. He sat patiently, gazing up at her with his delft-blue eyes. No one but Harold had ever looked at her like that. She stroked his hair and then he lifted his fingertips to her face, and drew her down to his, and kissed her.

'Maureen, you won't feel right unless you go,' he'd said.

'Okay, then. I'm going. I'm going, and nothing will stop me! Though, if you don't mind, I won't walk. I'll take the more conventional route, thank you very much. I'll drive.'

They'd laughed because they both knew she was doing her best to sound bigger than she felt. After that she went back to raking the leaves and he went back to watching the sky, but the silence was filled with all the things she did not know how to say.

So here she was, with Harold in her head, while she travelled further and further away from him. Only last night he had cleaned her driving shoes and set them, side by side, next to the chair with her clothes. 'I won't wake you in the morning,' she'd promised, as they got into bed and said goodnight. He had held his hand tight round hers until he fell asleep, and then she had curled up close and listened to the steady repeat of his heart, trying to take in some of his peacefulness.

Maureen drove slowly but there was hardly any traffic. If a car came towards her with its headlights shining, she saw it in plenty of time and pulled over in the right place – she even waved a polite thank-you – then the lanes were dark again, just the swing of hedge and tree as she passed. From there, she joined a dual carriageway and that was even better because the road was straight and wide and still pretty empty, with lorries parked in lay-bys. But as she got closer to Exeter, there were lots of roadworks, exactly as she'd dreamt during the night, and she got confused by the detours. She was no longer on the A38, but instead a chain of by-passes and residential roads, with many mini-roundabouts in between. Maureen drove for another twenty minutes before it occurred to her that the yellow diversion signs had stopped a while back and she had come to the edge of a housing estate. All she could see were blocks of flats and bony trees growing in spaces between paving slabs. It was still dark.

'Oh, well, that's great,' she said. 'That's marvellous.' It wasn't just herself she spoke to. She also had a habit of talking to the silence as if it was deliberately making things difficult for her. Increasingly she could not tell the difference between what she thought and what she said.

Maureen passed more flats and more tiny trees and cars parked everywhere, as well as delivery vans on the early shift, but still no sign of the A38. She turned down along service road because there was a row of bright street lamps in the distance, only to find herself at the bottom of a dead end, with a large depot to her left that was surrounded by a set of open gates and spiked fencing.

She pulled over and got out her road map but she had no idea where to start looking. She turned on her mobile but that was no use either, and anyway Harold would still be asleep. For a moment she just sat there. Already confounded. Harold would say, 'Ask someone,' but that was

Harold. The whole point of driving was that she wouldn't have to deal with people she didn't know. 'Okay,' she said firmly. 'You can do this.' She would take her map and be like Harold. She would ask for help at the depot.

Maureen got out of the car, and at once she felt the cold against her face and ears and inside her nose. As she crossed the car park, security lamps snapped on to her left and right, almost blinding her. She could make out light from a prefab cabin to the left of the main building but she had to go cautiously, with her arms shot out to keep her balance. Maureen's driving shoes were those flat suede ones with a bar across the top and special gripper soles; they were good on wet pavements but nothing was good on black ice. There were notices with pictures of dogs, warning that the premises were regularly patrolled, and she was afraid they might come running out. When she was a child, the local farmer had let his dogs roam freely. She still had a little scar beneath her chin.

Maureen rapped at the window of the hut. The young man on night duty wasn't even awake. He was hunched in a fold-out camping chair, the turban on his head crushed against the wall, his mouth agape and his legs sprawled all over the place. She knocked again, a bit louder, and called, 'Excuse me!'

He rubbed his eyes, startled. He pulled himself out of his chair and seemed to grow and grow. He was so tall he had to duck as he stumbled to the window, putting on his mask only as an after-thought. He had a thick brown beard, with hefty shoulders like a boxer's, and his hands were so large he had a problem undoing the catch on the window. He slid it open and crooked his neck side-ways as he blinked and stared down at her.

'I'm not going to pretend. I'm lost. I'm trying to get to the M5 but all those roadworks on the A38 sent me off in the wrong direction.' Her voice was louder than she'd intended because of the window, which she had to reach up towards, but also because she was anxious and he might not understand. Besides, she hated admitting she'd made a mistake. It wasn't as if she didn't know the route.

He gazed at her another moment, trying his best to wake up. Then he said, 'You're lost?'

'It was the roadworks. Normally I'm fine. Normally I have no problem. I just need to get to the M5.' She was doing it again. She was shouting.

He moved away from the window and opened the door at the side. She waited, not knowing what he expected her to do, just worrying about those dogs, until he called, 'Excuse me?' So she put on her mask and went round.

Now that she was in the cabin, the young man seemed even larger. The top of her head would barely reach his chest. He stood with his neck at an angle and his body hunched to make it smaller. Even his shoes – a pair of solid black lace-ups, the kind they used to put on children to correct their feet – couldn't get enough space. And it was obvious why he'd been asleep. An old electric fire blazed out orange heat from beneath the window. It was like being spit-roasted from the ankles upwards. Anyone would have fallen asleep next to that. Maureen swallowed a yawn.

He said, 'You don't want to go shouting at random strangers that you're lost. It's not safe. They might take advantage of you.'

His English was perfect. If anything he had a Devon accent. So there you were. That was another thing she'd been completely wrong about. 'I don't think anyone would want to take advantage of me.'

'You never know. There are all sorts of people in the world.'

'You are right, of course. But can you help me or not?'

'Yeah. Okay. I think so.' He tip-tapped a few things into his phone and held it out for her. It was no use: it was a map but tiny. He showed her where she was and all the roads she needed to take to get to the M5. 'See?'

'No,' she said. 'I don't. I don't see. That makes no sense to me.'

'Why not?'

'I don't know. It just doesn't.'

'Do you have a satnav?'

'We do have a satnav but I don't use it.'

He seemed confused but she wasn't going to enlighten him. The fact was she'd had the satnav disconnected. She couldn't bear that nice voice urging directions at her and telling her last minute that she'd missed the turn. Maureen was of the generation who had grown up with the phone on the hall table, and a map in the glove compartment. Even online shopping was a stretch. Twenty lemons instead of two, and all that kind of thing.

He said, 'Will you remember if I tell you?'

'I don't think I will.'

'I don't know what to do, then. What do you want me to do?'

'I would like you to read out the directions from your phone and I will write them down on a piece of paper. I'll take my route from that.'

'Oh, okay,' he said. He touched his beard and realigned his feet, as if this was going to take a whole different kind of posture in order to make it work. 'I see. Okay.'

Patiently, he told her to go to the end of the road, turn left, take a right, the second exit at the roundabout, and she wrote it all down on a page he had torn from a notebook. He paused at the end of each new instruction, to make sure she'd written it down. By the end she had twelve in all, and every one of them numbered.

'Do you know where you're heading after that?'

'Yes.' She pointed at the place on her road map.

'That's a very long way.'

'I know.'

'At least you'll get a change of scene.'

'I'm not looking for a change of scene. All I want is to get there.'

'Do you know your way after the M5?'

'Yes.'

'The junction numbers?'

'I think so.'

He looked at her for a moment, without saying anything. She got the feeling he didn't believe her. Then he said, 'Why don't you write those down too? You don't want to get lost on a motorway.'

He pulled his phone close to his face as he squinted a little and slowly read out the motorway exits she needed, plus the directions from there. There was no irritation in his voice. If anything, he seemed worried that he might get one of them wrong and mislead her. He shook his head as if he couldn't believe she was going to drive all that distance by herself, and in one day. 'It's so far,' he kept saying.

'Thank you,' she told him, once he finished. 'And I'm sorry if I woke you.'

'That's okay. I shouldn't be asleep.'

She thought he might be smiling behind his mask, so she smiled too. 'You've been kind.'

'Huh.' He shoved his hands into his pockets and turned to gaze out of the window. She was still on one side of the cabin and he was on the other, but their reflections were caught against the dark outside, like two see-through people, he so big, and she so short and trim, with her cap of white hair. 'That's not what most people call me.'

It came out of the blue. An honesty she didn't expect. She would have liked to be able to say something to make him feel better – she would have liked to be that kind of person, if only so that she could get back into her car and drive on with his instructions, without feeling she had failed. But she couldn't. She couldn't find it. That fleeting moment of goodness. People imagined they might reach each other, but it wasn't true. No one understood another's grief or another's joy. People were not see-through at all.

Maureen pursed her mouth. The young man gazed sadly at something or nothing in the dark. The silence seemed to go on and on. She looked at the floor and took in his black lace-ups again. They were such earnest shoes, like someone trying really hard.

'Well,' he said, 'I guess you should be okay now.'

'Yes,' she said.

'What's your name?'

'Mrs Fry.'

'I'm Lenny.'

'Goodbye, Lenny.'

'It was nice to meet you, Mrs Fry. Just don't go shouting at people that you're lost. And drive carefully. It's cold out there.'

'I'm going to see our son,' she said. Then she left and got into the car and made a U-turn to get back to the road.

02

The World's Guest

Ten years ago, Harold had gone into the world without Maureen. He had left to post a letter to his dying friend Queenie and, on the spur of the moment, made up his mind to walk the 627 miles to her instead. He had met many people along the way. Given up his wallet and slept in the wild. The story even hit the news and briefly made him famous. Left behind, Maureen had gone on a journey, too, but hers wasn't the kind people talked about or bought postcards of to send home. She *was* at home. That was the whole point. Harold was walking the length of England to save a woman he had worked with once, while Maureen cleaned the kitchen sink. And when she had finished cleaning the sink, she was upstairs, squirting circles of polish at his bedroom furniture. Keeping herself as busy as possible when there was absolutely nothing left to do She was even washing things she had already washed, just to find a little more washing inside them. And there were also days – though, again, who had known about them but her? – when she couldn't think how to get up in the morning. When she crawled out of bed and stared for hours at the laundry and the sink, and asked what was the point in washing or scrubbing when it made not one shred of difference? She was so alone she didn't know where to look or what to think about. She wasn't even sure that Harold would come home. The panic that had engulfed her was unfamiliar and frightening.

But that was in the past. Maureen didn't like to talk about that time any more. She knew it would sound sad, and it wasn't. There were far worse things. Harold had finished his walk to Queenie. Maureen had travelled to be with him when Queenie died. Together they had returned home and started again. Maureen nursed him slowly back to health, cooking all those dishes he loved when they were first married, bandaging the blisters and welts on his feet that no one else knew about. It was true they were somewhat shy of one another in bed to begin with because they had grown so used to sleeping apart, and she could still recall the bashfulness with which he had first called her 'sweetheart' as if she might laugh in his face. But she didn't. She liked it very much. They had taken daily strolls to the quay and he listened to her ideas for making new vegetable beds and redecorating the house. Sometimes people stopped to shake his hand because they had heard what he'd done, and she would wait, slightly to the side, not quite knowing how to set her face, not even quite knowing what to do with her hands, both proud and bewildered by how at ease with himself he had become. Now he was seventy-five and she was seventy-two: their marriage had arrived at a good new place, like their very own private creek. Once in a while, Harold received a card from one of the women he had walked with – Kate – but Maureen put it out of her mind and they got on with their lives. Then, five months ago, there had been more news about Queenie. The woman was back in their lives all over again.

Light was coming. Lenny's instructions worked perfectly. Maureen found her way back to the A38, and drove past barrow-shaped earthworks to merge with the M5. In the east there was a darkness that wasn't entirely dark, and the navy-blue horizon was rimmed with pink and gold, while Venus still hung high and bright. Shapes came seeping back to life. Scribbled outlines of trees. Black shadows she guessed were pylons. More depots and warehouses. A lifeless hump at the roadside that might be a badger or a muntjac. Ice patches along the roadside held reflections of the new light, like pieces of stained glass, but beyond them, the land was still flat and dimmed and empty. Maureen pictured Harold fast asleep at home. Later he would pad down to the kitchen in his bare feet, the way he did every morning, and open the back door to look at the sky. Hours he could spend, doing nothing but gazing upwards. He didn't even wear his watch. He preferred not knowing the time. On a good day he took his wooden cane because his legs were so weak he couldn't get to the end of the road any more, let alone the quay, and he watered the vegetable beds, entranced by the silver arc of water as it pooled over the earth, or he and Rex set up the draughts board and talked about this and that, but what he loved most was sitting on the patio, watching for birds. Whenever she felt a snatch of impatience, she told herself she was missing the point. At least he was happy, at least he was safe. And his health, too. At least he had that. It wasn't that he was losing his mind, rather that he was deliberately taking things out of it that he no longer needed.

Maureen indicated left and shifted to the nearside lane. The traffic was getting heavier. It made her anxious and she drove too slowly so that lorries came up behind with their headlights all blazing, and then went thundering past, churning up grit. Cullompton. Tiverton. The pin-sized silhouette of the Wellington Monument on the Blackdown Hills. Taunton. There had been a Slovak woman from Taunton who had been kind to Harold, but she'd got in touch a few years ago to say she was being deported. Harold had been very low about that. Rex asked local people to sign a petition, but it made no difference. And anyway he had three pages of signatures that all looked the same. 'Bottom line, Mrs Fry, the woman doesn't belong here,' one neighbour told Maureen. Another said he wasn't racist and he had nothing against the person in question, but it was time to look after your own. That was back in the days, of course, when she wasn't ashamed to show her face on the high street.

The sun rose, blooming over the frozen land, turning everything the red of a geranium, even gulls and traffic. The moon was still out but no more than a chalk ghost, reluctant to commit either to staying or going. At Bridgwater she passed the giant Willow Man caught in the act of striding south with arms outstretched like long fins. Anti-vax slogans were sprayed on the concrete underside of a bridge. *Fake News. Fake Virus.* England was a different country from the one Harold had walked through. Sometimes he would tell a story about a person he had met back then, or a view across the hills, and she would listen as if she was watching a film with her eyes closed, unable to find the right pictures. These days it was all safe motorways and Uber. It was paying with your phone, and please keep your distance, not to mention podcasts, milk made of oats and meat made of plants, and everything streamed online. Look for a bank spilling with primroses and you'd more likely find an old blue mask caught in the leaves. Ten years ago she couldn't have imagined all the change that was coming.

Maureen switched on the radio but it was a news story about a film star who had staged a hate crime against himself to boost his Instagram profile. She turned it off. People expected so much of the world.

I want to be the world's guest.

The words took her by surprise. It was her son who had spoken them, but she hadn't thought of them in years. He must have been only six. He had looked straight up at her with his deep brown eyes that seemed to know a sadness she didn't.

'What on earth do you mean?' she had said.

'I don't know.'

'Is it because you want a biscuit?'

'No.'

'Then what is it you want? A party?'

'I don't like parties.'

'Everyone likes parties.'

'I don't. I don't like the games. I only like the cake and the going-home present.'

'So what do you mean?'

'I don't know.'

She had felt pierced. Everything about David had saddened her – his solemn gaze and his slow walk and the way he kept himself apart from other children. 'Why don't you play?' she would say, when she took him to the park. 'Those children look nice. I'm sure they'll play with you.'

'It's okay, thank you,' he would say. 'I'll stay with you. I think they won't like me.'

But she'd had the sense, even then, that he did know what he meant about being the world's guest. That he was just waiting for her to catch up. Forever she had been running after this child. Even now she was doing it.

Maureen felt dizzy suddenly. Almost seasick. She needed coffee and the washroom.

03

Fried Egg

The waitress said it was okay for her to drink from her own flask but she would have to go to the counter and buy something to eat. Maureen asked if the waitress could take her order from the table because that was where she was already sitting, and the waitress said she couldn't. It was still early. The service station was empty, apart from Maureen and an old man whose hands trembled as he lifted his cup. Across from the Fresh Food Café, a woman in a hijab mopped the floor and another was opening the shutters on a shop.

'What difference does it make,' said Maureen, 'if you take my order here or at the counter? Show me the menu and I'll order something.'

The waitress said there was no menu, not as such, and anyway it wasn't waitress service. She wore a baggy black top with a sequin rabbit on the front. Her finger ends were chewed and her hair was oily and colourless. The happiest thing about her was that rabbit.

'This is silly,' said Maureen. 'You're standing at my table. Why can't you take my order?'

'I'm cleaning it,' said the waitress, and she gave it another antiseptic spray to prove her point. 'I'm only allowed to serve you at the counter. It's the new regulations.'

Maureen followed the waitress to the counter, but then she had to queue behind a family of five who had just arrived and were now ordering huge drinks from the coffee menu that had nothing to do with coffee. When it came to Maureen's turn, the waitress went through the breakfast options. It seemed to Maureen she was taking it slowly on purpose. There were pastries, muffins, iced doughnuts and sandwiches, as displayed beneath the counter. She pointed at each one. There was also a Full English, or a Gluten-free Vegan English, but those had to be done in the kitchen. There wasn't any more of the Winter Warmer Special because they had run out.

'If you don't have it, you should take it off the menu,' said Maureen.

'So what do you want?'

Maureen told her she certainly didn't want the full breakfast. It would be too much. 'I'll have an egg.'

'Without the Full English?'

'Yes.'

'Would you like the Full English to the side?'

'No,' said Maureen. 'I would like it not on my plate.'

'Okay.' The waitress picked up an iPad. 'How would you like the egg?'

'Poached.'

'We do fried.'

'That's all?'

'Yes.'

'If you only have fried, why did you ask how I'd like it?'

'People say fried.'

'Seriously?' said Maureen.

'Seriously,' said the waitress.

'Fine. I'll have fried.'

'Toast?'

'Are you going to ask what kind and then tell me you only do white?'

A blush stung the waitress's neck and spread right up to her hairline. 'No. We do brown. We also do ciabatta and gluten-free.'

'I want brown. Not too thickly sliced. And toast it properly. I don't want warm bread. Butter to the side. I will butter it myself.'

The waitress put something in her iPad that seemed to take much longer than 'fried egg and toast', then gave Maureen a wooden spoon with a number on it and took her order through to the kitchen. Maureen went back to her table with the wooden spoon. Outside, six seagulls were sitting in the children's play area and a long strip of plastic tape flapped from the arms of a tree. Then, on the other side of the café, a woman of her own age arrived with someone younger who must be her daughter, pushing a buggy. She nodded at Maureen as if to say hello, and Maureen nodded back, but she didn't smile. The younger woman hoisted out a baby, and lifted her up, so that Maureen could see she was dressed in a padded pink snowsuit with a fur trim around the hood. It looked too hot, Maureen thought. The younger woman said she would get coffees if her mother held the baby and her mother said, 'Sounds like a plan, Lou,' and took the baby on her lap. Maureen watched the way she unzipped the pink snowsuit while her daughter wasn't looking and pulled down the hood. She watched the way the woman drew the baby's head to her mouth and kissed it and, without even being close, Maureen knew that bread-sweet smell of a baby's head and the downy softness of its hair. For a moment she allowed herself to pretend she was this woman with her grandchild, and she could feel the love falling right out of her. Then pain, a kind of envy, seemed to flood her entire body, like a dark messy injection of poison. It was everything she could do to keep still and bear it. So here she was. Back in the same old place. She thought she had dealt with the past but there were times recently, there were times even after thirty years, when she hated the world for taking away what she wanted most. If only she were able to be more like Harold. Letting things go, piece by piece.

'Table thirteen?' The waitress put the plate in front of her. She said, 'Stay safe!'

Stay safe? Maureen wanted to ask. How exactly does that work? But instead she looked at the egg and said, 'What is that?'

It was so hard it looked made of plastic. It looked like one of those comedy eggs you bought in a joke shop. And the bread was not toasted – it didn't even look warmed up – with butter not to the side, but splodged thickly all over the top. 'No,' she said. 'You can't expect me to eat that.'

The waitress lowered her head so that her oily hair hung forward, all in one piece. She made a sucky noise, like a string of hiccups.

'You need to take it away,' said Maureen. 'You can't charge me for that. I want my money back.'

She poured another cup of coffee from her flask and unwrapped the clingfilm from her sandwiches and had those instead. The waitress pinched the plate away from Maureen as if she were dangerous, and took it back to the kitchen.

A short while later another woman came out. She walked straight to Maureen's table. She was twice the age of the waitress and her hair was cut in tufts that were dyed different shades of red, with pencilled eyebrows that didn't move.

'I hear you want your money back.' She dropped a pile of loose change on the table, not even in pound coins but ones that no one used any more, like 5p pieces and pennies. She made no apology for the egg. Then she said, 'I'm going to have to ask you to leave.'

'I'm sorry?'

'You can't consume your own food and drink on the premises. There's a sign.' She pointed to one at the entrance next to another that asked customers to respect social distancing and the wearing of masks, as well as being kind to staff at all times.

'But the waitress told me I could.'

'You were rude.'

'I didn't say anything.'

'It's exactly that tone of voice I'm talking about. The poor girl is in tears because of you. If you want to eat your own food, you can do it outside.'

Maureen was speechless. All she could do was sit there. The grandmother and her daughter turned their heads to watch what she would do next, and so did the man with trembling hands. 'Are you really asking me to leave?' When it came, her voice was shaking and shrill. It was the spike in her. She'd always had it, even when she was a child. Parenthood had come to her mother and father late – too late to rekindle a marriage that had gone cold. Her father doted on her, and her mother – though she criticized her frequently – was determined that Maureen should have the life she had not.

'Oh, little Maureen,' her father used to say, his eyes watery with pride. 'There's nothing little Maureen can't do.'

The woman with red hair was staring straight back at her. 'Correct,' she said. 'I'm asking you to leave.'

Maureen wiped her cup with a paper napkin and screwed it back on top of the flask, but her hands were shaking. She couldn't get the clingfilm to fit around what was left of her sandwiches, and when she tried to put on her coat, she kept missing the sleeve. As she left the service station, she thought of the grandmother gently cupping the baby's head and how she would never be one of those women. And she should never have told David that everyone liked parties: that was rot. She hated parties. She always had. You lied to children simply because their unhappiness was too much to bear.

Maureen picked her way across the car park feeling thin and pinched. Exposed. As if all the goodness was behind her, while she was in the cold. She tried to tell herself it didn't matter but something solid was lodged in her throat like a bit of cheese she couldn't swallow. She would not give in. She would not weep. A seagull tore at a McDonald's bag with its beak, holding it down with its yellow webbed foot, then lifting into the air with a French fry. She wanted to ring Harold, but if she did, she would wake him and he would hear the distress in her voice and begin to worry. Then, out of nowhere, came an old memory of a shop of people – all swivelled round, staring, appalled – and another shrapnel of shame went right through her.

'Maureen,' she said out loud. 'Spilt milk, Maureen.'

The grandmother would have eaten that fried egg. She would have smiled at the waitress and said, 'Thank you, dear,' and eaten every last plasticky scrap.

Another three hundred and fifty miles. Then this would be over.

04

Human Mouths

'You know what I missed most?'

'No,' said Maureen. 'I have no idea.'

'What I missed were mouths! People's mouths!'

'You didn't,' said Maureen. The sun was still low but strong, mists rising with perfect focus into the sharp air. Trees were pencilled in silver and light flashed between the branches in spokes. Ahead, traffic carried diamond sparks while the land stretched out, glittering and frozen-white. Maureen flapped down the visor. All that sunlight was giving her a headache.

'Months and months of masks! You know, I just hated not seeing what people's mouths were doing!'

'I know what you mean,' said a second voice. This one sounded older than the first and more solid. Maureen pictured a woman with grey hair and one of those linen shift dresses that hid things, whereas the voice of the first suggested someone who was altogether slimmer and more golden. She spoke in exclamation marks.

She was doing it again now. 'People say you read a person's face from the eyes! But that's not true!'

'You're right,' said Grey-hair. 'I've never thought that way before, but now you say it, I know exactly what you mean.'

'It's the mouth that tells you what a person is feeling!'

'Oh, you're so right.'

'You know what I find? I just want to hug people! I see them going about their lives and I just want to hug them! Complete strangers!'

'Well, that's it,' said Grey-hair. 'If there's one thing we learnt from the pandemic it was that people are kind. The kindness of strangers. It's what kept us going—'

Maureen reached for the radio. 'Oh, what utter tripe,' she said. And she turned it off.

Maureen was not an easy person. She knew this. She was not an easy person to like and she wasn't good at making friends. She had once joined a book club but she objected to the things they read, and gave up. There was always someone between her and everyone else and that was her son. This year he would have turned fifty.

After his suicide thirty years ago, her grief was so great she thought she would die of it. Really, she couldn't understand how she was not dead. She wanted time to stop. Paralyse itself. But it didn't. She had to get up every day and face his bedroom, the chair where he sat in the kitchen, his great big overcoat with no son inside it. Worse, she had to go out and face women with children, and young men who were high or drunk, and she had to walk past them without screaming. What had she been supposed to do with that unbearable burden? The incredible anger that was eating her alive? There had been a few cards of condolence – *We are sorry for your loss ; Our deepest sympathy* – a picture of a white lily, the embossed message in flowery gold italics. Harold had found some comfort in those cards. He even put them on the mantelpiece so that Maureen could find comfort in them too. But she stared at the words and despised them. Nothing about them made sense, in the same way that going to sleep made no sense either. And the more she looked at them, the more she felt accused – as if, without anyone saying it, they believed she must be to blame. In the end, she cut the cards into a hundred jagged shreds, and when that did not make her feel any better, she took the same scissors to her lovely long brown hair and cut that off too. Oh, she felt mad. Absolutely hopping. She didn't even recognize who she was. She was just this new person, this raging sonless mother, the shadowy figure you glimpse behind a pair of net curtains. The future she'd meant to have was gone. She had no idea how she was living this kind of ghost life instead, in which she could do nothing except watch the person who had taken her place and hate her. All she wanted was her son. All she wanted was to see David.

'So if you think you want my husband, take him,' she had said to

Queenie, when she paid a visit a few weeks after the funeral. It was the first and only time they met, though Harold used to tell stories about her at work – they seemed to share the same sense of humour – and Maureen could smell her in the car sometimes, a mix of violet sweets and cheap scent. Queenie had found Maureen hanging up the washing in the garden. She had come up the path holding out a bunch of flowers that Maureen put straight in the laundry basket. 'But if you don't want him,' she'd told her, 'clear out of our lives.' They'd stood, the two of them, either side of the washing line while Maureen continued to peg out clean T-shirts that her son would never wear, and Queenie wiped away tears. 'Haven't you gone yet?' Maureen shouted.

In her grief, she had said the worst things. Queenie was Harold's friend. She would never have taken him. But Maureen no longer cared in those days whom she upset. She wanted to upset them. She wanted to drive them all as far away from her as possible, to the other end of the earth, if she could. Even Harold. 'Call yourself a man?' she'd railed. 'Call yourself a father? It was your fault! I don't even want to look at you!'

It was only after Harold's walk that Maureen had finally been able to apologize. 'Forgive me,' she had said, and he had taken her hand and clutched it for a while as if he had never held anything quite so precious and said, 'Oh, Maw, you were never to blame. Forgive me, too.' She thought they might dare to have conversations about David and all the things they had got wrong. All the lurking, shadowy things she wanted to say and for which she could not find the words. But Harold was so exhausted in the weeks and months after his journey that those conversations never even started. She got the impression he had found some kind of release, an absolution of a kind, while she – who had gone nowhere – was left high and dry. She took up gardening again, though, because he had once loved to see her in the garden, almost as much as he'd loved her long brown hair. She redecorated the sitting room with patterned wallpaper and had the lino on the kitchen floor replaced. She chose a new colour for the bedroom and made curtains to match the counterpane. She even cleared David's room, wrapping his things up, one by one, and placing them in a box for the loft. But she still kept a space for her son inside her. It was where he came from, after all. That small creel inside her.

Weston-super-Mare. Clevedon. The early morning was a tenderblue, fading to milk on the horizon, and the frozen land rose and sloped away with white glowing spills. Gulls reeled, yawing and screeching, so many they were a broken criss-crossing of lines, while above them vapour trail stacked a path across the sky. Bundles of mistletoe hung in a line of trees, like oversized handbags. Approaching Bristol, she reached the stretch of motorway that was raised on columns, carrying it above woodland and the bowl of a valley. She passed over the River Avon, and saw light glinting on all the hundreds of cars parked at the compound of Portbury Dock, while far out there were the tall cranes and liners at the Severn Estuary. Maureen stopped at another service station, but only for water and the washroom. It wasn't as clean as it should have been and she had to put paper on the toilet seat. She washed her hands carefully.

A woman in a coat with big flowers all over it was crying and saying, 'I don't know why I bother. I don't know why I keep going back,' and her friend was holding her and saying, 'The trouble is you're a saint. You're your own worst enemy,' while she pulled paper towels out of a dispenser and passed them to her friend. Maureen made a deal of stepping round them because they were also in the way of the hand-dryer.

'Your mother is a saint.' It was something her father had often said. 'She is a saint for putting up with me.' And Maureen would wish he wouldn't because it made him sound so old and given-up.

The service station was busy. There were families everywhere, with children running all over the place. Twice she had to stop in her tracks. A man in a T-shirt with the words *Dining Area Host* was picking up trays of leftovers, one at a time, and trudging with them towards a screened-off section in the middle. Maureen didn't know when that term had come about. She didn't know why it was a better word than 'cleaner'. She passed a Lucky Coin game arcade and a Krispy Kreme doughnut display beside a row of those large grey plastic armchairs that gave a massage if you put money in the slot. An old man was asleep with his feet curled up and his face mask over his eyes. Maureen had hated the first time she wore a mask but that was only because it was like being squashed. She had grown used to it very quickly. And she liked the anonymity. The polite keeping of one's distance. After all, she'd never been what you would call a hugger. She didn't even like people calling her by her first name – that was another thing she'd disliked about the book group, apart from the trash they chose to read. It was all Deborah this and Alice that. So if Maureen had to wear a mask for the rest of her life, she could think of worse things.

'Could I interest you in a book?' said a woman, arranging a table of second-hand paperbacks in aid of Help for Heroes.

'Not my thing,' said Maureen. She didn't even stop to browse. You never knew what you might find. It was enough to bring a fluttering feeling to her chest.

In the shop, she went in search of a bottle of water. Blue feet-shaped arrows directed customers in single file, which Maureen followed, though the couple coming towards her in matching animal-print fleeces did not, so she had to step aside for them and they didn't even say thank you. 'Well, thank *you*,' she said, under her breath.

There were more notices about social distancing and hand sanitizer stations, with spots of gel on the floor. But there was still nothing to make her want to go round embracing complete strangers, or even understand humankind any better. She paid for her water and a crossword magazine and no one asked her where she was going or if she was making good time.

The cashier had beautiful long fingers with green nail varnish, and a name badge that said 'Moonbeam'.

'Can I interest you in the special offer?'

'That depends,' Maureen said. 'What is it?'

'Three air fresheners for your car for the price of two.' Moonbeam pointed at a display of them.

'But I only have one car,' said Maureen. The air fresheners confused her. They were a selection of neon-coloured tropical fruits, like pineapples and melons, and all of them with sunglasses on.

'It's still a bargain. If you lose one of your fresheners, you'll have another two.'

'But if I have three fresheners, it means I'm waiting to lose one. And if I'm waiting to lose one, I will.'

'It's up to you. I'm just telling you the special offer. You don't have to buy it.' Maureen had barely turned before the cashier looked at the four young women behind her in the queue and gave a rolling of the eyes.

Harold had met kindness on his journey. Or he had brought out love in other people. But it was not like that for Maureen. 'A difficult child,' she heard her mother saying. Now she thought of them, the words seemed so clear, and she could see her mother in her patent shoes with three straps, which she was always polishing because of the mud outside. She could remember the smell of her mother too, always the same, always redolent of everything most longed for and most elusive. Her mother had been beautiful once and had airs. She came from good stock, was what she liked to say, but her husband had poor health and little money and they had been forced to retreat to the countryside. Her mother hated everything about the countryside. The smells, the dirt, the isolation. It mortified her that they couldn't afford extra help. 'You think a house cleans itself?' she would say, in her sliced accent, holding a mop as if her dislike for it was personal, and Maureen would watch her and vow, *I will never be that person.* She was her father's child.

Yet these days she experienced a faint shock when she met her reflection in the mirror. Despite her short white hair, Maureen had her mother's mouth and chin. Even her way of holding her head high. You think you will be different but the blueprint is still there: Maureen looked into the mirror and saw the ghost of her mother, staring back.

Mid-morning. Signs for Stroud, then Gloucester, Cheltenham. The Cotswold hills were a dust-blue shoulder to her right. She passed a broken-down HGV, its cab jack-knifed forward like a broken neck. Already the day was losing its sharpness. Vast scarps of cloud lay ahead, while the air felt full and there were still dark borders of ice on the hard shoulder where the sun had not reached. Fog was coming. A coach swung in front of her, St George flags at the windows and football fans waving. She overtook a convoy of trucks carrying ready-made prefab homes, each with a set of net curtains at the window, and a woman whose car was packed to the roof with bin bags. By the time she reached the M42, the fog was so thick she could see it flickering towards the windscreen, like grains of sugar. The only colour now was the smudgy red of taillights ahead; wind-crippled trees at the roadside appeared to grow out of water. The world had become a strange emptiness of road and mudbanks, where things had no connection, dissolving then solidifying, and she thought that this was how it was with her mind. That it was a series of puzzle pieces that could never be put together.

WARNING. M42 CLOSED. Maureen was pulled back to the present. A sign flashed above the motorway, the orange letters spilling into fog. QUEUES AHEAD. She drove another few miles and tried to focus on the road but it was like driving into nothing and she kept losing concentration. She was faraway again, thinking of David and his tablet at the crematorium that she visited every month and polished with a cloth, and the little green stones around it that she tidied with a hand-sized rake, even though other people did not tidy their little stones, so that they fell into David's and then she had to tidy those too. She was thinking of the large woman with loud make-up whom she had approached recently, because the stones on her plot were all over the place, and the urn was rusted over, and how Maureen had said it surely wasn't too much to ask her to look after it properly. The woman had told Maureen to mind her own bloody business, and in her panic, Maureen had replied that if the woman ate a better diet, she might not be so unhappy. She had actually said that. Those very words had come out of her mouth. One moment, they were safe in her head, offensive, yes, but somehow not seeming that way – because this woman was big, no question, she had many soft chins, all coated in that terrible make-up – and the next, there the words were, slap in the air, like great big posters. Too late, Maureen realized her mistake. The woman had come up close, so close Maureen could see the clogged orange pores of her skin and the creases in her purple eye shadow, and shouted that Maureen was a fucking insane bitch. So now, when she went to the crematorium, she wasn't able to think only of David, she was also thinking of that large woman with the make-up, and hoping she would not be there, and the whole place was tainted in her mind, in the same way the bookshop on the high street had become tainted a few years ago. Carry on like this, there wouldn't be anywhere left.

Maureen hummed to stop thinking. This was the problem with the car. Too much time trapped in her head. Better to be doing things with her hands. She hoped Harold was managing with the dishwasher. She hoped he could find the coffee and the cups. She should have left those Post-it notes in the kitchen, after all. She would come off at the next service station and phone home. Besides, she needed the washroom again. She had only to think about it and she needed it. In fact the more she thought about it, the worse it got. A kind of burning low down, a tight heat. She needed to stop thinking about it. She thought about Harold instead and the skin on his back that was still as smooth as ever, and how the first time she had seen him naked, she had been afraid even to touch him because she wanted him so much. She had never seen her parents so much as kiss. The road curved to the left and Maureen kept driving in a trance of red taillights, her mind with Harold, until it dawned on her that something was wrong and the thing that was wrong was that those lights ahead were not moving, while she was. She was moving towards them and they were stationary.

Maureen pressed the brake. Nothing happened. She cramped it harder but missed and got the footwell. The car kept travelling forward. She jammed her foot down but too fast because this time the car seemed to lose traction and instead of stopping made a swerve to the left, and then, despite everything she did, she was heading very slowly but at the wrong angle towards the hard shoulder, and for a matter of moments she could no longer remember how to stop a car, or even which pedal was which, she knew only that it was out of control, that she was sliding towards the barrier and there were other cars all around her, none of them moving, and beyond that, a wall of fog, and all her turning of the wheel and pumping of the brake made no difference.

There was a strange moment of stillness, an almost welcome realization that what she was trying to prevent was already happening and there was nothing she could do any more except sit very still and see what happened next. She badly needed the washroom.

05

Sea Garden

Queenie made a sea garden at her home in Embleton Bay. Locals now call it the Garden of Relics because of the things people leave there. But I only heard recently that she created a monument to your son. I thought you might like to know that. Much love, Kate x

To begin with, it had been a postcard that arrived in the summer. Harold had read it out loud and they'd got on with their morning. Maureen weeded the strawberries while he sat in the sun. But her mind kept going back to it. 'I didn't know Queenie had a garden,' she would say to Harold, trying to keep the snag out of her voice, and he would smile and say he didn't either. The fact was it was just a garden. A garden that was four hundred and fifty miles away. If there was a monument to David, so what? Queenie had worked with Harold for all those years. They must have talked about David sometimes. But from there the garden grew in its awkwardness, like a splinter you don't attend to. Why had Queenie made a monument to David? What right had she to do that? And what was it like, this monument? Had Queenie known David? The questions came back to Maureen as she put out the washing or forked the vegetable beds. They returned to her in the lulls when she brushed her teeth or made Harold's breakfast or even as she lay beside him at night, wide awake while he slept. Time went by. The days shortened. The leaves changed. But her head didn't. She couldn't forget about the garden; it only became more insistent. It was out there and yet it was stuck inside her too.

'Are you sure you didn't know about Queenie's Garden?' she asked Harold, one evening over supper. 'The one Kate wrote to you about?' It was autumn by this time. She tried to put the question in a casual way as if it was something that had just occurred to her.

'Queenie's Garden? I'm not sure. I don't think so.'

'But she was a gardener, was she?'

'I don't remember that she was a gardener. We never spoke about gardening. At least, I don't think we did.'

'Then why is David in her garden? Did Queenie know David? Why didn't I know she knew him?'

The impatience in her voice betrayed her. She was asking too much too quickly and now he was looking pained, as if he suspected he had done something terrible that he should remember without knowing what it was. 'Oh dear,' he said. 'Oh dear.' He touched his head with the heel of his hand and tapped it, trying to wake things up. 'It will come back, it will come back, give me a moment.' But it didn't. She picked up the dinner plates. Scraped his leftovers on top of hers. Took them to the sink and rinsed the plates with hot water.

'Can I help you, Maureen?'

'It's fine. You just sit there.' She hadn't intended it to come out like that. The blow was cheap. He came up behind her. Snaked his arms around her waist and rested his chin on her shoulder. He was tired and she felt it, then. What she'd done to him, bringing all this back about David.

He said softly, 'It was a long time ago, you see.'

'I know it was.'

'The garden is nothing to worry about.'

'I know.'

'We're happy.'

'We are.'

'So let's not worry.'

'No, Harold. We won't.'

He kissed her and the subject was closed. But even though she'd agreed not to, she did. She did worry. And the fact that he didn't want to made her double-worry – as if she had to take it on for both of them. It had been the same after Queenie died and the director of the hospice sent on Queenie's letter. Harold hadn't wanted to worry about that either. It was Maureen who had pored over the pages, trying to understand from the packed script that held no words, only dashes and squiggles, what

Queenie had been so desperate to tell him. Trying to understand what he didn't wish to know. In the end she had tucked the letter into a shoebox and stowed it in the loft, along with David's things. But she was too old for this now. They were both too old. She didn't want it all welling up again. Only it had already begun. The ghosts had entered the room.

Alone, Maureen searched for images of the garden on the computer. She was shocked. There were all these people who had visited it, people she didn't know. Taking selfies and family portraits, or artistic wide shots. So they must have seen Queenie's monument to David. They had seen it, and Maureen had not. Where was it, then? What did it look like? Was it an exact image of him? Or something more contemporary? She looked and looked, and she tried to make the images larger, but she couldn't find him anywhere. She couldn't find anything that looked remotely like her son.

The truth was it wasn't just David she couldn't find. She couldn't make sense of the garden, full stop. It didn't even appear to have a fence. It simply came out of the dunes. There were stretches of shingle, interspersed with circles of stones and flowers and metal sculptures that were all kinds of shapes – funnels, tubes, spirals, spindles and whorls – alongside pieces of driftwood, some the size of wooden spoons but others as tall as posts, and dominated by one huge baulk of timber at the centre. There were strange sculptures too, made out of plastic bottles, guttering, tin cans, old furniture, rope and brushes – the kind of things, in fact, that she wouldn't think twice about throwing away. There were even poles with weather-bleached animal skulls on top. She looked at all this as if she was staring at life from the other side of a steamed-up window that she couldn't rub clean. Banners of seaweed and cork floats were strung between sticks, or hung like necklaces over single pieces. Ribbons were tied to branches. There were seed heads as bold as pieces of ironwork and grasses the size of sprouting fountains. In summer, all this was thrown into relief by the bright splashes of yellow and orange and red from gorse, marigolds and poppies. (You could tell it was summer because the sky was blue and the people visiting the garden wore sunglasses and T-shirts.) On other occasions, it appeared to belit by hundreds of tiny candles. At the back stood an old painted wooden chalet with a falling-down roof.

Winter came. Harold and Maureen got on with life. They ate together and slept together but they were in separate circles all over again. He was happy watching for birds, and playing draughts with Rex, while she was cooped up by herself with the computer, searching for Queenie's Garden online and getting more and more agitated. Besides, as far as Maureen was concerned, a garden was a garden. It was for growing things to eat. Swede and onions and potatoes and spinach and fruits to freeze or bottle and take you through winter. It wasn't for bits of junk and wood and metal. So it wasn't simply that David was there, but more that he had been made a part of something from which Maureen was excluded. It was like looking at those cards of condolence all over again. And then she'd had a nightmare that disturbed her so much she'd had to go downstairs and turn on every single light in the house until day came and Harold woke.

'What happened, Maw sweetheart?' He put his arms around her and she rested her head on his shoulder as she began to tell him her dream.

It was about digging in a vegetable bed and finding David all alone beneath the earth, though she stopped short of talking about the worms that poured out of his mouth and ears, or the side of his face that was so decomposed it was a black layer of rotting leaves. She couldn't bear to say those things about their only son, even after all this time. Best to keep those dark thoughts to herself.

'I'm sorry. I'm not like you, Harold. I can't stop dwelling on Queenie's Garden.' She described all the images she'd seen online that she couldn't make sense of.

It was then that he gave one of his smiles that still unbuttoned her slightly and told her he'd been wrong. She needed to go and see it.

'Oh, no,' she said quickly. She got up. Straightened a few things. Wiped her hand on a chair, checking for dust that was not there. 'No, no. There's no need to do that. No, no. It's much too far. Who would look after you? No, no. I'm just talking about it. That's all.'

'You're right, of course. It's a very long way. But why don't you think about going? You could do it over a few days. Kate's a kind woman. She lives about twenty miles away. You could stay at least one night with her.'

'Oh, no. No, I wouldn't want to do that. I wouldn't want to stay with

Kate. I don't know Kate. She's your friend. Not mine.'

There were so many reasons she couldn't go, she said. It wasn't just the distance. There was the house and the washing and everything else: she was even thinking of replacing the old pink bathroom suite with something more neutral. The truth was she was slightly scared of Kate, though she had never met her, just as she was scared of Queenie's Garden. Kate was in her late fifties, and some kind of activist. She had decided to give her marriage another try after walking with Harold but it hadn't worked and now she lived alone. That was all Maureen knew. Of the many people he had met, Kate was the one he cared for most, which was another reason Maureen felt insecure when she thought about her. Maureen wasn't sure she would even know what to say to an activist.

But she had got herself cornered. And, true to form, she'd achieved it all by herself. In the end she had to agree. Harold was right. Yes, she would go to see the garden, but she would get the drive over and done with in one day. Rex agreed to look after him while she was gone, though privately she suspected that, with Harold's forgetfulness and Rex's heart, it would be more like two small boys holding hands.

'I won't visit Kate. I'd rather keep this to myself. I'll order a shop for you and Rex online. And I'll show you how to use the dishwasher. It isn't difficult. It's just some buttons. I'll leave a Post- it note . . .'

This time he laughed. 'Even we can work out how to wash a few pots and pans.'

She wrote instructions anyway and found a nice guesthouse called Palm Trees near Embleton serving early-evening meals, and booked it for two nights. She would drive there on the first day, see the garden the following morning, and set off for home early the next. She made so many meals for Harold and Rex, there was barely room for them all in the freezer. If she kept herself busy, she felt more in control. The evening before, she packed a few necessary things, then pressed her best blue blouse to the thinness of a paper cut-out, while Harold found a wire brush and cleaned her driving shoes. Like preparing armour, she thought briefly, except no one was going to war. It was just a garden with some driftwood in it, and that was all.

He smiled at her and maybe he caught hold of what she was thinking, because he said, 'It's okay. There's nothing to be frightened of.'

'I know.'

But she watched him later as he slept, his hand loosened from hers and now neat on his chest, his breath going pop, pop, pop, and she envied the peace it brought him. He is the brave one, she thought. The complete one. Not me.

06

Accident-Accident

By tamworth, the fog was so thick she could barely see beyond a few yards. The watery outline of trees seeped into air, with crows roosting in the branches like big black buds. There was no horizon and no sky. You might have thought this was the only place left in the world, a service station on the M42. Maureen phoned Harold from the car park, once she'd had a change of clothes. The coach of football fans spilt out of the entrance, holding their flags above their heads and singing, 'Eng-a-land! Eng-a-land!'

Harold said, 'An accident? What do you mean, an accident? Are you hurt? What happened?'

'No. The car is fine. There's not even a dent on the bumper.' The air wrapped itself around her, like a wet bandage.

'I wasn't worrying about the car. I'm not worried about the car at all.'

'Well,' she said, 'that's because you don't drive any more.'

He gave a soft and slightly creaky noise that she knew was him smiling. 'No, Maureen. It isn't because of that. It's because you're my wife and the car isn't. The car is a car.'

'Well, I just wanted to say I'm fine. Nothing broken.' She was talking in an oddly bright voice she didn't like, but she couldn't bear to tell him about the other car that had stopped or the young man who had got out to help her. From the motorway she heard sirens and saw flashing blue lights within the fog as police and ambulances wove north. 'Now they've closed the M42 completely. There's been an accident.'

'Another accident?'

'Yes. Not like mine. Mine was nothing. I only hit a patch of black ice and swerved into the hard shoulder. This was a lorry. I have to follow a detour.'

'Poor you.'

'It could add another hour. More, maybe. I don't know.' She held tight to her mobile. She didn't want him to hang up. Not yet. But she also didn't know what to tell him. Out of nowhere, she had a picture in her head of him tying back brambles once on an overgrown path, so that other people would not get hurt. It was such a Harold thing to do. She wanted to cry but she could not let herself. 'How is Rex?' she said. 'Is he with you?'

'Yes. Rex is here. We're playing draughts.'

'Hello, Maureen!'

'Ask him if he took his pills.'

'Maureen says, "Did you take your pills?" '

'Yes, Maureen!'

'Have you been eating properly?'

'Very well.'

'Don't just eat sandwiches.'

'We won't.'

There was a moment of silence that felt longer than it was.

Harold said slowly, 'Are you all right, Maureen?'

'Of course I am. I've had a bit of a shock, but I'm fine.' 'You're sure?'

'I'm positive.'

'So long as you're sure. You know I'm here whenever you need me.' 'So am I, Maureen!'

'Thank you,' she said. 'Tell Rex thank you too.'

'We know you can do this.'

'You can do this, Maureen!'

'Make sure you drive carefully.'

'I will. And don't forget to eat.'

'We won't.'

'Promise me. Not just sandwiches all day. Sandwiches are not enough. They're not a proper meal.'

And he said yes. He promised. 'Not just sandwiches,' he said. 'We will eat proper meals.'

*

This was what she did not tell him. Could not, in fact. About the kindness of the young man who had stopped to help her. The kindness that had made everything a hundred times worse. Because there she had been, with the front of her car at an angle and right against the barrier of the hard shoulder, shocked but not injured, and not a disgrace either, when a young man pulled up behind and leapt out. He signalled at her to unwind her window and leant down to ask if she needed an ambulance. He was wearing no coat, in her distress she somehow noticed that, but he looked clean, his chin shaved soft and pink, his parting straight, and his sweater ironed – the sort of young man her mother had once hoped Maureen would marry. She insisted nothing was wrong but he wouldn't go away. He was hell-bent on being helpful. Suddenly all she could think about was a tight-bunched feeling in her bladder.

'You might be in shock,' he was saying. 'Is there anyone you would like me to ring? Are you sure you can move your legs?' 'I need a washroom,' she said, in her best telephone voice. 'Come again?'

Too late. She had wet herself. Right there in front of the lovely clean young man with no coat. She moved her legs to keep him happy and it all just happened. An involuntary dissolving of her body that briefly felt delicious, followed by a terrible warm flow between her thighs. Afterwards the traffic began to move again, but slowly, and she had to reverse into the waiting queue, with this man now in his car behind her, knowing full well what she had done, and she had to drive twenty miles in that slow procession of traffic, sitting in her own wetness. She was disgusting. She said it aloud, 'You are disgusting, Maureen Fry.' And then she had to walk into the service station with something from her suitcase, hiding her behind with her handbag. She headed straight for the washroom and there she yanked out a wedge of paper towels and soaked them with water before locking herself inside a cubicle.

'Pooh-ee. That old lady stinks,' she heard a child say.

She could have died. She could have died of the shame. She waited for someone to use the hand-dryer before she stuffed her soaked underwear into one of those bags for sanitary towels and shoved it into the bin. Then she had dressed – all the while balanced in that tiny cubicle – in her clean underwear and slacks that were supposed to be for tomorrow, trying her best not to get them on the tiled floor because it too was wet, while everywhere she looked there were poster adverts for period-proof underwear. Oh, the world made no sense. She walked out of the washroom with her chin high, but feeling scorched. In the shop, she found antiseptic wipes and took them to the self-checkout because the last thing she wanted was any kind of conversation with another human being.

And now here she was, back at the car, cleaning the driver's seat. She should have listened to the assistant with green fingernails. She should have bought those three air fresheners.

'Okay,' a man was saying to his wife, as they passed. 'Okay. I may not know what I'm talking about but anyone with any sense would agree with me.' They each nursed a tiny dog in the crook of their arms.

Maureen drove on. From Tamworth the traffic was directed to Atherstone, but then there were roadworks and yet another detour. A detour of a detour. She didn't know that was even possible. Worse, the smell was still on her and it was in the car too and all she could think of was a hot shower. She tried to keep her mind on the road ahead and not allow her thoughts to drift but it was hard when everything looked the same. 'I want a dog! I want a dog!' David used to say. There was a Christmas they had given him a fluffy toy that went, 'Woof! Woof!' when you pressed a button, and even sat on its back paws, as if it were begging, and he had said, 'Oh! A dog!' But she had caught him afterwards, staring at the garden with the toy dog back in its box, and she had known, with a dropping away in her heart, the disappointment.

The traffic reached a standstill on a dual carriageway. The banks were littered with plastic. Fly-tipping: a row of ten bin bags someone had arranged in a line. She was behind the coach of football supporters again. They waved their flags out of the windows and she watched anxiously, not wanting them to notice her. People began to get out of their cars and lorries and walked where pedestrians were not allowed to go. They climbed the central reservation and tried to see what was going on ahead. They got out their phones and even spoke to one another, complete strangers. Then the football fans jumped down from the coach, carrying beers and waving their flags, knocking on people's car windows. Maureen sat very tight and still. A car of young women waved to the football fans and got out too, laughing, even though they were dressed in tiny tops that were more like bras, and began sharing beers with them, as if they were in a club. Young people, thought Maureen. There was something about the glint in their eye, and the carelessness. And yet she had been the same once. Hard to believe, but she had thought she was on the cusp of the future. She had honestly believed history was all a kind of rehearsal and the real business of life would begin, with Maureen at the centre. She would pass her school exams with flying colours and go to university to read French – no one else in her village had gone to university – and life would happen. She would meet other people like her, gifted and exalted, clever people, who wore berets and smoked those French cigarettes and talked about philosophy. Not that she had read any yet, but she would. Hadn't her father always told her? She could do anything if she put her mind her to it.

Ahead, the traffic began slowly to move. People got back in their cars. Beyond the fog, she saw nothing but industrial units the size of hangars.

On and on. So slow it would have been quicker to walk. Briefly the fog cleared and the sun threw out pale arms as if it were drowning in cloud. A gorse bush flashed yellow sparks. After another half-hour, Maureen pulled over at a lay-by to stretch her legs. There was one of those vans where you could buy burgers and kebabs and the smell was of overheated rubber and hot fat. She was too exhausted to eat but she finished her flask of coffee.

At the opposite side of the lay-by, a man was sitting alone in the back of his car, with the windows steamed up. He seemed not to be doing anything. She even wondered if he was asleep. Suddenly he opened the door, walked to the bin and emptied a plastic bag of water bottles and polystyrene food trays into it, then smoothed his plastic bag and folded it into a neat square. He pulled a toothbrush out of his pocket and a tube of toothpaste, cleaning his teeth and spitting onto the ground, before returning to his car and getting once again into the back seat. He was wearing smart casual clothes. If he had seen her, he didn't acknowledge it.

As Maureen drove on, she thought about the man in the car and wondered how long he had been there. Days, probably. It was possible he had no home. But there was only so much you could see of another person's trouble without getting lost yourself. Better not to get involved in the first place. A truck slowly overtook her, piled high with discarded Christmas trees. A flock of crows flew out, like charred scraps.

In her mind, Maureen was back in David's room. After Harold's walk, she had decided to redecorate that too. She had chosen a bright shade of yellow and taken down the blue curtains and made flowered chintz ones instead. It had felt right. Like a fresh page. Peaceful, even. She put a desk in there, thinking she might try her hand at poetry, though the few times she tried, she gave up. The words she wanted would not come, or lost their colour the moment she put them together. It was no wonder she'd flunked her exams at school and ended up at secretarial college instead of university: it turned out she was not so special after all.

David's room had stayed the same for several years, sherbet yellow and empty. She could go past his closed door without hurting, or even feeling the need to go inside and talk to him the way she once used to. It was the pandemic that changed things. Everyone forced to stay at home. She found herself going back into the room, if only to be in a different space. And it had struck her then with a force that made her weak how ferociously empty it was, and how ghastly and yellow, and how much she did not like those flowery chintz curtains. She did not like them one bit. So she had begun to fetch things of David's out of the loft and put them back. His books, his trinkets, his photographs. One by one. She even found his old blue curtains and re-hung them. Harold had said nothing. Maybe he didn't notice. Sometimes she thought they were heading in opposite directions – as if she was now responsible for carrying all those things he felt free to let go. And yet the room was all wrong. Even if she made it blue again, she would still see the yellow. She would still know she had tried to pack David's things away. It left her with a bitter, vinegary feeling. The only thing she had left of David was his room and, look, she had vandalized it.

From far away came a fresh memory of looking at him as a baby when he was so small and black-haired, and realizing, with a sense of responsibility that terrified her, that nothing lay between him and the loneliness of the world except her, all her love and her fear, but mostly her fear, because if anything happened to him, she would not be able to bear it. She would not survive. She had never known such silence as the moment she found out he was dead.

Maureen pictured the trinkets she had placed back in his room – a china zebra and a wooden horse and a glass deer, the photograph of him as a baby. Such meagre scraps on which to heap all her great love. The emptiness stretched between them on the shelves. Where were all those words he had once told her that she must have forgotten, or misunderstood, all those stories, all those ideas, never realizing how little she would have left of him one day? How was she supposed to bear the weight of so many things she still couldn't understand?

The traffic poured back onto the M1. Loughborough, Kegworth. Nottinghamshire at last. *Welcome to Robin Hood County!* Maureen shook her head. She groaned. All this relentless thinking and remembering, and she had still over two hundred miles to go. Stuck in the car, she was exposed only to herself, with no Harold to dilute her. Smoke tumbled upwards from chimneys. The coach of football fans was back and they pointed down at her and laughed, and even though it surely wasn't possible they knew what she'd done earlier, she couldn't help feeling that they did. She thought of home, where everything was clean and in the right place, and the pink bathroom suite with its brass taps and matching pink tiles, which didn't need replacing, not really, and she thought of

Harold padding downstairs in his bare feet that still bore the scars from his walk to Queenie. She thought of the man living in his car and how much she did not want to dwell on other people's sadness.

Maureen swung off at the next exit, and pulled over at the first garage. She didn't even make it to a proper parking space. She reached for her mobile and as soon as he answered she told him she'd made up her mind. She was turning round.

'But why?' he said. 'Why?'

'Harold, I had an accident-accident. It wasn't just the car. I wet myself. I actually did that. And now I'm wearing my clothes that are supposed to be for tomorrow and I want a shower, Harold. I want a shower. I can't do this. I'm not like you. And I've only just passed Nottingham. I won't even get to the guesthouse in time for dinner. I'm coming home.'

There was a pause during which he said nothing and then there came his voice with its familiar soft creakiness.

'Oh, Maw. We're getting older. That's all. But you wanted to see the garden. You couldn't get it out of your head. And now you're more than halfway. So why don't I look for Kate's number and ask if you can stay there for the night? It doesn't matter if you arrive late. You won't feel right unless you do this, Maureen.'

Listening to him, she felt her heart swing wide open. He understood and accepted her for who she was, in the same way, many years ago, that she had watched him dance as a young man, all arms and jumping about, ignorant and out of place, and she had accepted him too. Maureen had not known what she was for until the day she met Harold: all she wanted after that was to stand between him and the rest of the world. In love and loved. It would be fanciful to say the fog was clearing but she thought there was a thinness to the cloud where she hadn't seen it before. A promise of blue, even if it wasn't there yet.

So Maureen did what he told her. She got back on the road. Rex texted her a list of directions to Kate's home and a smiley emoji.

Ten minutes later, her phone gave another ping from the passenger seat and there came one more text from Rex. This time it was an attachment to a map, with an arrow showing where she could stop at a service station and take a shower.

The emoji he chose was a unicorn with hearts for eyes. She didn't understand the point of it. But still. She smiled.

07

North and Further North

North, said the signs. Always north. Early afternoon and the fog was lifting. Chesterfield, Sheffield. Far away, the white-patched Peak District. Fields of wind turbines, like majestic blades on giant egg beaters, so strange close up they didn't look quite real. The land rose and fell, the earth giving way to houses and warehouses, slate-grey rooftops, and the outline of further cities and towns on the hinterland. Maureen drove below snatches of sky where sunlight glinted on the road, steel blue, spun gold, as rich as the glances off a crow's wing. Harold said there were as many different types of birdsong as countries in the world. He said it often, as if he had never said it before, always with wonder in his voice.

Sometimes Rex recorded a bird call they didn't know on his phone, then went home to identify it on his computer. 'Listen to this!' he would say later, rushing back and holding out his phone for her to listen. 'What do you think it is, Maureen?'

'Sounds like another bird to me,' she would say. 'Who would like coffee?'

'Could I ask for two sugars, please, Maureen?'

'Oh, Rex,' she would say, starting to laugh. 'You honestly think I haven't learnt after all these years how you like your coffee?'

At Tibshelf, Maureen had taken a shower. This was why she was happy. Who knew? Who knew there were showers in service stations? She had never so much as noticed one before – but there it was, a clean cubicle, behind a grey door with a picture of a showerhead on the front, and inside a set of hooks to hang her clothes. There was even a vending machine selling everything a human body might require, but in miniature form, including a doll-size bottle of body wash, a sachet of shampoo, a condom and a tampon. She had stood in that deluge of steaming hot water and it was almost as wonderful as the shower back at home.

The M18 and then at last the A1. Doncaster, Adwick le Street. Pontefract. Ferrybridge power station, with its disused cooling towers, like overturned pots. Maureen was entering North Yorkshire. An exit for Leeds. Wetherby. The sun sent down streamers of silver and gold light between clouds. A heron lifted into the air, as unlikely as a carpet bag taking flight. When she stopped at the service station, she was careful to be polite. She made a point of smiling at the young man mopping the floor in the washroom and telling him what a lovely clean place it was. When she bought a cup of tea, she thanked the barista a number of times, even though her hot drink was technically no more than a paper cup with some boiled water inside it, and a teabag in a separate sachet, and when the barista asked if she wanted anything else, she said, 'No, thank you. That's perfect. Thank you.' She found a table beside the window and asked the couple near by if it was free, although it was very clearly empty and there was a plastic screen between them. She took out her puzzle magazine while she drank her tea and managed a whole cryptic crossword without being bothered by anyone. She even smiled at a table of four children who were all dressed as superheroes and eating KFC from buckets, while their mother swiped her phone and sipped a fizzy drink.

'I like your coat,' she said to another woman, as she left.

'This old thing?' said the woman. But she tugged at the lapels and laughed.

'Yes, it's a lovely coat,' said Maureen.

Back in the car, it struck her that really the coat was quite ordinary. It was Maureen's mood that was so likeable. She switched on the radio, and when there was a song she knew, she hummed. A flock of geese flew overhead, their long necks straining north.

Already the day was over. That low January sky closing down. The spilled red of a winter sun. The land unfolded and cantilevered outwards, like breathing deeply. Ripon. Bedale. Scotch Corner. Durham. By the time she reached the Angel of the North it was dark again, the sky high-starred. The sculpture appeared before she expected it, leaning out of a hilltop ahead. It was hard to see, but the moon caught the span of its wings and she saw how wide out they stretched, how horizontal, not like ethereal wings at all, and she had the fleeting impression that if this angel came from anywhere, it would not be the heavens or the sky, but somewhere more human and earthbound. Maureen made her way round Newcastle, crossing the Tyne, and finally turned off the A1 to head west. There were granite farms, scattered and isolated, their windows a buttery yellow. She passed beneath a tunnel of trees, and the light from the street lamps shone through the branches and made mosaic crystals on the way ahead. At last there was the sign for Hexham.

Maureen had been on the road for almost fourteen hours. She was so exhausted, and had seen so much, she felt bruised, marked all over, and the sound of the car engine seemed to have taken up residence inside her head.

She pulled up to check Rex's directions one more time, and applied a small amount of lipstick, then drove on to meet Kate. She could do this. She could.

08

Truck

When maureen was a child, her mother dressed her in frocks and white socks. The frocks she made herself on her electric sewingmachine and added details by hand like smocking to the bodice, or puff sleeves. The only time Maureen really remembered her mother laughing was when she ran her fingers over a new roll of organza. And Maureen had liked those frocks. She had believed her father when he said she looked like a princess, as if looking like a princess was a good thing when you're five and live in a farming hamlet slap bang in the middle of nowhere. It was only when she started school that it began to dawn on her she had been gravely misinformed. That a child in white lace, with a rosebud trim at the waist, or a moss-green silk sash with a bow the size of her head, is a walking target for other children, less fortunate, who will lie in wait for her as she skippetty-skips home in her little-girly frock, and they will splatter her with mud pies and worse. Similarly, that a child who carries a satchel and keeps her pencils sharp, and lays them on her desk in order of colour, from dark to light, or who talks as if she has a plum in her mouth, or insists on telling the kind of long stories that so delighted her father, will never be popular. Will, in fact, become a laughing stock.

As Maureen approached Kate's, she experienced the same feeling she'd had all those years ago as a child, that same low-belly horror at having got everything wrong. Until that day, it had not occurred to her – because why would it? – that other children would not admire her superior clothes and her nice neat pencils and the way she believed she knew the answers to absolutely everything, even when she didn't, in the same way she had assumed Kate would live in a dear little cottage that she would have cleaned extra-specially since Maureen was coming to visit. In her mind, she had placed a casserole in the Aga that Kate would surely own – because even if she was an activist she still had to eat – and she had laid a table with a clean white cloth. In anticipation of these things, Maureen had stopped to buy wine and a box of chocolates.

Her mistake was obvious now she thought about the directions. No house name. Not even a number. Nor, come to think of it, a street name. Just instructions to follow a lane that turned out to be more of a wild track, and a few references to suspicious landmarks, like a disused phone box, and the old gates to a farm. Why had Kate never mentioned to Harold in any of her postcards that her home was no longer a home-home, in the traditional sense of the word, let alone a cottage, but actually a converted truck? And why had she omitted to say that it was not on its own, this mobile home, but part of a community of other campervans and trucks? All inhabited by the kind of women Maureen read about in the paper, who lived in trees to stop them being chopped down, or sat on bridges to protest about global warming?

She had driven for what felt like miles down the track, easing the car in the dark around a pothole only to bump it into a stone, and passed these trailers and caravans without giving them so much as a second thought – until she reached a gate that said 'No trespassing'. She'd had to reverse, because it was too narrow to turn, hitting all the potholes and stones a second time, but this time with more force because she couldn't see them properly in the dark out of her rear windscreen and, anyway, reversing had never been her strong point. She stopped close to the group of caravans and campervans, but she had no signal to call Rex.

'Can I help?' A blue woman had knocked at her window, with a rainbow shawl. The blue, Maureen later realized, was because she was heavily tattooed. The rainbow was her hair.

Maureen wound down her window but not too far and said she was looking for a person called Kate but she had made a mistake.

'No. You're right. Kate is here,' the young woman had said. Her voice was as sweet as a child's. She could only have been in her late twenties.

'Here?' said Maureen, unable to disguise her shock. 'That's right.'

'I don't know where to park.'

'Yeah. Here is cool.'

'Here?' said Maureen again.

'Cool,' said the young woman.

So Maureen straightened the car and parked, though she straightened it again, because with nothing to align it against, like a garage wall, it was hard to get it correct. Then she stepped out of the car, straight into mud in her driving shoes, and opened her boot, wondering if the rainbow-haired young woman might help with her suitcase, but apparently not because she had already drifted ahead.

Maureen followed her past the other caravans. Not wanting to dirty the wheels of her suitcase, she was forced to carry it. They passed about ten in all and she could see lights inside them and the silhouettes of other women. She hoped none of them would come out. She had no intention of meeting any more strangers.

'That's it,' said the young woman.

'That's it?' Maureen repeated.

'Yeah. Mum lives there.'

'Your mother?'

'That's right.'

'Kate is your mother?'

So this was Kate's daughter. Kate had a daughter. Another thing no one had thought to mention to Maureen. And her hair might have been rainbow-coloured but it would have benefited from a wash. Then Maureen remembered she was trying to be nice, so she said, 'I do like your hair.'

'Cool.'

'I'll just go ahead, shall I?'

'Sure.' Away she had drifted.

Maureen picked her way in her driving shoes past a group of empty plastic chairs, a firepit, stepped around a pile of wooden pallets, and squeezed past a child's purple bicycle. She thought of Harold cleaning her shoes only the night before and felt unbearably tired. Fossebridge Road seemed like another country.

The door opened before Maureen could knock on it. An unexpected blessing because until that point Maureen was not clear it was a door. From the truck came the cry, 'Maureen!' A woman appeared, with wild grey hair woven with ribbons of fabric. She wore a thick green cardigan and large earrings that were feathers and beads, as well as many necklaces and something else that resembled a dream-catcher.

'Maureen, you poor love!' cried the woman, as she heaved down a steep set of steps and then threw her arms around her. 'I'm Kate!' She kissed the side of Maureen's cheek. Completely uninvited. Maureen recoiled.

'It's such a joy to meet you. Come in, darlin', come in.'

Maureen followed her up the wooden steps while Kate said over her shoulder how truly wonderful it was to meet her after all these years and how much she loved Harold. He had been such an inspiration, she said. She apologized that the truck was so cramped, and hoped Maureen wasn't surprised. Maureen made herself say no, no, it was a very nice place. 'Very unusual,' she said. She was aware of the artificial strain in her voice, and also the awful splodges of mud over her driving shoes.

Inside the truck, there was not one single place for the eye to rest that hadn't already been claimed by something else. It was like looking directly into a migraine. Tiny Buddha ornaments, chakra stones, hanging quartzes, crystals, candles, exhortations to find your inner goddess and your angels, shelves draped with purple curtains. Everything carried a thin layer of filth and was either broken or about to be. And the smell. Dear God. She'd thought she'd smelt bad. Incense sticks were puffing away in every corner. She could barely breathe. There was no Aga. There was no casserole.

Maureen produced the wine and chocolates from her bag and offered them to Kate, who said, 'You shouldn't! You shouldn't!' and placed them on top of a unit covered with so many other things, Maureen was not certain her gifts would ever see the light of day. She felt a pang of remorse for them.

The place was a hovel. She could try as hard as she liked to be nice but there was no nice way of saying it. There had been the holiday chalet they'd stayed in every year in Eastbourne when David was a boy and towards the end, it was true, the place had seen better days. A smell of mildew when you opened the front door, and dirt-coloured carpet to hide stains. There had been the roadside motel where she'd stopped with Harold on the way home after his walk, which she hadn't realized until too late was in the middle of a red-light district. But they could have been anywhere; he had slept and slept. It was Maureen who had eaten alone in the motel bar with a number of women who did not seem to be there for the pleasure of dining. But this. It had never occurred to Maureen that a person who sent postcards to Harold could live like this. It wasn't even clean. It especially wasn't clean.

The truck was designed like an open-plan studio – an idea that had never appealed to Maureen – with a miniature kitchenette near the door, the cupboards made of hardboard, with a tiny sink in the middle, and on the other side, a single wardrobe space, hung with another purple drape, alongside a shower that was a plastic-curtained cubicle, so narrow you would only be able to stand in it sideways. Then there was yet another purple drape, beyond which there appeared to be the world's most uncomfortable sofa – more of a ledge – and a Formica table with two chairs and a stool. An incongruously large wing-back chair was covered with an old eiderdown that Maureen would honestly fear to disturb. 'What a lovely place,' said Maureen again. 'Isn't this charming?'

She took off her coat, but there was nowhere to hang it so she put it back on again.

'How long are you holidaying here?' she said. Her voice was on its brightest setting.

Kate bustled through to the other end of the truck. She seemed to be saying to Maureen that this was her home, not a holiday let, and that it was also home to her daughter and the other women living there. They had decided to exist as a community, sharing whatever they owned. It was the best decision she had ever made, she said, apart from walking with Harold, of course. At the front of the truck, Maureen could see now there were two seats and a steering wheel.

Maureen was still holding her suitcase. Kate was only a step or two away from the man in his car. She could not understand why anyone would choose to leave their home to live in a vehicle, and her confusion made her panicky. She and Harold had been in the same house for more than fifty years. The idea of not living at 13 Fossebridge Road, with all her things safe in the correct places, appalled her. Kate switched on the kettle and reached for two chipped mugs.

'So how are you really?' she said, as if there were two versions of Maureen, one behind the other, and she didn't believe the one who was standing at the front.

'I'm fine,' said Maureen.

'Harold told me you've done the whole drive in one day. I can't believe you've done that. You must be exhausted. He said you're going to visit Queenie's Garden. I guess that's tough, huh?'

'It isn't really,' said Maureen.

'Darlin'. You must be hungry.'

Maureen was. She was starving. Her limbs were almost hot and shaking with it. She hadn't eaten since her sandwiches. But her mouth said she wasn't. 'I'm fine, thank you. I don't even need a cup of tea. I'll just go to bed. Maybe you could show me to my room? It's been a long day.'

Even as she said this, she experienced doubt and felt foolish, as if once again she was missing the point. There was clearly no other room, beyond the one they were standing in. Also, there was no bed.

'I thought you could have mine tonight,' said Kate. She pointed out the thing that was a ledge, not a bed, and explained it folded out. She spoke again about how great it was to get to know Maureen at last, and how meeting Harold had changed her life, while all the time Maureen stared at the ledge and thought of her bed at home with lovely pressed sheets and Harold inside it. Kate was still talking. She was telling Maureen about her marriage now and how it was lockdown that finished it, though things were good with her ex, and he still lived in their old house.

'I don't understand,' Maureen said. 'You gave him your house?'

'Yes, Maw. I wanted a clean start.'

The truck did not strike Maureen as a clean start. She tried to smile.

'And I wanted to be with my daughter and my granddaughter, you know?'

No, Maureen did not know, not until Kate pointed outside to the young woman Maureen had met earlier, caught in the light from the other trucks and caravans. Maureen could see she was holding a scrap of a child with long black hair. The little girl had her legs tucked around her mother and her head on her shoulder. Maureen experienced a coldness, a drawing-in. So Kate was a grandmother.

'Maple,' said Kate.

'I'm sorry?'

'She is the light of my life.'

'But her name is Maple? As in the syrup?'

Kate gave a polite not-quite smile, as if she wasn't sure whether Maureen was being deliberately offensive. 'No, not the syrup. More like the leaf.'

Oh, Maureen was exhausted. She was inside-out with it. All that driving and then all the people. People who had green fingernails and people who lived in cars and trucks and people who named their children after parts of nature. Harold had told her strange stories about his journey but he'd never mentioned anything like this. Her head was hurting. 'You should come and visit us some time,' she said. 'Harold would love to see you.' She imagined Kate's truck parked outside 13 Fossebridge Road and knew she didn't mean it.

'Yes, I will,' said Kate.

She knew Kate didn't mean that either.

Nevertheless Kate showed Maureen how to unfold the ledge into what was basically a larger ledge and passed her sheets that were not ironed, but smelt clean enough. She said goodnight, though this time, thankfully, she did not attempt to hug her. Alone, Maureen unpacked her nightdress and put it on and cleaned her teeth. She got out her puzzle magazine but dropped it onto the floor and she was so tired she couldn't be bothered to bend and pick it up. She lay on the bed.

Bed was a kindness. There was nothing bedlike about the pull-outy thing with its lumpy mattress on which Maureen was now doing her best to relax. She was beyond tired. She lay rigid and uncomfortable but she must have fallen asleep without noticing because she was woken by voices outside the truck, and heard a faraway clock strike ten.

'You okay, Kate?' It was Kate's daughter, the sweet-voiced woman covered with tattoos. Maureen opened her eyes wide in order to hear more clearly.

'Yeah, sure,' said Kate.

'Where will you sleep?'

'I'll hunker down with someone. It's no problem.'

'So what's the story? With Maureen?'

'Well, it's been hard for her.' At this point her voice dropped and Maureen couldn't make out any more words. Then she heard doors closing and the voices of other women calling to one another and laughing, asking how they were, if they needed anything.

'Goodnight, hon! Goodnight!'

It was quiet again but Maureen was too ill at ease to sleep. She had that feeling that she'd had as a child of being completely wrongly dressed, and with her things all precious and silly, but unable to change because her world presented no alternative. She thought of the kindness with which the women at the camp called to one another, the easy intimacy, and Kate, who had willingly given up her own bed, even if it was a ledge, and how she would never be like that. She got up and opened her handbag for a tissue and found the piece of paper on which she had written Lenny's instructions. Another invitation to connect that she had failed.

Maureen sat stiff in the wing-back chair, taking care not to trouble the eiderdown. She had no idea what to do with herself. If only she was back in her own kitchen, where everything was clean and stowed away, even the cups, their handles all pointing in the same direction. In her mind, she allowed herself to creep along the beige carpet of the hallway, passing the hooks where she and Harold put their coats, to the sitting room with its patterned wallpaper, its matching upholstered chairs, and the mantelpiece where she now kept a framed wedding photograph and a portrait of David, along with a china shepherdess that had belonged to her mother. And from there she began to think of the house in which she'd grown up that was always cold, and suddenly she could see her mother, industrious at her sewing machine, while her father apologized so much for being a burden that he became one.

If only she had been more like the other children. If only she had learnt how to dress like them and talk like them, instead of being kept apart. She remembered now walking across the fields with her father, even though the farmer let his dogs run loose. How the dogs had come at them and barked at her father, who held out his hands to placate them and told her not to run but to be calm, and how she had refused to listen as the dogs came close and decided to run after all, so that one had jumped up then and, when her father put himself in front of her, had taken a bite at her chin and mauled her father's hand. Her mother had railed and railed at him and he had sat, so full of remorse he couldn't even look at Maureen. Her mother had called him weak and good for nothing, and he had shaken his head, bearing it all, and Maureen had wished that for once he would stand up for himself. And yet, after he died, her mother had lost all interest in life. She was dead within three months. It struck Maureen that a person could be trapped in a version of themselves that was from another time, and completely miss the happiness that was staring them in the face.

For a few hours, Maureen managed to doze. She woke with her body stiff, but at least it was morning. She dressed in her slacks and afresh blouse, straightening the sleeves of her cardigan, then put on her coat and driving shoes and picked up her suitcase. She would have taken her wine and her chocolates if only she could find them.

Outside the first shade of pale was coming but it wasn't so much light as a little less dark. There was an atmosphere of stillness across the camp. Each of the trucks and mobile homes was closed up and unlit, except one where Maureen heard a woman's voice softly chanting. Briefly she felt an intense longing for everything to stop so that she could go back and give it one more try. But how could she do that? It wasn't in her. It was not how she was made. Nothing for it but to do what she had learnt as a child and hold her head high and walk away. In the distance, traffic gave a muffled glow along the horizon, moving north. Maureen clicked the fob on her car key and the car popped alight. Its enthusiasm struck her as frivolous. But she got in.

Maureen went without leaving a note. She went without saying thank you or goodbye. It wasn't as if she would ever see Kate again, or her awful truck. So she just left.

09

Garden of Relics

The morning sky was torn and tattered by the wind, and golden light shone through, flashing, then vanishing, yet she saw everything, the land and the light and the cloud – even wink snatches of the sea ahead – through another kind of fog, because the only thing she could think of was David. Thirty years. Thirty years of waiting and searching. And now she was finally going to see him. He was her one thought.

Maureen had driven straight from Kate's to Embleton. She'd rung Harold to check he was awake but she said nothing about what had happened. She didn't even mention the truck. She took care to talk only about the driving and the weather, and when he asked her what she had made of Kate, she told him that she had gone to bed as soon as she arrived. There hadn't been any time to get to know her.

'Oh, what a shame,' he'd said, and she could hear the regret in his voice. 'I always liked Kate.'

'I'd better get going now,' she'd said.

At Embleton, Maureen located the Palm Trees guesthouse, and

stopped to check in. The receptionist was a friendly young woman sitting in a little booth with a toy plastic palm tree on the desk. She said Maureen's room was ready for her if she wanted, but Maureen explained she was just dropping off her suitcase before she went to visit a garden. 'Queenie's Garden? The Garden of Relics?' said the girl, with her singing Northumberland accent. 'Just past the golf club! You can't miss it! When my mother died, we scattered her ashes there! It's a lovely walk!'

The walk could be as lovely as it liked but Maureen had no intention of doing it. She took the car to the golf club and when the road became a dead end, she parked as close as she could and made the very last stretch on foot, never looking back, not once, but always forward. She tied on a headscarf but the wind still flapped her slacks and got at her ankles. Beyond the dunes lay a horizontal blade of sea, and a vast expanse of sky.

She followed a track that crossed alongside the golf course towards the shore: a number of wooden chalets stood on the dunes ahead, looking tiny beside the sea, and it was towards these that she made her way. At the end of the golf course, the path swung to the left with a hand-painted plywood sign for Queenie's Garden, shortly followed by another sign pointing the way over a small bridge. The signs irritated Maureen. She knew the purpose of them was to be helpful, but she felt she should instinctively know where to go without the help of plywood, and the fact that she didn't – the fact that she actually needed these signs – made them all the more irksome.

Once she got to the sand, she had to take care in her driving shoes because it gave way abruptly to soft, sludgy patches that might wet her feet. The tide was a long way out. Gangs of gulls and oystercatchers scattered through the sky, and the wind threw up balls of foam from the sea that skittered and tumbled across the land and finally broke into nothing. In the distance to her left, Dunstanburgh Castle was a jagged ruin on the horizon, shaped like the tricky piece of a jigsaw puzzle. And all the time she was thinking, David, David, David, where are you?

The signs pointed along the foot of the dunes, offering a welcome, each one decorated with seaweed banners and plastic flowers and shell necklaces. *Bienvenue! Willkommen! ¡Bienvenido! Välkommen! Hoş geldin! Witaj!* She didn't see why they needed all those foreign languages. It was just showing off.

From the beach, the signs directed Maureen up a flight of wooden steps set into the edge of the dunes, leading to a cluster of chalets. The steps were so steep they were more of a ladder, and scattered with sand; even though there was a blue rope to hold onto, it wasn't enough and she had to reach out to the thick grass for support. There were already tributes. A plastic wreath decorated with bright red baubles. A bunch of fake lilies. The wind was getting stronger and made a gushing sound all round her. Maureen approached the first of the chalets, a wooden house with rickety steps and a veranda, its door and windows boarded up with shutters and a padlock. The next chalet was painted green, with matching curtains at the windows, while another was more like a bungalow with slate roof tiles. The signs to Queenie's Garden kept pointing ahead. She could make out the outline of some of the shapes she had seen on her computer, like totem poles, and she slowed. Suddenly she had no idea what she was going to do. All this time she had been thinking about seeing David and never once had it dawned on her to question what that actually meant. What would happen when she was finally standing in front of Queenie's Garden.

Nothing Maureen had seen online had prepared her for seeing it in real life. Nothing she'd imagined either. The garden was even more of a mystery now that she was here. She had no idea where to look for David.

Beneath her feet there was rough grass, but ahead the ground became intricate patterns of shingle, flint and stones of different colours, set in squares and circles, and interplanted with skeletons of plants that had died back over winter, as well as gorse bushes shaped like candle flames. Between these stood pieces of driftwood, dominated by one tall piece at the centre, while other monuments surrounding it were no bigger than spoons. They were made of all kinds of things. Spiralled pieces of iron, twisted links, rusted chains, with chimes of keys and holey stones, and scraps of plastic and wood. There were also banners that flapped between poles, and many, many glass jars containing candles. But the thing that astounded her most was the number of people.

Two men stood at the back of the garden, pointing out its vari- ous features, and nodding as if they agreed it was beautiful. A young couple were hand in hand, speechlessly absorbed in a pyramid of stones. Another woman sat on her coat with a notebook and pencil, sketching what she saw, while a man in a biker's jacket was fixing a padlock to a chain. Maureen could see now that there was a kind of path through the garden that she had not noticed before, leading to the painted hut at the back. It was like looking at something you have never seen, such as the bottom of the ocean, where nature is a vast and infinitely more exotic version of what you imagined, and you feel very small for having given it such a poor expectation.

There was movement from a corner of the garden, and Maureen realized with a jolt that another woman was very close by, bent over, wearing a hat with two pompoms, one on each side of her head. She was probably in her early sixties and she seemed to be digging at the stones with a trowel.

Maureen stayed on the periphery, unwilling to go any further but not yet able to leave, hoping the garden would make sense to her if she just kept staring, while other people continued to enjoy it. At last the woman put down her trowel. 'Can I help?' she called.

'No, thank you,' said Maureen.

So the woman stayed where she was and Maureen stayed where she was. She tried looking for David among the sculptures but she still had no idea what she was searching for – there was nothing that looked like David here – and just when she really needed them, there were no signs either.

Besides, with all those other visitors in the garden, Maureen felt awkward and self-conscious. She tried walking a few feet to the left but it still made no sense to her so she went back to where she'd been before. The woman in the hat with two pompoms put down her trowel again and stood. 'Excuse me? Are you lost?' she called.

'No. I'm fine.'

'Is there something you're trying to find?'

'It's okay. I can manage.'

The woman looked at Maureen a moment. Her hat seemed to accentuate the wrinkles in her face, like slashes in her cheeks. 'Why don't you come in?' she said. 'Take a proper look round?'

A strange thing to say since there was no fence to separate what was inside from what was out. And yet instinctively Maureen understood what the woman meant. That there was a hallowed space, which was the garden, while everywhere else was not — everywhere else was ordinary dunes and marram grass. Maureen stayed pinned in the same spot, her hands tight-knit, until the woman came right up close, then took a step to one side, making a gesture with her hand as if inviting Maureen through an unseen gate.

'This way,' she said. She turned and made her passage through the garden.

Maureen dipped her head as she followed. Yet another thing she did not understand. Like crossing yourself when you enter a church, except that she was not a churchgoer. She did not even know where the woman was taking her.

The path was not a straight one, but went in curves around the boulders and pieces of driftwood and stone circles. Things flicked in the wind, like tiny pieces of washing, but as she passed, she saw they were photographs of many different faces and that there were written messages too and other strange mementos, like shoes and crosses, and keys and padlocks tucked between the stones. Candles were everywhere, as well as further sculptures made of bottle tops and pieces of coloured plastic and foam. A gust of wind took up from the sea so that the ribbons and pieces of seaweed flew out and there was a clinking sound of bells and many chimes.

Maureen went slowly, as if she did not trust the stones beneath her feet – as if they might give way without warning. All she could think of was the day Queenie had come to visit with her flowers and waited while Maureen hung out her dead son's washing. The other people in the garden looked up as she passed and some smiled. Once again, she experienced that old feeling of being the wrong shape for the situation in which she found herself. Of being an intruder. She wished that – all those years ago – she had been kinder to Queenie.

The woman said, 'I'm Karen. I'm a volunteer. I work here twice a week. It's your first time, isn't it?'

'Yes.'

'I thought as much. I remember my first time. I cried and cried. It has that effect.'

Karen smiled sympathetically at Maureen as if she were expecting her to weep, and Maureen turned away. The sun had broken through the cloud again and flared over the garden, catching the pieces of driftwood so that they appeared especially bright, their sides gold and purple. The chimes flashed silver.

'Are you a gardener?'

Maureen said she was, but just vegetables.

'Queenie grew vegetables too. She especially liked ornamental gourds.'

'Oh, I never tried those. I'm more – ordinary. Beans and, you know, potatoes and things.' She tightened the knot of her scarf.

'Most people come to visit in the summer, when the weather's good. But Queenie loved it best in the winter. I feel the same. Of course, when you work in a garden all year, you get to know it like a person. Every part has a story. Did you meet her?'

'No.' She said it quickly.

'She was a very special woman. She left the garden to the people of Embleton Bay. At first no one was sure what to do with it. But it's become a tourist attraction. Visitors come from all over the world. Even China.'

Maureen had no idea people might come that far. And no one would describe her as special, apart from her father when she was a child, and look where that had got her. She tried to smile but it didn't happen.

'Then people began leaving things of their own here. Padlocks at first. We had so many padlocks. After that they brought more personal things, like photographs and poems in bottles and even their own sculptures. We took them all away. But we began to think that Queenie would have wanted those things to stay. She was a curator, after all.'

They passed several boulders that had been carved with names and a bright blue bird made of fragments of glass. Karen said, 'Someone told me once that the garden was about love. Since then, I've heard a few people say that. They even say it makes a noise of its own but people will believe all sorts of things. It's just the wind.' Her voice was quiet, as if she was talking to herself. 'Now this little shoe?'

She pointed at a child's shoe, so small it must have been a first one. It was weather-beaten to the point where the leather had lost its colour and it was woven with ivy into a larger driftwood cross. There were shells too, all threaded with the ivy. 'I am glad someone felt they could leave that here.'

Karen showed Maureen another sculpture, a heart shape, made of barbed wire. 'I wonder what went on there,' she said.

After that she moved to a line of photographs and touched each face with her finger, marking its presence. There were totems made of driftwood and old garden tools and one with a model of a dog and another with a bird skull. She talked about the people who had brought memorials to the garden, like a man whose husband had died in a car accident and a farmer who had lost her home because of mad-cow disease back in the eighties. People from all walks of life, she said. 'I love to hear their stories.'

'You mean they leave things?' Maureen still did not really get why the garden was considered beautiful. But even more she did not understand why people would feel free to leave pieces of themselves there. Things that were so deeply personal and private and could not be replaced.

Karen said there were still the original tributes in the garden that had been Queenie's. She had found a place for her mother and father – she pointed at a monument that was made of a spade, and another that was a sturdy branch – and also a curtain of feathers. 'These were some female artists she once lived with. But they're flighty things. They're always blowing away.' She laughed. 'We have to keep finding new ones.'

They were in the centre of the garden now, standing beside the tallest driftwood piece. Karen glanced up at it and said, 'There was a man Queenie cared about, I believe. Yes. I think this might be him.'

Maureen was no longer hearing the words. She felt the shock in her own face. A kind of dropping away behind her eyes and mouth.

She looked at where the woman was pointing. It was a huge baulk of timber. Ten feet or more. It was so strong it might have once been part of an old ship. Nevertheless she also knew that what Karen was saying to her was the truth. If Harold was anything, he was that piece of wood. Steadfast and solid. She would have liked to touch the surface, all those wrinkles and twists. To rest against the tall bulk of him and feel his goodness.

'But the only piece she ever gave a name to is the one she called David.'

Maureen was not ready. Her thoughts had slipped over to Harold; the words came to her as a blow, like being hit when you're not even looking. To hear David's name from the mouth of a woman she did not know was as shocking as visiting his body at the funeral parlour.

'David?' she said.

'He died young. He took his own life, I think.'

Maureen did not know what to say. She did not know how to arrange her face. She didn't even know where to look.

'Which one is that, then?' she said. 'Which one is David?'

'Well.' Karen smiled. 'For a long time I got it wrong. I thought he was the figure over there.' She pointed to a piece of driftwood that was set apart from the others, with a hole worn right through it. It must have been about four feet tall, but so slim it was hard to see how it had not split because of the hole: you could see through it to the other side. 'That's not the saddest thing I've ever seen,' Karen said quietly. 'But it is one of them.'

'But it's not David?'

'No. I don't think that's anyone. It's just a piece of driftwood Queenie took pity on. David is the one over there.' She pointed to another figure, fastened in the shingle. 'You see?'

Maureen was nothing but nerve endings. Oh, it was the most appalling thing. Crueller even than the rings of bruises around his neck that the undertaker had tried to cover with make-up. There were no words. There were no words for the horror she felt on looking at that terrible piece of driftwood. She felt dizzy. Mauled. The monument was a knotty V-shape, in height only about two feet, the wood weathered to dark grey, crooked and complicated, like a broken lyre, and worn away into sharp points at both ends. It was not a tragic structure, like the holed piece Karen had already shown her. This was angry; it was violent; it was separate and undeniable. Maureen thought of his bedroom that she had wrongly painted yellow. She thought of the tablet at the crematorium and the little green stones she was always tidying, and how he was not in either place, no matter how much she tried to find him. But this was David. This was him. Too fragile for the world and yet full of youth and complication and pomp and arrogance. She did not know how such a piece of wood could have survived the wind and rain and yet, secure in Queenie's Garden, it had held fast. All those years she had been calling for David, all those years of waiting, and he'd been here all along. Queenie had taken him.

'Would you like to see more?' said Karen. 'Or have you found what you were looking for?'

Maureen's heart seemed to shrink inside her chest, trying to defend itself. It was the same sensation she'd had as a child, and during Harold's walk, and again in Kate's truck, of being measured against something she didn't understand and would never get right.

'Are you sure you're okay?' said Karen.

Maureen couldn't speak. She nodded.

'Can I get you something? A glass of water?'

She managed one 'No.' She managed one 'Thank you.'

But she was almost not able to walk in a straight line as she hurried along the dunes and down the steps to the beach. And all the while she could feel Karen's eyes on her, so that Maureen had the strangest feeling of watching herself from a distance, as if she had become a person alone and apart, even from herself.

10

A Bad Night

That evening, maureen ordered a light early supper in the Palm Trees guesthouse. After seeing Queenie's Garden she had walked towards Dunstanburgh Castle because she wanted to keep moving, but nothing pleased her. Nothing took her from her own thoughts. She hadn't even felt able to manage a crossword puzzle. The dining room was brightly lit with a bewildering number of plastic palm trees in all shapes and sizes. At another table, a well-dressed couple were talking to their son about working harder for his finals. Even though Maureen tried to get on with her own meal and not listen, she might as well have been sitting right with them. Their son kept pushing his hands through his shaggy hair and saying it was cool and not to worry, while the woman said, in her voice that cut through the room, 'I don't understand. How is it cool, if you fail your finals? Tell him, Peter. If you don't put in the effort, you'll never get anywhere.' Maureen thought, Dear God, how much longer must I endure this kind of thing? She folded her napkin and left her meal barely touched because her mouth had given up trying to eat.

Her room was nothing like the one on the website. It was narrow and draughty, with a loud carpet that must have been laid in the fifties. She took a shower and afterwards she found an extra red blanket wrapped in polythene and put her clothes back on with the red blanket on top. She looked like someone rescued from an accident. She had no idea how she would sleep. The minibar was empty.

Maureen rang Harold and told him she was going to have an early night so that she could leave Embleton first thing.

He said, 'So? Did you see Queenie's Garden?'

'I did,' she said.

'How was it?'

'Well, it was, you know . . . It was fine.'

'What about . . .?' He couldn't do it. He couldn't say his name. She had to do it for him.

'No,' she said. 'I didn't see David. Kate was wrong. He isn't there.'

'Oh.' She could hear the sadness in his voice. The disappointment yet again. She should never have gone on and on about the garden. She should have let it be. He would have happily forgotten, if it hadn't been for her. 'Oh, well,' he said.

'To be honest, I don't really know why I came.'

'You wanted to see Queenie's Garden.'

'Well, yes,' she said. 'But I don't know why I thought that was a good idea. I don't know what I thought would happen.'

'So what is it like?'

Maureen thought of the tall driftwood sculpture, and the V-shaped one close by. She thought of how she had wanted to touch the tall one, and feel the solid strength of it; surely it had once been the same for Queenie. She remembered the final letter Queenie had written to Harold that was all dots and squiggles, the pen nib pushed so hard sometimes it had stabbed right through the pages. To think Maureen had stored that letter in a shoebox. To think she had kept it safe when what she should have done was tear it up. Oh, she should have gone at it with the scissors. She had been right that day by the washing line: Queenie had wanted to take Harold from her all along. Maureen felt that old stinging bitterness. That ancient jealousy. She took a pause. A deep breath.

'Maureen?'

'Harold, I don't think I can talk about Queenie and her garden. I know I said I wanted to come here. But I was wrong. It's been a wasted journey. We just need to forget the whole thing.'

Even as she said it, she knew it was not true. It might be possible for Harold to forget but for her there was no such way out. She might forget her entire life story. She might forget the dogs that attacked her and her father because she had not listened to him, even though he later bore the blame, and she might forget the humiliation of not getting into university or the beret that she subsequently threw away. She might forget seeing Harold for the first time as he danced like a madman and she watched transfixed, knowing her life had changed and there was no going back. She might even – God help her – somehow lose her most recent mistakes, but she would always see Queenie's monuments to Harold and David. Because they were beautiful. As much as she didn't want to, Maureen knew it. She knew it so deeply it was seared into her bones. Queenie had taken them both and rendered them beautiful while all Maureen had managed was a vacant bedroom and a tablet with little green stones. Surely it wasn't too much to ask that you get to the end, and looking back, you don't fill with horror and bitterness at all the things you got wrong. The mistakes you made, over and over, like falling repeatedly down the same old hole.

'Are you still there?'

'I'm still here,' she said.

'You seem quiet.'

'I'm tired. That's all.'

'Did you get on well with Kate?'

'I told you already. I didn't stay long.' She pursed her mouth. Changed the subject. 'Did you eat?'

'When?'

'Today.'

'Yes. We ate very well.'

Another pause. Another not knowing what to say. 'Well. Goodnight, then, Harold.'

'Goodnight.'

It seemed to Maureen that in the space of two days she had aged ten years. She felt ancient and ruined and empty.

It was a sleepless night. The third in a row. More like hovering above the surface of repose. She lay there, wide-eyed and restless, a prisoner of her own thoughts, alert to every creak in the radiator and alien banging of a door. It reminded her of the months following David's death when to give in to sleep had felt like a betrayal, and she had spent hours in his room, cocooned within his blue curtain, refusing to believe what she knew to be true. But she must have dozed in the end because she came to hearing wind beating at the window, and had no idea where she was. Red numbers were floating in the dark, telling her the time was 05:17. She knew something had happened that made the world different, but she didn't know what it was until she felt the blanket on top of her and knew with a fresh influx of pain that she had driven to Embleton Bay to find David in Queenie's Garden and ease something inside her, like taking out a splinter, yet what she had found had only filled her with hundreds more spikes.

It was no use. She couldn't sleep. She switched on the lamp and reached for her crossword puzzle, but all she could think about was the garden. Her eyes felt gritty and tight, and her head was a clamp. 'Not the saddest thing,' she heard Karen the volunteer saying, as she pointed to the holed piece of driftwood. 'But one of them.'

Maureen recalled the way Queenie had looked at her all those years ago as she pegged out her washing. Demeaning and full of pity. A chill went right through her. She threw on her clothes, ramming her arms into her coat and her feet into her shoes, barely pausing to switch off the lamp, pulling her suitcase out of the room, even though the silly wheels got stuck on the meeting point between the carpet and the landing, and she had to yank it. She looked for the receptionist in her booth but all the lights were off, so she placed her room key beside the toy palm tree and pulled open the front door.

Maureen couldn't leave that guesthouse fast enough.

11

Anna Dupree

Rage. oh, such rage. Like a blazing column in her chest. How dare Queenie? How dare she? Maureen had not felt this way since the book group. The moon was a silver-white fragment, flooding the land in cold light. She followed the path of her own shadow, her driving shoes stumbling over the sand. Ahead, the skin of the sea heaved and waves rolled out of the dark. A salt smell pricked her nose and the wind came at her face. The noise was terrible. She crossed to the end of the bay and made her way up the steep wood steps, grasping at marram grass, but it burnt her hands and that hurt too. She moved past the closed-up chalets towards the garden. Her car was parked at the golf course, ready to go, with her suitcase and handbag. Queenie could do whatever she liked for other people, she could even take Harold if she must, but she could not have Maureen's son. She could not have David.

In the dark, the garden was transformed. Things generally became smaller once you knew them but moonlight shone among the driftwood figures, magnifying each one. The wind made sounds she did not know, hissing and seething, followed briefly by silence. Maureen felt her way between the sculptures. A flutter of something caught her hand and she flinched. All around her rose the statues and pieces of driftwood and she was frightened, as if they were watching. She needed to get this over and done with. She needed to hurry.

Maureen moved towards the figure that she knew now to be her son. She placed her hands firmly on either side of the V-shape, as though grasping a pair of horns, and she pulled. Nothing happened. The wood slipped through her fingers, grazing them. She tried again. Same thing. If only she had gloves.

'Okay,' she said. 'Well, if that's what you want.'

This time she stooped right over, cradling him beneath her so that the V-shape was either side of her body and she was at the very middle, and she wrenched yet again, really hard, but her balance wasn't right. Instead of freeing him, she lost her grip again and this time she stumbled backwards. The ground seemed to shoot away from beneath her, sending her down. She heard a sharp crack and experienced an unforgiving pain. Oh, God, she thought. Please let it not be my son.

It took moments to work out what had happened. Moments that didn't flow from one another but happened in a more staccato way like a series of full stops. Everything was in the wrong place. She was on her back. Sky. She was looking up at the night sky. Stars, tiny and flickering. Something had slammed against the back of her neck. The vertebrae of her spine felt numb. She tried to breathe. It hurt. She stopped. She moved what might be her leg. It *was* her leg. That hurt, too. She couldn't be sure she still had toes. She tried to move and heard a noise like an animal stuck underground and realized it was coming from herself. She stopped trying to sit. She stayed lying still. She took one breath. She took another. She was beginning to feel cold.

'Maureen,' she said. 'Move.'

But she couldn't. She couldn't move her arms or her feet or her head because the moment she tried, there it was, astonishing pain in her neck. Suddenly all she wanted was to close her eyes and sleep.

'Maureen,' she said again, louder this time. 'Move, you fool. Move.'

It was no good. She could be as impatient with herself as she liked, but it made no difference. She couldn't do this. She was in too much pain.

'Help!' she called. 'Help!' Nothing answered or arrived.

The driftwood figure that was Harold was only a few feet away. Maureen shuffled towards it, bit by bit, still on her back. Her body seemed to be made of fragile pieces that were badly put together. Keeping her neck rigid, she tried to reach for the wooden structure, but sparks of pain stopped her. If she didn't move her neck, she could do it. She rolled over. She clung on with one arm, then the other, dragging herself to her knees, all the while not moving her neck, holding it as if it were welded to her shoulder blades, then crawling herself upwards, until she managed to stand. She leant her body against the driftwood piece. If she as much as twitched a muscle in her neck, the pain flashed.

There was nothing to do but wait for daylight. She stayed with her spine pressed against Harold because without him she knew she would fall apart, like a pile of stones, and she tried to imagine him behind her as she washed the dishes at the kitchen sink, but it was no good. She was caught in the very middle of Queenie's Garden, like a living relic, while the figures and statues watched her and whispered. All she could think of was the night in the bookshop.

Had she known? Did some part of her head know what was going to happen even when she bought her ticket for the event? 'Oh. Don't you just *love* that book?' the bookshop owner said, and she pressed it to her chest as if it were attached to her vital organs. No. Maureen did not love that book. Reading it for her new book group, she had felt so wounded – she had no idea where to place herself. It was a story about a woman whose twenty-year-old son hanged himself. The only reason she finished the damn thing was because she wanted to be part of a book group. Otherwise she would have flung it out of the window. It was a vile book.

On the night, the shop was packed. Maureen chose a place at the end of a row, wanting to be alone, but an assistant asked last minute if she wouldn't mind moving in case there were latecomers. She had squeezed past other people to a seat in the very middle, and her new acquaintances from the book group – Deborah, Alice, and so on – were smiling at her in a polite way from their rows. Maureen's heart felt tight, as if someone had wound it in plastic bands. She was finding it hard to breathe.

To her surprise, the writer was even younger than she expected. She might only have been in her late twenties, wearing a leopard-print dress, a pair of cowboy boots and a wide belt that accentuated how neat and small she was. She turned to the audience and the first thing she did was bow her head with her hands clasped in prayer. Oh, Maureen hated this safari/cowgirl writer.

Throughout the evening, she had a strange feeling of not being there, as if she were dreaming, or as if she was remembering a bookshop from a dream. Her heart still felt compressed, while strangely the rest of her body felt emptied. Almost without any bones at all. The writer spoke about the book and her life, and gave some observations about grief that made the room go silent. The bookshop owner said this had been the most important and moving interview of her life, and after that there were questions from the audience. Someone asked whether the writer believed in God, and the writer said she believed in what we could not see, and the audience nodded and a few wept. All the while Maureen remained absolutely still, both present and somehow not there at all. Then a woman in the audience put up her hand and said, 'What I want to ask . . .'

A shuffling of chairs. Rows of faces turning, wary, confused. The owner saying she was sorry, but no one could hear, and a young man with a mic now wriggling past knees to get to Maureen. Because she was the woman in the audience with her hand in the air. She was the one whose legs were shaking as she took to her feet and whose voice was too shrill – but at the same time it did not seem to be her.

'What I want to ask, Anna Dupree, is how dare you?'

Maureen could no longer recall her exact words. The memory was a series of stains on her mind, as if a shutter had come down between the place in her brain where words formed and the other where they took on meaning. She was rigid, on the edge of avoid. She knew she had asked if Anna Dupree had ever lost a child, if she really thought she knew what that was like, when look at her, she was barely old enough to have a baby, let alone a full-grown adult son. She asked exactly what right she had to write about something she did not know and sell millions of copies all over the world to other people who did not know either. Had she called Anna Dupree a tourist? Probably. Had she accused everyone else in the bookshop of being a tourist? Chances were, yes, she'd done that too. Now she had started speaking she didn't feel able to stop, though stop she must, but to stop would mean there would be consequences, there would be the terrible thing that must happen next after a woman says something like this, so she kept ploughing on, closer and closer to the void. A member of the book group with pretty hoop earrings had shaken her head, as if to say, No, no, Maureen, please don't do this to yourself.

Meanwhile Anna Dupree listened with her hand to her mouth. Her face looked stretched.

Maureen wanted to leave. More specifically, she wanted not to have come in the first place. She wanted none of this to have happened but she was stuck in the middle of the shop, in a jungle of fold-up chairs and kind people who were doing their best to look elsewhere, with her face so red she could feel it burning, and she wanted to say, I am sorry, I did not mean this, but she had already said it. It was too late. Besides. She did mean it. That was the trouble. She really did. Every terrible word.

A difficult child.

She made her way to the door, crushing her knees into the backs of chairs, pushing past people's elbows and shoulders and, as she hit the warm air of the summer evening, she overheard someone murmur, 'Yes, that's his *wife*,' and she knew they were talking about her and Harold. She knew she would never come back to the bookshop. She knew that when emails came about the book group, she would feel so conflicted that she would delete them without a first glance. She didn't want to pick up another damn book, not ever. She knew, too, that people would move away from her in the supermarket – even though Harold would say she was only imagining that, which irritated her because it made her sound paranoid. She would shop online instead.

A few months later, Maureen read an interview in a Sunday magazine where Anna Dupree talked about her worldwide bestselling book and how she was going to stop writing fiction because of something a reader had said to her. *I realized I could not make it up any more.* Maureen buried the magazine in the recycling bin. 'Serves you right,' she said. But she no longer knew if she was talking to herself or Anna Dupree.

It was not the worst thing, what she had done that night, just as the unnamed figure in Queenie's Garden was not the saddest. But it was worse than a leaking bladder, worse even than falling as you tried to steal something from a garden, because Maureen had laid her deepest loss at the feet of the world and experienced nothing but an affirmation of her left-outness and her shame. David's loss was her secret. It was the rock against which she was for ever shattered. And Maureen was a loose cannon, firing herself in all directions. She was sundered from life, irrevocably and completely. She would never be free.

At first light, Maureen shuffled her way through the garden. The figures and sculptures were barely shadows. She could just about walk if she didn't move her neck but any slight turn of her head sent pain shooting down her arms. The rising sun gave orange and pink flashes and the sea held its light and so did an inlet of water winding its passage through the sand. The beach was littered with kelp, their roots like knuckles, and driftwood, and plastic bottles. She felt weak. She couldn't remember when she had last eaten. In the distance, sunlight struck the windows of the line of houses of Embleton, and briefly they flamed. She longed to speak to Harold but he would be asleep and, anyway, she had no idea how to explain what she had been trying to do. She didn't even know how to get into the car.

In the end Maureen lowered herself, piece by piece. She started the engine, and inched the car at a snail's pace away from the bay. She could manage if she didn't look down at the pedals or the gear stick, though she couldn't move her neck either to check her rearview mirror. All those years of holding her head high and now it was doing it all by itself. She concentrated on the road ahead, forcing herself to stay awake, but the pain was coming in wheeling patterns that made her drowsy. She knew she should turn round and drive back but she could not bear another night in that guesthouse. She heard the roar of a van behind, too close. As he overtook, the driver swore and shouted at her to get off the road.

It was too much. She couldn't do it. She didn't even know where she was going. The truth was, she could go where she liked, but she would never get away from herself. Because it wasn't Anna Dupree she hated. Not really. It wasn't even her damn book, or the many people who loved it. It was the fact that this young woman had been able to conjure something beautiful out of grief, while Maureen, who lived and breathed it like a full-time professional, could not. And now she knew Queenie had found a way to do the same with her garden.

Maureen pulled over at the next garage and rang the only person she could think of.

12

Coffee Beans

'Maureen? what happened?'

Kate was calling Maureen's name even as she lowered her foot out of the driver's door and bundled down from the truck. Her granddaughter Maple was in the passenger seat, sitting on her mother's lap. They had parked right up close to Maureen at the garage.

'I can't move.'

'Where does it hurt?'

'I don't know. My neck. Everywhere.'

'Will you let me help?'

Maureen felt Kate's hands reaching towards her and asking, 'Okay? Okay?' as she began lifting her gently out of the car. What was happening did not feel right but she let Kate help her while she also wondered where she should put her hands. She didn't want to push her away but neither could she hold her arms around Kate so she just left them dangling mid-air. Kate was smiling but Maureen had no idea if it was for her and she still had no idea what to say. She noticed Kate's hands were warm and very strong. She guided Maureen carefully towards the truck and flung open the rear door, while still holding Maureen, and supported her as she took the steps, one at a time, all the while saying, 'Okay? Okay?' From there she shuffled Maureen right to the back of the truck, where the bed was already pulled out. In the passenger seat, Maple turned to watch, her eyes very dark and round over her mother's shoulder, as Kate guided Maureen's body on top of the eiderdown and lifted her feet. It was so good to be lying down. Maureen kept herself rigid. She closed her eyes. I could die now, she thought. Truly, I am done.

'Is that lady going to hospital?' she heard Maple ask.

'We're going to look after her,' said her mother. 'We have to be quiet.'

Kate's face was so close, Maureen could feel her breath. It smelt of something like toothpaste and earth. Maureen kept her eyes shut as she heard Kate's voice saying, 'Okay, darlin'. This is what we're going to do. Sarah is going to drive your car back to the camp before she goes to work. I'm going to take you to the hospital and get you checked out and after that you can rest with me. You don't have to say anything.'

She was speaking to Maureen slowly, and even though she was so close, her voice sounded as if it were a long way off. Maureen kept her eyes closed. She gave the softest of murmurs to show she had understood but she didn't move and neither was she ready to reply. She wanted to stay very still like this, being spoken to kindly as if she were a child, while deep down the waves of pain pushed through her.

Maureen felt something firm on her head and realized it must be Kate's hand, touching her short white hair. 'You've had a hard time, but it's okay now. You don't have to go anywhere until you're ready. You're going to be fine.'

Her neck was not broken, but the muscles were sprained, her back was badly bruised and her blood pressure was too low. Maureen needed to rest for a few days and limit her movement. She certainly wasn't fit to drive. Kate had waited with her at the hospital. She held Maple on her lap and read stories, over and over again, while Maureen sat ramrod-straight beside her, wishing someone would stuff a baking tray against her spine, not daring to move unless she shifted her entire body, not even daring to speak. She had forgotten how children could listen to the same story and find something endlessly comforting in the repetition of it.

'Are you in pain?' the nurse asked.

'I can manage,' she said.

He smiled as if he knew better and gave her the first of a course of strong painkillers. He showed her some exercises to ease her neck and shoulders.

'You were lucky, Mrs Fry,' he said. She did not ask what he meant by that because she knew he was right.

Kate said she had rung Harold to explain that Maureen had taken a fall but was going to be okay if she rested for a few days. She had reassured him Maureen was not seriously hurt and there was no need for him to come because Kate would look after her. 'He wants to say hello,' she said, and she rang his number again and held the phone against Maureen's ear.

'Oh, Maw,' she heard him say. All that love in his voice. 'Oh, sweetheart.'

And she nodded, and said, 'Uh, uh, uh,' because that was the only thing she could do without hurting.

'Are you okay? Will you be okay?'

She said, 'Uh uh uh,' again.

'Shall I come?'

'No,' she said. 'It okay. Kate here.' The drugs were kicking in.

Afterwards she allowed Kate to guide her back into the truck and already she felt she knew a little more of the way Kate held her, so she trusted her to take her weight. Kate drove them slowly to the camp, then heated a pan of soup that they ate at the table. Maureen was so exhausted she could barely lift the spoon to her mouth. Kate fetched the eiderdown and helped her get underneath it. The bed no longer felt lumpy or alien. Kate pulled the eiderdown right up to Maureen's chin and said, 'There, there, darlin',' until Maureen's eyelids drooped. Sleep came suddenly. Maybe it was the painkillers. She was aware she was thinking of Harold and wanting to speak to him again but couldn't summon the energy to open her eyes.

When Maureen woke, she felt she was coming up from somewhere like a black hole. She wasn't sure why she was there, or even where 'there' was. And then she made out Kate in the wing-back chair reading a library book under a lamp and wearing a pair of big glasses. Briefly Maureen was alarmed, as if she had been absent for some time, during which things might have happened that she didn't know, and she tried to sit up, but the pain was too much and she stayed lying down.

'Rest,' said Kate, glancing up once from her book. 'I've spoken to Harold again. He sends you all his love. He's with Rex.'

'Did he say what they were doing?' said Maureen. She closed her eyes before Kate answered.

When she next woke, Maple was curled in Kate's lap and Kate was reading her another story, but her voice was low, more like a chant, and Maureen couldn't make out the words. She didn't need to: it was a comfort just hearing them, and not being alone. She pulled Kate's eiderdown over her head and fell asleep once more. The next time she woke it was morning and the sky was a band of silver beneath purple cloud. The truck was empty.

Kate brought coffee on a tray and arranged two cups on the table. She helped Maureen sit and gave her cushions and another painkiller. They successfully avoided talking about what had happened during her previous visit and spoke instead about inconsequential things, like coffee. Kate told Maureen she ground her own beans and Maureen said she always bought instant powder and Kate paused and said, with steeled intensity, that no one should drink that crap. It was full of shit, she said, you might as well as drink washing-up water. She served her own coffee from a silver pot that looked like something you would find in a Turkish bazaar and she poured it into two small blue cups, like a ritual. Maureen managed one sip – she couldn't move her neck enough for more – and found what Kate had said to be true. It was the most delicious coffee. Hot and milky with only a hint of bitterness; a sweetness of chocolate, too. And this way they sidestepped their differences to move forward.

'Shall I lift the cup for you?' said Kate.

'You don't have to. I can manage.'

'Oh, Maureen, why won't you let another woman help you for once?'

So she lifted the coffee towards Maureen's mouth and placed the saucer beneath Maureen's chin and this time she took a good proper drink.

'I feel I owe you an apology,' Maureen said.

Kate smiled. 'You don't owe me anything. But I'm glad you rang me, Maureen, when you needed help. I'm glad you gave us another chance.'

When their cups were empty, they sat for a while not saying anything until Kate reached for Maureen's hand and spread her own firmly around it and kept it over Maureen's so that she could feel its weight and the calluses on her palms. Kate said, without looking at Maureen, but towards the window: 'How do we do it? How do we accept the unacceptable?'

After the quiet, her voice filled the room and so did the question. It came over Maureen how tired she was, as if it was evening again instead of morning. Kate closed the curtains. 'Can I get you anything else?'

'No, thank you. You've helped me more than enough.' 'I'll let you rest.'

In the dimmed light, Maureen lay under Kate's eiderdown and fell into another deep sleep.

Later, Kate knocked on the door of the truck and asked if Maureen was feeling any better. She had a favour to ask. She and her daughter had a women's meeting to go to – it would only take two hours. She wondered if Maureen would let Maple sit with her. 'I don't know, Maureen. I feel bad about asking. I just wondered if you'd think about it.'

Maureen said, 'Yes. I'm glad you asked.'

'Do you think you could manage?'

'Maybe. I'm not sure Maple likes me.'

At this Kate laughed. 'Oh, Maureen,' she said. 'Listen to yourself for once. She's a child. If you're kind to her, she'll like you.'

Before Kate left, Maple brought her book and colouring pencils into the truck. Kate had put on red lipstick that Maureen wasn't sure about but she held her tongue and said nothing. Maple hugged her grandmother hard, hanging from her neck like another vast necklace, and Maureen began to think the whole plan would not work, but Kate kissed her and said Maureen was a good woman and then goodbye. To begin with, Maple was wary of Maureen. She sat at the table but kept her arms around her book and her things, as if she feared Maureen might steal them. The best thing was to give her some space.

Maureen made her way to the kitchenette and washed a few plates. These are very good painkillers, she thought. She found a cloth and ran hot soapy water into the plastic sink.

From the table, Maple began to talk. She was still colouring in, but she went on without stopping, speaking about whatever came into her mind, with no need for Maureen to remark on any of it, though she listened to everything Maple said, entranced, because it was so long since she'd been alone with a child like this. She had forgotten how they could talk and talk. She spoke about a girl who was her friend and a black-and-white dog that barked on the farm as well as her bicycle and so many other things, none joined together except in the sweet place that was Maple's head. Then the little girl slipped down from her stool at the table and carried it to Maureen's side and asked if she could see what Maureen was doing.

Without moving her neck, Maureen helped Maple stand on her stool and let her swish her hands in the soapy water and wash a few spoons, with Maple still chattering away, until Maureen realized she was no longer listening to the words, only the tune of them, because she was wiping everything in the vicinity. She was wiping the taps, the rim of the plastic sink, and the lip where it met the draining-board, the unit surfaces, the pots of utensils, the kettle, and the splashback behind it. She was even scouring the dirt from the plug and the knobs on the drawers, and the hooks for the tea-towels. She worked on, calmed by the cloth in warm water, the rinse and squeeze, calmed by Maple's sing-song voice, but most of all calmed by the experience of those surfaces becoming uniformly clean – even though there was no disinfectant spray, and no canister of Pledge or Mr Sheen, and no rubber gloves either. She tidied the mugs, arranging them with the handles pointing all to the right. Already she felt exhausted. Then Maple got down and lay on the bed and asked Maureen to read her picture book.

It was about rabbits. Rabbits who lived in a house, not even a burrow, and wore hats and coats. Three pages in, Maureen was falling asleep. But Maple called her name and Maureen felt an old crease of pleasure, hearing her name spoken by a child, 'Maw- weeeen.' It sounded so sticky and exact. So she went back to the book and managed another page – the rabbits appeared to be making soup – before closing her eyes, until this time she stretched out beside Maple and fell asleep.

When Kate and her daughter returned, the old woman and the child were both lying on top of the bed. Maureen was snoring loudly, her mouth wide, and Maple was also open-mouthed and flush-cheeked, tucked into the crook of Maureen's arm. Sarah lifted Maple and Kate moved an extra cushion closer to Maureen. She left a packet of painkillers and a glass of water in case Maureen needed them when she woke.

In the morning, Maureen asked if she could take another look at

Maple's picture book. She wanted to know how it ended.

'That was quite a good story,' she said. 'I liked it.'

There. The nice words just came out.

13

Moonlight Sonata

It was a long time since anyone had looked after Maureen. She stayed for three more days in the cave-like truck that was filled with dream-catchers and Buddha statues and chakra stones and rose lamps, and smelt of incense. Kate made meals and washed her clothes, and when Maureen looked out of the window, she saw her comfortable slacks flapping on the washing line beside Maple's little clothes. She watched the girl riding on her bicycle or playing with her mother with her rainbow hair. Sometimes she watched the other women, stopping to talk to one another outside, or sharing a coffee. Occasionally Maple curled up next to Maureen with one of her books, and Maureen would manage to hold her neck upright enough to read to her. The outside world was contained by that one window, sometimes dawn-pale, sometimes cloudy, sometimes hidden by the curtain. She slept in away she had never slept before, deep and free, looking at the clock and no longer knowing if it was morning or evening, but closing her eyes and sleeping again. She phoned Harold often and he told her the things he was doing with Rex, which were the same things they always did – playing draughts and watching for birds. She asked if they were remembering to eat properly, and he told her, yes, they were doing splendidly, they had finished a goulash and a stew, but they still had a pie left, and a soup. The thing he wanted most, he kept saying, was for her to get better.

'I'm glad you're with Kate,' he told her on the third day. 'I knew you'd like her. Of all the people I walked with she was my favourite. Did I ever tell you that?'

'Well,' said Maureen, 'maybe you did. But I like hearing it again.'

'I miss you.'

'I miss you too.'

'But you'll be home soon.'

'Tomorrow, I hope.'

'Guess what?'

'I don't know.'

'We saw a black redstart.'

'That's a bird, is it?'

'Yes, Maw. It's like you. It's a beauty.'

*

That night, Maureen opened her eyes and knew she had been woken by the slight noise of a door. The curtains were open and the room was lit by the moon, as bright as daylight, but everything luminous and slightly blue.

There he was, watching her from the wing-back chair. He had placed her clothes on the floor, carefully, though, so as not to crumple them.

'David,' she whispered.

'Hello,' he said.

He was sitting the way he used to, legs sprawled, like a tall person inside a body that had grown too small. He was wearing his old greatcoat with the wide lapels that were pinned all over with badges, and his favourite black boots. His hair was long and thick and brown, just as it had been before he shaved his head. He looked the way he always looked, which meant that he was a little dishevelled and roughed up around the edges, but there was a sharpness to his eyes. He wasn't high or drunk or anything. He was holding a winter bouquet of twigs that looked like witch hazel and scarlet dogwood, along with some fern and ivy berries and crimson haws. His fingernails were green.

'Is it really you? Is it really my son?'

'It's me.'

'I began to think I would never see you again.'

'Well,' he said. Two or three times he shrugged in a bashful way. 'Here I am.'

He was quiet for a while, just watching her with those beautiful dark eyes, and she remained in stillness too, not wanting to do anything that would break the moment. She wondered if the winter twigs might be for her or just something he happened to be carrying.

'Are you all right?' she said at last.

'I'm all right.'

'Is that a mad thing to say?'

'I don't think so.'

'There was a time I used to talk to you. I talked to you all the time. I talked more to you than anyone else and that's the truth.' She was speaking softly, rapidly, afraid the words would dry up if she didn't get them out. 'I told you everything. About what I was doing and what I was thinking and you listened. You were so patient with me. I know I'm not being clear. I wish I could explain it to you. Maybe I don't need to.'

He nodded. Then he looked down at the bouquet and touched a seed head of old man's beard, which was soft and white, like a wispy ball of thread.

'In the end I stopped. I stopped talking to you. Did it hurt you that I stopped? Should I have kept talking? Would you have liked that?'

'It's okay.'

'I know. I know. I'm asking too many questions. It's just seeing you again. There's so much I want to say.'

He lodged the bouquet beneath his arm and reached for a cigarette from his pocket. He lit it with a match, and the smoke turned from grey to blue as it hit a shaft of moon from the window. He said, 'Did something happen to your neck?'

'Oh. It's nothing.'

'It looks like it hurts.'

'I'm taking pills. I sleep a lot. I'm a bit drugged up.'

He smiled and gave a long pull on his cigarette, squinting slightly as he exhaled.

'There is a woman here. She's looking after me. I thought I didn't like her but I was wrong. Kate is a good woman. So I'm fine, honestly. I'm just stuck for a few days. Holed up. Isn't that what people say?'

She was afraid that if she stopped talking, he would disappear. God help her, already he seemed less present.

'I don't know. I don't know what people would say. I was never very good at all that.'

'David?' she said. 'If I stayed here longer, would you stay too?'

He smiled again, but this time as if she was asking something too painful to answer, and then rubbed his eyes with his knuckle. She remembered how as a child he would rub them while he did his homework until his face flamed and his knees would twitch, and how she would worry that learning the way he did, ferociously like that, and wanting to excel, was a kind of punishment. And she remembered then how she had wanted the same when she was young. How she had wanted to be more than the place she came from. They were the same, the two of them. David had only taken up the thing that she started.

'I wish I'd got you a dog.'

'A dog?'

'Yes. But I was frightened. Of dogs, I mean. The farmer let his dogs chase me when I was small. But you always wanted a dog.'

'I don't remember.'

'You went on and on about a dog.'

'Ha,' he said. 'Did I?'

'Don't you remember the dog we gave you for Christmas?'

'What dog?'

'Oh, it was a hideous thing that went woof. You kept it in the box.'

He laughed again and now she laughed too, and it was so good to be laughing again with David. They had always understood each other.

She said, 'I saw Queenie's Garden. Did you?'

'Why would I have seen her garden?'

'I don't know. I'm coming to the conclusion I know very little. I'm a silly old woman. That's all I know.' She thought of the emptiness that was still inside her, even after all these years. Now that she was with him at last, she did not know how she could bear to give him up. 'Oh, David. I can't move on. I'm sorry. I'm thinking of myself. I don't want a life without you. Don't leave me again. Stay.'

He flinched as if she had struck him. She had said too much. Yet again her mouth had gone and said completely and utterly the wrong thing. Her damn mouth. And this time it wasn't to a stranger, it was to her own son.

David slid off the chair and put down his bouquet and sat hunched on the floor, with his chin against his knees. She had thought the bouquet must have been tied together with string but it wasn't, and now the twigs and flowers had fallen apart. It didn't look like a proper bouquet any more but instead a bunch of winter things he might have snapped off in passing because he liked the look of them. Or maybe he hadn't even given it a thought. Maybe his hands had just snapped off the twigs for something to do.

He began to cry but very quietly into his arms, rocking himself, as though he didn't want her to know what he was doing.

Maureen got off the bed and sank on her knees beside him and lifted her arm around his shoulders, pulling him close until he leant the full force of his weight against hers. Her shoulder gave a twist but that was nothing. You can twist yourself right inside out, she thought, but I will stay put. His hair was soft on her cheek and smelt of the shampoo he had used as a teenager; as lightly medical smell. He had seen an advert for it on the television and gone on and on at her to buy it. It was years since she'd smelt it or even thought of it, yet now it felt the most real thing in her life, more real even than the floor she was kneeling on or the moonlight at the window. She wanted to get the smell right inside her so that she would never forget it. She thought of the many things she wanted to say. *I missed so much. How could I have let you go?* She wanted to be able to buy him that shampoo he loved and ask in the morning show he had slept, and cook him an egg the way he liked it, sunny side up, and understand what he had meant as a boy when he'd said he wanted to be the world's guest.

But none of this did she say because he got there first. He asked if she could just listen. He had things he needed to tell her because he knew they were in his way but they were such terrible things. He kept saying, 'Sorry, sorry, sorry.' Almost every other word was an apology.

'It's okay,' she said. 'It's okay. You can tell me, son. I'm here. Of course I'll listen. You tell me whatever you want to say. Tell me everything. I'm not going anywhere.'

He told her he used to steal money from her purse all the time, and he was so sorry about that. He wished he had not got into drinking and the pills but it was only because he had believed for a while he could be something special, and he needed to quieten the voice in his head that was saying he was no one. He said he remembered running into the sea at Bantham Beach when he was a boy and he didn't know why he had kept running, except that he thought he could swim, and he was sorry for that, and he was sorry, too, for the day he'd graduated when he'd kept them waiting two hours in the hot sun so they missed the whole ceremony.

And Maureen said, 'I know, I know. It's okay, son. It's okay. But, oh, my lord, you are not no one. Do you hear me?'

He told her the truth was that he hadn't actually finished his course at Cambridge, he had been sent down, so the whole graduation thing was a lie, and he was a shit because she had bought a dress and Harold had bought a jacket, and they were so proud of him. He had watched them, he said, from a distance, and now he felt sick to think what that must have been like for them, waiting in their best clothes.

'I know,' she said. 'It's okay. And, anyway, that was one terrible dress I wore that day. I don't know what I was thinking of. Really. I looked like a boiled shrimp. I would have stood me up.'

He said he wished he had never shaved his head because he knew how much that pained her. He said did she remember the hat he loved with a feather in it, and she laughed and said, 'Oh, yes, son. Yes, I remember that hat. That was such a fine hat. So dandy. You were a peacock in that hat. It's okay, son. I know, I know. It's okay.'

There was so much more he wanted to tell her. He couldn't unburden himself fast enough. She had barely taken hold of one thing, and he was handing her another, yet everything he said chimed with something that was buried inside her. He said how much he loved his first pair of shoes when he was three ('I know, I know'), and did she remember the bonsai tree he tried to grow, and she said, yes, as she held him. 'It's okay, son. I know, I know. It's okay.'

She drew him closer. When they were standing, she barely used to reach his shoulders, but she spread herself wide around him. I would become the size of the world for this boy, she thought. Then she brushed back his hair and lifted his face towards hers, but already it was lapsing away, his dark eyes more blurred and even his shoulders a little thinner. 'You are someone,' she said. 'Do you hear? Goodness me, you are someone.'

She stayed at his side, listening and holding him, though she could no longer make out the words, and later she heard the first birdsong and found she was lying in the bed. The truck was empty.

The curtains were drawn. She was wearing her nightdress. David was not sitting in the wing-back chair and she was not beside him and there was no winter bouquet. There was no sign whatsoever that he had been there, not even a smell of shampoo or sprinkling of cigarette ash. Her clothes were folded on the arm of the chair, just as she'd left them.

She lay on the bed, as the sun came up and filled the truck with winter light, and the birds kept calling, *Tchink tchink, Haw haw haw! Tsee tsee!* Good morning! Good morning!

14

Winter Bouquet

After she left Kate, Maureen did something she did not understand. She drove into Hexham and asked a stranger where she might find a bookshop. She bought a copy of Anna Dupree's paperback, and then she found a florist and chose a winter bouquet. She did not understand but she still went and did those things. After all, they were only two more in a whole journey of things she did not understand. She put them on the passenger seat, and drove back to the golf course. She carried them to Queenie's Garden for her third and final visit.

Her parting with Kate had been affectionate and slow. Maureen had not spoken about her night but she believed Kate might have sensed something, without fully knowing what it was, as she straightened the wing-back chair and paused a moment to smooth a ruck in the upholstery. She helped Maureen pack her suitcase and made one of her pots of coffee, which they drank in their coats on the plastic chairs outside. She gave Maureen a bag of freshly ground beans to take home for Harold, and they promised to keep in touch and see one another again. Then, to Maureen's surprise and pleasure, Kate had taken Maureen's face between her palms and kissed it with a completeness that reminded her of putting a stamp on a letter. 'I won't forget you lying in my truck,' she said. 'Whatever happens, I will always keep that memory of you here.'

By the time she was walking past the golf course towards the dunes it was already mid-afternoon, though the sun had broken through and lit the land crosswise, throwing long, spindly shadows, and catching a nearby cloud, so that it glowed like a tangerine above the bay. There was only one other person in the garden – a man sitting in the far corner – dressed in a robe under an anorak and hat, his head bowed, holding prayer beads. There was rain in the air, but only light. It wouldn't hurt her.

Maureen made her way past Harold's driftwood sculpture, and David's, towards the unnamed one with a hole for a heart. She found a good place for the book beside a statue made of bottle tops and corks, with an additional garland of bright pink paper flowers, and she laid it there.

'I hope you write another blockbuster, Anna Dupree,' she said. 'I really do. But I hope you don't mind if I don't read it.'

She turned now to the holed piece of driftwood that people believed had no name. Because it was Maureen. She knew it. She had known it since that night in the guesthouse. She knelt and placed her hand where the hole was, and for a moment it was full again. The hurt was gone. Her anger too, and her resentment. At last they were not there. She had been wrong: this brittle piece of driftwood was not an act of unkindness on Queenie's part, or even pity. It was one of forgiveness. Queenie had understood Maureen's grief that day they'd met beside the washing line, and done the best she could to give it a place, just as Maureen now knew her letter for Harold had been a letting go of love. She was glad she had kept it in a shoebox. Without any exchange of words, they had taken up each other's loss, and given meaning to what was unbearable.

Maureen remained kneeling, all alone in that garden she did not understand. Once again there was a rip-split in the cloud and the light shone down on the sea, catching flecks of rain, so that the air was filled with specks of snow-white brightness. A kestrel breasted the sea wind and hung, wings hooked. Maureen watched it for so long she suddenly felt able to see as far as the bird saw, and beyond.

All of Northumberland stretched away, swelling and wimpling towards the south – over the patchwork of low hills and plains, flint walls, patterns of fields, the valleys and fells, over the Cheviot Hills, the backbone of the Pennines, the limestone gorges of the Peak District, the western velvet spur of the Forest of Bowland, the Yorkshire Dales, the rolling Cotswolds, the Mendips, the chalk coasts, the mighty rivers, Tyne, Ouse, Trent, Thames, Exe, the wetlands, forests and woods, the trees that were so various they appeared beneath her like moss and algae, the network of roads and railways and canals, the factories and warehouses, the sprawling cities, the sewage works and toxic heaps, the asbestos, the plastic, the landfill – all the way to the heather-purple peaks of Dartmoor, and a blue estuary, and a road of little houses, each with a garden, where Harold gazed up at the sky, watching for birds. She imagined the edges of the world shifting slowly and she stayed in its mysterious motion as her mind made windings deep into the earth through holes and runnels, where closely woven grasses hid the sky. She followed the ancient path of water and saw the curlicues of buried shells, she followed beetles into scrolls of leaves, and on and on, deeper and deeper, through to where larvae were buried, and she was no more than an eyeless globe in the dark, or a mantle of roots creeping out its threads. Then the kestrel dropped out of view, and once more she was in Queenie's Garden.

'Well,' she said, coming to, 'Maureen, Maureen. Now you've finally lost your marbles.'

Maureen stared at all the driftwood sculptures and the seed heads like umbrellas. *I am the world's guest,* she thought. And suddenly she understood. She understood what David had meant when he was a boy. She had lived her life as if she was owed something extra because he had been taken away, and other women's sons had not. She thought of Harold watching for birds and how his face lit up when he saw a bluethroat. To have lived a whole life and then find wonder in a tiny creature covered with feathers, weighing no more than a coin. What was it all for, if not for that? She felt the painful shock of joy that floods in, like blood pushing into a limb that has been starved. It was about forgiveness, the whole story. Harold's pilgrimage and Queenie's letter, and now Maureen's winter journey too. The chimes and necklaces of stones moved in the wind and so did the seed heads. Yes, they said. Yes, Maureen! Everything was about that. She thought of all the strangers who had found a resting place for their losses that were too terrible to bear. The padlocks for love, the paper crosses, the photographs, the keys and flowers, homemade relics and hundreds of candles, the poems and messages. Forgive me, forgive me, for continuing to live when you are gone. The essential loneliness of people was there, wherever you cast your eye – it was in a service station, it was in a bookshop, it was in a parked car by the side of the road – so the things they did to try and bear the loss were choices that required respect. Such acts of love were only so many different ways of saying the same thing, because really there were no words to say.

Maureen got to her feet and laid her winter bouquet against the V-shaped monument. Queenie had been right to place David in her garden. He was not Maureen's lost son, he was himself. He belonged to no one but himself.

'Thank you, Queenie,' she said, and she found, to her surprise, that she was weeping.

From the car park, Maureen rang Harold. She told him she would drive through the evening and be home very late, though she wanted to drop off a card for a night-security man who had been helpful near Exeter. To all this he said yes. Yes, of course, goodness, yes. She must drive carefully and stop whenever she needed. If she wanted to, she must find a place to sleep. He couldn't wait to see her, but the most important thing was that she was safe. Then she asked, 'What have you two eaten today?'

'Oh, we've eaten like kings. Rex and I had sandwiches.' 'What did you put inside?'

'The sandwiches?'

'Yes.'

'I don't think we put anything inside them.'

'So they were bread, then? Really they were bread.'

'Yes,' he said, laughing as if this was a happy new word he hadn't come across before. 'Did you hear that, Rex? Our sandwiches were bread!'

Maureen took one last look across the bay towards Queenie's Garden. Brave things had been happening in the world, even though she hadn't noticed. Tiny black packages of buds on the branches and the smallest of shoots from the ground, as green as jewellery. The wind felt sharp and there was still a low ache in her neck, but she experienced no pain.

Maureen stayed a while longer, reluctant to give up the last of the day. Reluctant even to give up her solitude. It was so peaceful. In the distance, Queenie's Garden waved and sparkled. She watched the clouds frill with gold against the bracken-red sky, and the light that tipped upwards in floods, even though the sun was no more than a lozenge on the horizon. A flock of tiny brown birds swooped down to a winter bush, chit-chattering away, like gossips on a street corner. What was it they were saying? Whatever it was, she liked it. So busy, so loud! *Tchink, tchink, Haw haw haw! Tsee, tsee! Choo choo!* She couldn't say how and, even if she could, she didn't need to, but she knew she was the happiest she had been in along time.

'Maureen,' she said quietly. 'Maureen. Maureen.'

Then she got into the car to make the journey home.

Acknowledgements

A little over ten years ago, my first novel had the good fortune to fall into the hands of Susanna Wadeson, editor at Doubleday. Since then our book output has grown in size, and so has our friendship. My thanks are, as always, to Susanna for her faith, wisdom, questions and dedication, and for giving me the freedom to write about the things that move me. This book is for you.

Thank you to my wonderful agent, Clare Conville, and all at Conville & Walsh. Thank you to Hazel Orme and Kate Samano and the copy-editing team, Cat Hillerton in production, Beci Kelly in art, Emma Burton and Lilly Cox in marketing, Oli Grant in audio, Laura Ricchetti and Natasha Photiou in international sales, Tom Chicken, Laura Garrod, Emily Harvey, Neil Green and Elspeth Dougall in UK sales. Thank you to Andrew Davidson for the exquisite illustrations. Thank you to Clio Seraphim and Kiara Kent and the entire Random House team. Thank you to those who championed Harold Fry all those years ago – Erica Wagner, David Headley, Cathy Retzenbrink, Fanny Blake – and have continued to be so generous over the years. Thank you for your unequivocal encouragement, Larry Finlay, and thank you, too, to Alison Barrow, because without your spark, guidance and friendship, none of this would be happening.

Thank you, as always, to my family, for your love. To Sarah Edghill, for casting an eye over a nearly draft of the first chapters of this book and having the courage to tell me it didn't work. (She was right. I started again.) Thank you to Niamh Cusack for reading every one of my stories over many years, even the ones that were emails.

Thank you to my husband, Paul Venables. In truth, the thank you is a private one. But Paul has been involved with my writing from the very start and I couldn't do what I do without him. Sometimes it is good and right to shout about things like that.

Lastly, and above all, my thanks are both to the readers who have read with such kindness over the years – asking me questions that inspired more thinking, generously sharing their own stories – and the booksellers and librarians who kept getting books to us, even when we were all locked inside. The gate-keepers of reading. Where would we be without you?